T0279128

NUBIA

THE RECKONING

Books by

OMAR EPPS AND CLARENCE A. HAYNES

Nubia: The Awakening

Nubia: The Reckoning

OMAR EPPS
CLARENCE A. HAYNES

NUBIA
THE RECKONING

DELACORTE PRESS

Text copyright © 2023 by 72073 Inc.
Jacket art copyright © 2023 by Adeyemi Adegbesan
Map copyright © 2022 by Maxime Plasse

All rights reserved. Published in the United States by Delacorte Press,
an imprint of Random House Children's Books,
a division of Penguin Random House LLC, New York.

Delacorte Press is a registered trademark and the colophon
is a trademark of Penguin Random House LLC.

Visit us on the Web! GetUnderlined.com
Educators and librarians, for a variety of teaching tools,
visit us at RHTeachersLibrarians.com

Library of Congress Cataloging-in-Publication Data is available upon request.
ISBN 978-0-593-42868-9 (hardcover) —
ISBN 978-0-593-42870-2 (ebook) —
ISBN 978-0-593-70994-8 (int'l. ed.)

The text of this book is set in 11.5-point Adobe Caslon Pro.
Interior design by Jen Valero

Printed in the United States of America
10 9 8 7 6 5 4 3 2 1
First Edition

To my rock and pillar, the Queens of my Kingdom
and matriarchs of our family, my beloved mother,
Bonnie, and my beautiful wife, Keisha . . .
True Goddesses in the flesh . . .
—D.E.

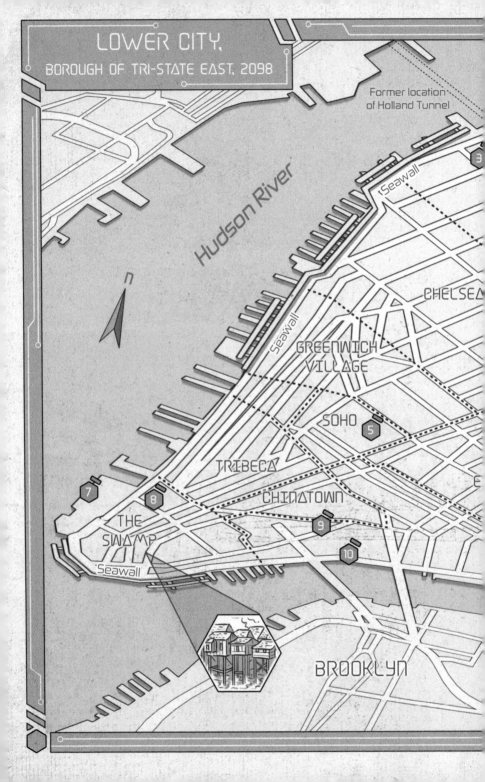

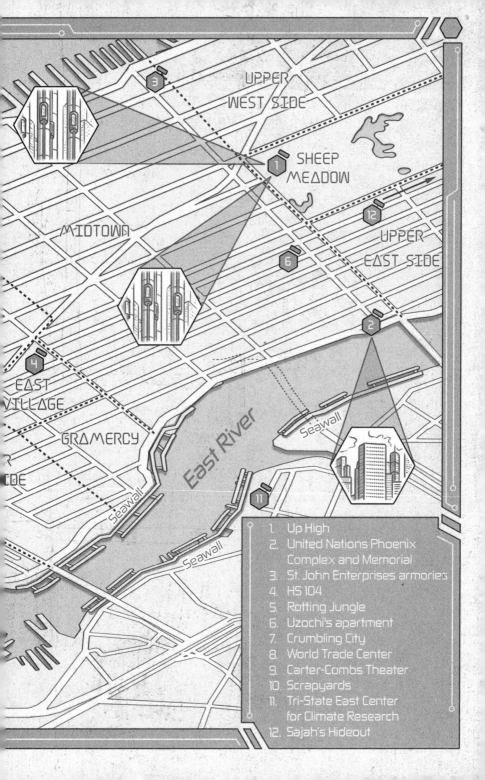

UPPER
WEST SIDE

SHEEP
MEADOW

MIDTOWN

UPPER
EAST SIDE

EAST
VILLAGE

GRAMERCY

East River

Seawall

Seawall

Seawall

KEY MOMENTS IN NEW YORK HISTORY

A Special Timeline Presented by Helios News

2059— first New York City seawall built in Inwood area of upper Manhattan

2061— strict protocols placed on use of artificial intelligence in personal and professional walks of life after errant program completely takes over Brooklyn power grid for a week

2067— construction begins on the Up High, the world's first sky city created with antigravity tech; seen as residential option for the wealthy concerned about rising sea levels

2069— Helios News founded by Myrtle St. John; soon becomes most popular holo-news network in United States

2071— first New Yorkers move to the Up High, soon joined by host of other residents from around the world

2072— the term "ascension" used for the first time by Helios News commentator to describe process of moving from lower city to the Up High; becomes part of popular speech

2076— New York, New Jersey, and Connecticut break away from the United States to form a new independent government, Tri-State East (TSE); its coastal counterpart, Tri-State West (TSW)—consisting of California, Oregon, and Nevada—is founded at the same time

2077— nu-raves first appear in city, a highly intelligent avian species cloned from traditional ravens; pigeon population radically decreases

2078— the United Nations Massacre occurs; scores of hostages are murdered, with terrorists apprehended by private militia later dubbed St. John Soldiers; militia helmed by Myrtle St. John's nephew, Krazen

2079— St. John Soldiers become primary peacekeeping force for TSE, which becomes only nation-state in Western Hemisphere to have fully privatized military/police force

2080— a group of female migrants from Mumbai working in education incorporate the principles of sexual consent into high school curricula across the city

2081— under second amendment to TSE's constitution, firearm possession made illegal nationwide with only specialized militia forces having access; mass transition made to stun gun and Taser tech

2082— series of storms descend on region, destroying parts of lower New York's infrastructure, including subway system; additional seawalls immediately built by St. John Enterprises; host of Nubian refugees arrive

2083— large influx of lower city refugees arrive from Caribbean, including Jamaica, Haiti, Dominican Republic, and Virgin Islands

2084— experimental Conway Protocols tested on Up High convicts, utilizing memory alteration to eliminate recidivism; deemed successful but abandoned after accusations of human rights violations from United Nations

2086— the Nubian Quarter, aka the Swamp, is created in lower Manhattan next to city's largest seawall; notable for being the only fully governmentally subsidized neighborhood in New York

2087— Starlight Greenhouse opens on easternmost
        edge of the Up High; noted for its extensive
        collection of near-extinct plant and bird life

2089— clusters of Dutch climate migrants arrive;
        responsible for design of vehicular hover
        system that replaces subways

2093— the UN awards TSE biannual Lighthouse Prize
        for its high rate of acceptance of climate
        refugees; damaged lower-city economy
        stabilizes due to real estate investments from
        St. John Enterprises

2098— Myrtle St. John dies; Krazen St. John and
        daughter Sandra only living members of
        illustrious St. John dynasty

2098— a wave of Nubian teens allegedly "awaken" to
        a host of mystical abilities; Swamp rendered
        barely inhabitable after partial collapse of
        local seawall

Prologue

He knew his powers were gone long before he opened his eyes.

Beneath the castaway, the beach was coarse, his lacerated skin burning. Sand raked his fingertips, filled his mouth. He heard the easy lap of the water nearby. He supposed he should have felt relief that he had washed ashore, though he had no idea where he was. The man slowly opened his eyes, the air thick against his skin as he spat an errant braid from chapped lips, a gesture that required more energy than he had. He couldn't move his hands or limbs, couldn't lift his head, his body a wasted, corpselike thing almost devoid of life. How long had it been since he'd eaten, since he'd had fresh water, his days defined by the thrashing of the ocean?

He shifted his gaze, trying to discern the surrounding landscape. The sand on the horizon was a brilliant gold even with overcast skies. The castaway lifted his eyes slightly, barely making out the thick copse of palm trees dotting the horizon.

A hole opened in the castaway's chest, an agonizing chasm of regret and grief. As much as he wanted it to be, he knew this land wasn't Nubia. And even worse, he knew he'd lost the glorious, wondrous thing he'd cherished above all else.

He closed his eyes, his mind racing to the recent past, to the hurricane he'd chosen to create as an exercise of power. Doing so was his divine right as both sovereign and catalyst, a ritual that would have strengthened his connection to the kinetic. Never had he dreamed that he'd lose control of the storm, that the thunder and winds and rain would become a rampaging terror, destroying everything in its path. His people barely had time to get to the boats as they shrieked and moaned and wailed, sounds that hadn't desecrated his land in eons.

The ache in his heart burst forth again as he thought of the other elemental Nubians who'd rushed to his side to try to stem the storm so others could flee. How many people had escaped? Had his wife made it to safety? His brother?

"You have to leave with us, you numbskull," his brother had begged, running up to him during the storm. "You must come now, or you'll drown."

In response, the man had tried to make light of the situation, letting forth a small smile, trying to convey that this absurd situation would soon be resolved, that Nubians would never be run off their land by a storm. Anything to get his stubborn sibling onto the boats to watch over their family.

He remembered seeing the last of the vessels leave the shore of his island home amid the wind and rain. He whispered a quick prayer for his pregnant wife as the small league disappeared on undulating waves. The rain grew thicker and he could barely see the hands he held in front of his body, trying to focus his gifts. He finally grasped that all was lost when the gigantic wave reached the shores of the only home he'd known and battered his head and arms and torso and filled his lungs and swept him away, drowning out the screams of the other elementals who'd stood by him.

He didn't know how long he'd lost consciousness for, how his body had managed to rise to the ocean's surface from the depths. But when he awoke, he was shocked to find that life still throbbed within his veins. He was even more shocked to find that he was surrounded by floating debris. A Nubian boat, he was sure, destroyed by the hurricane. No survivors to be found.

And so he'd clung to a large piece of driftwood as day turned to night, shame eating away at him as he cried, a being once heralded for his power reduced to such vulgar circumstances. His head pounded. He could barely stay awake, much less call forth his gift. And then, after two full days had passed and the storm had subsided to reveal a bright blue sky, it had happened. The man had felt the break in his heart that cracked and splintered through his entire being. The splitting of his body, his mind . . . *everything*. The exquisite power that had lived and breathed within, sliced and gutted from him for no reason he could discern. The pain of losing his connection to the kinetic had been unlike anything he had ever known, even though the castaway was a hardy man, having withstood regular beatings over the years from Thato during their blasted fighting-forms sessions.

My gift has vanished, the man thought.

No . . .

He'd clung to the driftwood in disbelief, trying to settle his mind and heart, thinking the watery abyss might offer him true peace. But still he'd held on, even as the storm returned more ferocious than ever, so unrelenting that he eventually succumbed to sleep even while being battered by waves and rain.

The weight of these memories seized the man as he lay on the beach, pulling him in so many directions that, at any moment, he thought he might shatter, might disappear. He was spent. He had no voice to cry for help, no strength to rise. If night fell, he would be easy prey for any manner of beast. *This is it, then,* he realized as the last bit of energy left his frame, as his powerless body succumbed to whatever the fates decreed. He felt the darkness closing in like a heavy blanket, the kind his wife would drape over him when they lay down.

"Sleep, dear heart," she would tell him. "Sleep, and when you wake, you'll find me in your arms."

But that tenderness was gone. That life, his beloved . . . all gone. The tears came again. Nubia, their paradise, their oasis, swept away, all because he hadn't been good enough.

The drums of failure beat a sharp, staccato dirge in Siran's mind. And as he closed his eyes to welcome death, a bead of rain fell upon his cheek.

Chapter 1

Uzochi

"Hey, Uzochi, you with me?"

For a moment, Uzochi didn't realize he was touching his cheek. He blinked a few times, quickly understanding that the air around him was dry, not a drop of moisture to be found falling from a sunny, bright sky. He was whisking away a phantom raindrop, something that was no longer part of reality.

"Uzochi," said the voice again, softer now. He turned to its source, finding the strong, warm eyes of Zuberi looking back at him as they crouched in a narrow alley across from one of the entrances to Central Park. He readjusted to his real-world surroundings, noting that Tasha, his former classmate from HS 104, was with them as well.

Both of the girls were dressed in all black in a militia-style vest, shirt, and pants. Zuberi's locs were pulled back and covered by the standard cap that most St. John Soldiers wore. She had a backpack by her side that he knew carried her trusted staff, which had been modified so that it could be collapsed into three parts, making for easier transport. Even if Uzochi hadn't had the power to read her thoughts and experience her emotions, he'd have known how to discern the determined expression on her face. She reached out and touched his hand, and he gripped hers in return.

"Another vision, buddy?" Zuberi asked.

Yes, Uzochi wanted to say, a vision more confusing than any of the others. He could only hold on to scraps from this one, bits of memory that made no sense even as he tried to put them together. Still, he could feel the sensation of sand between his fingers, the smell of the ocean invading the alley where he and the girls hid. In the memory, there was a figure on the beach . . .

Adisa, the great Nubian elder who had shared his consciousness with Uzochi in the moments before he died. Adisa's memories had risen often, random and unbidden, in Uzochi's mind over the past several weeks since the elder had passed on. And he wasn't sure why.

"I'll take that as a yes," Zuberi said, her soft lips curving to a half smile that drew Uzochi's attention back to her.

"You're right. Yes," Uzochi said, straightening up. Like Zuberi, he was cloaked head to toe in militia black that allowed them to blend into the shadows of the alleyway. He found the thick padding on the clothing bulky and cumbersome, not at all to his liking, but he didn't complain. He knew why they had to appear to be St. John Soldiers. Once they moved from their spot in the alley, they would need to be able to get to the massive elevator towers that would ferry them to the city's wealthy Up High quadrant with as little drama as possible. They had gone over the plan extensively and trained and drilled and practiced and trained some more for days, practically to the point of exhaustion.

"Don't worry," Uzochi told Zuberi, dipping forward so that their foreheads touched. "I'm here. We'll get Vriana. I promise."

Zuberi clutched his hand just a bit more tightly. Even though she nodded her head and gave a faint smile, Uzochi was an empath. He could sense her concern that his eerie visions were becoming a distraction right as they were embarking on their mission. He would never intentionally read her thoughts without her permission, but he felt her pressing other emotions toward him. Emotions she wanted him to feel.

Gratitude. Trust. Worry.

A sense of it all being too late.

A sense of it all not being enough.

"Your plan, it's a good plan," he reminded her, even though he wanted to say *Fuck the mission* and take her in his arms. "We've practiced, prepared for all sorts of contingencies. We know what to do."

Uzochi quickly turned back to the gleaming silver towers, noting once again how they dominated the landscape of Central Park. Not too long ago, he had come to the park every few weeks and stared at the elevators. He would stand there, grasping the straps of his immaculately clean scholarpack, ignoring the people surrounding him, and daydream. He imagined that he would soon earn a scholarship to a prestigious Up High university and become one of the few lower-city New Yorkers to ascend, to establish a life for himself and his mom in the sky, free of the threat of flooding and nonstop work and the taunts and insults routinely hurled at Nubians.

His dreams of ascension came to an abrupt end when waves of teenage Nubians began awakening to extraordinary powers, gifts that were in fact their birthright. Adisa and Uzochi's mom and others had revealed that back in their ancestral homeland, Nubians were defined by their connection to a primal, universal force known as the kinetic, which bestowed them with uncanny abilities. The existence of these gifts was kept hidden by the adults in their lives after fleeing the storm that destroyed their island home, having lost their own connection to the kinetic and arrived on the shores of New York as refugees with no power. A sixteen-year-old academic star, Uzochi had awoken to his abilities as an empath, a telepath, and, apparently, a telekinetic. But most importantly of all, he was a so-called Nubian catalyst, the individual who would guide his people to the next stage of their evolution. Adisa had proclaimed this almost immediately after learning what Uzochi could do. According to the elder, Uzochi's powers of the mind were tremendous, as evidenced by how he had guided dozens of young Nubians to more easily awaken to their powers. They were now known to many as the Children.

The awakenings had attracted the attention of Krazen St. John, the tycoon security specialist responsible for running so many of the businesses that comprised the Up High, the sparkling oasis of a city that floated above Central Park. The technologically advanced Up High was heralded by the world as the treasure of Tri-State East. And Krazen's private militia of St. John Soldiers was seen as key to maintaining the peace both in the Up High and in lower New York.

But Uzochi and most Nubians knew the truth: Krazen was a ruthless manipulator, having managed to get scores of Nubian kids who were part of the gang known as the Divine to join his forces, training to work as a special unit of his militia. The sky king had sent the Divine to attack the theater that the Children had called their home, and then had blown up the seawall that protected the Swamp from the seawaters that were a perennial threat to Nubians. It was all done so that Krazen could send a message to all of Tri-State East: that powerful, dangerous beings were now in our midst, and that the only way New Yorkers and the rest of the nation would be safe was for Krazen to have them under his control.

Though Uzochi and Lencho and a couple of other Nubians had managed to seal the breach in the wall and protect the Swamp from being completely destroyed, saving countless lives, many of the surrounding structures had been damaged. Shacks precariously perched on stilts had collapsed into the flooding water, leaving countless people homeless, and the outdoor Nubian market had been swept away. Even though the Children had used their powers to clean up the quarter the best they could, the Swamp felt like an even more dangerous place than before, with a compromised seawall flanking fragile homes that seemed to be on their last legs.

Crowding into a small Swamp apartment that was undamaged, the elders had deliberated on this state of emergency with Uzochi at their side, as befitting his status as catalyst.

Zuberi and her father, Thato, stood among the group as well. Within hours, the elders had decided that the community had no choice but to leave the Swamp and seek shelter in whatever structures were available. They considered the area just west of their location, the collection of tall, empty buildings known as the Crumbling City. But it was quickly decided that the once-monumental edifices would be far too dangerous to set up camp in, having become nothing but hollowed-out, water-logged skeletons.

And so they looked slightly north instead, zeroing in on the huge building known as the Rotting Jungle. The space was notorious, having been the former headquarters of the Divine, but that didn't matter now. The elders had decreed that Nubians who lived in structurally sound buildings could stay in the Swamp if they so chose, but the bulk of those who lived in shacks on stilts would move to the Jungle and the surrounding abandoned buildings.

"But . . . but that area is, like, almost completely gang territory," Uzochi said, his mind still spinning from the recent turn of events. And then he remembered the other issue they'd have to contend with—Elevation, the addictive lower-city drug that supposedly made people feel like they were flying free and living in the sky, like those who'd ascended to the Up High. "And what about all the people there who're Elevated out of their minds?" he added. "There're dealers and junkies all over that neighborhood."

"Which is why staying in the city is not a viable option," Thato chimed in, pounding his fist in his palm. "It's far too dangerous. We must make other plans. As a collective, we must *flee* this cursed place or we will most certainly be hunted." Ever since the awakenings had started to occur, Thato, an entrepreneurial security specialist, thought that Nubians had to abandon New York entirely. It was only at Zuberi's behest to stay with the others that he hadn't upped and left with his daughter.

The elders had stared at Thato and Uzochi after their remarks, Uzochi feeling waves of annoyance mixed with deference directed at them. Then someone stood up, an elder known as Beka, a bespectacled woman with a round, full face and smooth skin who had her salt-and-pepper hair pulled into a bun atop her head. Uzochi abruptly realized that she was the only elder wearing makeup.

"Uzochi, Thato, your concerns are noted. Thato, we continue to weigh your wishes on this matter of our relocation. This will take time, as you know. And Uzochi, revered catalyst"—Beka bowed her head slightly when she said this, as did most elders—"our community has awoken." She spoke with a slight smile on her face. He could've sworn her eyes were smiling as well. "The world knows who we are. Do not fear. Dealers and these junkies, as you say, will not bother us."

And so, just days after the flooding of the Swamp, most Nubians moved en masse less than two miles north to the SoHo area of the lower city. It was a weird time, with individuals and families occupying rooms and apartments directly across from other New Yorkers who had abandoned any semblance of a functional life, having given themselves over to two or three glowing purple pills a day. The promises of Elevation usurped all else.

11

Uzochi, Zuberi, and the rest of the Children suddenly found themselves in the odd position of being protectors of their people. Uzochi scanned as many buildings as he could with his mind to make sure there was no immediate danger, doing his best to ensure that no Nubian would take up space already occupied by someone who was a gang member, Elevated, or otherwise unhoused. Uzochi's days were full of fear and revulsion and confusion, as he navigated the emotions that came from Nubians and non-Nubians alike. But Beka was right. Miraculously, even though Nubians faced prejudice from all corners of New York, not one gang member or addict attacked the Nubians moving in their space.

Uzochi knew why. A glimpse of the holo-news headlines that appeared on billboards in the lower city told the story.

**NUBIANS DISPLAY POWERS IN
FIERY THEATER DISASTER . . .**

**SPECIAL-POWERED NUBIANS APPEAR
ON SCENE AS SWAMP WALL FALLS . . .**

**SWIFT-FOOTED NUBIAN SAVES
CITIZENS FROM RISING WATERS . . .**

**DAWN OF A NEW AGE: THE MYSTICAL
REALITY OF NUBIANS . . .**

What had happened at the Carter-Combs Theater and the Swamp seawall had been the stuff of news and social media coverage for days, nonstop, 24/7. Nubians were all anyone could talk about. Were they really displaying special powers? Was this some sort of media or public relations hoax, remembering the wave of deepfake videos that informed the mid-2030s and how specialized tech needed to be created to identify clips as legit?

Still, even with the skepticism, Krazen's press conference statements that Nubian powers were real were all that some people needed to hear. And so the folks who lived in the abandoned tenements, who'd learned what it took to survive under the harshest of circumstances, knew better than to be starting something with a whole bunch of people with crazy powers. Better to make peace and learn how to live side by side with rotten Nubians than to have a bunch of scary African sorcerers take them out.

As ugly as that was, after all that had happened, Uzochi was grateful. There simply weren't enough hours in the day for all the work that needed to be done, especially considering most Nubian adults had decided to homeschool their kids to better safeguard them from the larger world. And he was still responsible for helping other Nubian teens awaken to their powers and understand their connection to the kinetic, something that took time and energy. It had become rewarding, spiritually fulfilling work, though there were failures as well. Keera, the girl whose fiery gift had destroyed the Carter-Combs, had left a note saying she feared her power was too dangerous to other Nubians and it would be better if she went away. They had no idea where she'd gone, and her absence weighed heavily on Uzochi.

But there was good news as well. Thankfully, he and a few others were starting to notice that some of the kids seemed to be coming into their gifts more easily without tons of his telepathic coaxing. Uzochi found he actually had moments to breathe.

But it was tough. Many Nubian families and singles had taken up residence in the Rotting Jungle, which had been wholly unoccupied, as almost all of the Divine had joined Krazen's militia. Uzochi and most of the Children had set up shop there as well. Abdul, an elemental, had created flowing streams of water with lots (and lots) of soap to wash away the grime from all manner of surfaces, trying his best not to shriek when legions of roaches and rats scurried out of their hiding places. Uzochi had tried to help by using his telekinesis as well, realizing that he'd prevented so many deaths because he'd been able to create a field of force with his mind. But telekinesis was difficult for him to wield. By the time he'd levitated a whole bunch of junk to lay outside the Jungle in a huge pile, his head was throbbing. He felt far more comfortable in the realm of thought and emotion. Using his power as a hard, physical thing was . . . odd.

Even with all the dangers they faced, Nubians still had moments of pleasure. Abdul and others had used their gifts to help clean out other buildings besides the Rotting Jungle, prompting their new neighbors to bring over food galore for the recent transplants. And then there were two kids who'd just awoken to their gifts, making a difference. One, a girl named Veronique with long silver hair and an aura of tranquil self-possession, could accelerate the healing process with mist from her fingers, mending cuts and bruises for people in the area. And another, a smiley boy named Leonard with a purple Mohawk and multiple piercings who loved electronic punk music, could accelerate the growth of flora. Suddenly the neighborhood around the Jungle, usually putrid and barren, had become an oasis of plants and flowers. And the media was taking notice.

These moments of joy were welcome but didn't ease Uzochi's mind. He found himself thinking constantly about Krazen St. John and his plotting. News had surfaced right after the Swamp Wall explosion that Krazen would be running for mayor. Dread had filled Uzochi's heart: What would this man resort to for the sake of having Nubian gifts under his control? If he'd been willing to kill scores of people just to make a point about how unsafe the Swamp seawall was, what would he be willing to do to get to Nubians? The answer to Uzochi's question had appeared soon enough when reports surfaced of a Paranormal Registration Act being considered by the city council, with a similar law on the table for all of Tri-State East. If passed, the act would require every single Nubian in New York to register their name, location, and powers with the government and possibly be detained by the authorities. The prospect of this chilled Uzochi to the bone.

His thoughts immediately went to his history classes, where he'd learned about Black people being enslaved for centuries in the former United States, which was soon followed by convict leasing, and then decades later, the internment of Japanese Americans in camps. Was this what awaited Nubians? Uzochi couldn't prove it, but he was sure that Krazen had something to do with the act even though he wasn't an elected official yet.

The other thing that occupied Uzochi's mind constantly

amid all his duties . . . Zuberi, and a yearning to connect with her as much as possible, to get to know her even better and try to unburden her of her grief over losing Vriana. (Uzochi's big secret was that he found himself kneeling at his bed in his little room at the Jungle and thanking Goddess every night that a spectacular girl like Zuberi had come into his life.) One of Krazen's militiawomen had approached the two girls when they were close to the theater and taken Vriana away to the Up High under false pretenses. Zuberi was certain that was where she was still being held and wanted nothing more than to run up to the elevator towers, take on a league of St. John Soldiers by herself, and make her way Up High, using Nubian fighting forms to subdue whoever got in her damn way, bashing in heads and forcing someone to reveal "Where the hell is Vriana Anan?" A nice fantasy, sure, but even headstrong Zuberi knew she couldn't get Vriana back by herself.

And so, as Uzochi and Zuberi got to know each other under stressful circumstances, as they made sure to find time each evening to sit with each other and talk and experience each other's emotions or thoughts, the two started to hatch a plan.

And now that plan, after weeks of strategizing and diligence, had finally come to fruition.

Uzochi took a deep breath, trying to unburden himself of all that he carried on his shoulders. He let go of Zuberi's hand and beckoned for her and Tasha to move forward, to leave the confines of the Seventh Avenue alleyway and cross Fifty-Ninth Street to enter Central Park. They hooked a left and nonchalantly made their way to the Sheep Meadow section of the park, just a trio of St. John Soldiers heading back Up High. Nothing to notice there.

Then Uzochi glanced across the street, his heart sinking when he saw the holo-news billboard displaying breaking news.

EMERGENCY LEGISLATIVE SESSION CONVENES . . .
PARANORMAL REGISTRATION ACT PASSED . . .
OFFICIAL PROTOCOLS TO BE ANNOUNCED . . .

Shit, shit, shit.

Uzochi shook his head, remembering he had to stay on mission. He glanced up at the sky city elevator towers yet again, never having dreamed in a million years that these would be the conditions under which he would ascend. He'd made so many mistakes since awakening, been so self-absorbed since getting his powers, but today, he could at least right one of the wrongs Nubians had endured.

Today, they would get Vriana back.

Chapter 2

Zuberi

As Zuberi walked through Central Park with Uzochi and Tasha, she felt the same hum in her body she experienced when training, which was good. Exactly what she needed for what they were about to accomplish. When she'd been learning the fighting forms with her father, Thato had told her to keep the final goal in her mind at all times, whether it was taking down an opponent or seeking to flee or simply exulting in exercise. *Hold your goal like a target,* he would command, *and visualize yourself achieving it with every blow or kick or turn or twist.*

Each day that your muscles ache after a day of training is a day that your body is breaking and building itself anew, he would say. *And remember, the body and mind can do seemingly impossible things.* Of course, Zuberi hadn't known then the *seemingly impossible things* her father had been describing. She hadn't known that being Nubian meant more to him than just hailing from a particular land. Zuberi had learned, as she came into her own precognitive powers, that Thato had once been

18

tied to the kinetic energy that flowed through Nubians. It was only a few weeks ago, right before the fire that destroyed the Carter-Combs, that he'd finally revealed what his gift was before it was taken from him like all adult Nubians.

For most of his life, her father had possessed heightened senses, being able to see the color of a condor's feathers soaring high in the sky, or hear the roar of a waterfall leagues away, or detect a coming earth tremor by the minute tilting of the ground. Zuberi wasn't exactly surprised, as this sort of gift made sense considering her dad's on-guard persona. But she did feel like she was getting to know another side of him, which filled her with a type of astonishment.

"I have observed you, daughter," Thato said that evening, causing Zuberi's eyes to snap up as they sat among the stands, the theater nearly deserted. "You have a limited view of what your gift can do."

Zuberi didn't understand. She opened her mouth to respond, indignant that she was hearing such a rude critique from a man who'd harbored major secrets for most of her life. But before she could say anything, Thato stood up and gestured for her to do the same. He assumed one of the standard fighting-form stances. And even though, after a long day, she was so tired that even her bones seemed to ache, Zuberi mirrored him. True devotees of the forms never turned down an opportunity to practice.

Thato didn't tell her when he was about to begin. He simply danced, arms and legs striking out as she parried him. She was slower than she wanted to be, struggling to keep up with each of his fluid, perfectly executed moves.

"You're using the forms well, as usual, Zuberi," he said, though he didn't sound as impressed as she wanted him to. "Now, look for my phantoms."

Zuberi nodded, knowing that her father was referring to the visions that came to her when she used her Nubian gift of precognition: she would see ghostlike images floating above the bodies of her subjects. These phantoms, as she often referred to them, represented the potential future selves of whoever she was focusing on.

She tried to do as her father requested but found herself unable to track Thato's future selves while volleying against his blows. His phantoms moved in an unmistakable blur above him. When he landed a hit to her stomach, she stumbled back in frustration.

"It's impossible," she said, frustrated, hating that she felt like she was going to cry. "I can't focus on your future selves and our sparring at the same time."

"And that's precisely the problem," Thato said. "You're treating the future and the fight as two separate things, your powers and the forms. But they're one and the same."

He struck for her face, and she instinctively blocked him with her forearms, trying to grasp what he was getting at. He moved for her stomach, and she kicked up with her knee.

"You've heard this from Adisa. When Nubian children are trained, they're taught that their gifts should be as natural to them as breathing, will *become* as natural to them as breathing," Thato continued. "Your power is an extension of you, of the wisdom you will gain. When you move your arm, use your opponent's future self *to guide* your movement."

She missed blocking one of his kicks, which landed on her side. Zuberi winced at the pain. Thato stepped back, gesturing at her face as she breathed hard.

"Let go of the dimensions of this world and embrace your second sight," he told her. "Rely on your ability."

Her mouth dropped open. "What?"

He grinned. "Trust your dad, all right? Ignore this world and focus on the phantoms in your mind. Follow them. Close your eyes if you must."

"But how will I know the path you'll choose?" Zuberi countered. "Whenever I use my gift, I see the different paths someone might take. You have different futures—"

"You're a fighter, Zuberi, a warrior, someone whose instincts are practically second to none," Thato said. "You *know* how to fight, how to effectively use your intuition. That's part of you, part of how you interpret your visions. Or rather how you should. Look for the clues that will allow you to predict the future when you fight."

Zuberi didn't get a chance to fully absorb her father's advice. He came at her again, striking out with his fist as she barely managed to block him.

"Focus on your second sight!" he bellowed. "Let my phantoms guide your actions."

Zuberi groaned, trying to understand his orders even if it meant she'd be knocked on her behind at any minute. Her father could be a real pain. How the hell was she supposed to fight him if she only focused on his phantoms, if she wasn't fully in the real world, here and now? That was what the forms were supposed to be all about.

Your power is an extension of you, of the wisdom you will gain.

She watched Thato as she shifted from side to side, readying for his attack. She tried to pay close attention to his tells, how he liked to stay nimble on the balls of his feet, how he favored his left arm slightly over his right.

As per usual, his potential future selves appeared above him. But this time she gathered herself and blocked out the present, following her father's advice, focusing all her attention on his phantoms. The change was immediate. They were no longer the intangible, faint blurs she thought might be ghosts the first time she saw them. They were fully formed, almost as clear as Thato himself in the real world. They each enacted different motions, one squatting down for a swift swivel kick, another leaning into a left hook, and another leaping forward.

There . . . the one preparing to kick . . . that phantom was a bit more solid, a tad brighter.

Yes.

That was her father's most likely path, clear as day. She knew it in her heart.

Zuberi processed all of this in seconds, barely leaping in time to dodge his attack, counterattacking with a light elbow jab on his right shoulder. Thato rolled forward, stood up, and turned to his daughter, his face stern.

"Do you understand?" he asked.

Zuberi nodded. She did understand. She had far more control over her ability to predict the future than she'd thought.

Zuberi was reenergized, ready to spar all evening if she had to now that she'd unlocked this new understanding of her gift. It was unbelievable. Her father suddenly had a hard time landing most of his blows, clearly amused as he realized how quickly his daughter had understood the lesson he'd meant to impart. And Zuberi realized a wonderful truth: It didn't matter which path Thato wanted to choose as they fought. It mattered which path she could force him down, the one that would work best for her.

As they continued to spar, one of Thato's phantoms came toward her, punching straight-on, but then wavered backward. He'd been hit. Zuberi knew what to do. She moved forward, feinting left and then right, before drawing him into making another punch straight-on. She ducked and landed a hard blow to his chest that sent him stumbling to the floor. Zuberi stood still, the air seeming to crackle around her.

She'd done it. She'd effectively combined her power with the fighting forms.

Zuberi had spent the entire night sparring with Thato, relying on this new knowledge of her gift, too amped up to sleep. She was faster now, gaining confidence in differentiating which of her father's phantoms indicated a more likely future. She was finally beginning to understand her power in a way that could be useful, that would make her a contender.

Before everything that had happened two months ago, Zuberi had thought she knew exactly what she wanted. She craved revolution, to use the fighting forms she'd sewn into the fabric of her body and spirit to challenge the system that Krazen St. John had imprisoned Nubians in. She was ready, especially after she'd seen Uzochi face his own challenges head-on at the theater and at the Swamp seawall. Zuberi had worried that he was going to turn his back on the Nubian community, but then, on that day, he'd proven to everyone that he truly deserved the title of catalyst, that he would prioritize the needs of his people above all else.

Her feelings for Uzochi had developed into more than admiration, if Zuberi was being honest with herself. She saw in him a boy who wasn't afraid of her strength and assertiveness, a boy who found her power and prowess with the fighting forms genuinely thrilling. He never asked her to be small for the sake of his own ego, and in fact always seemed to be cheering her on. The awakenings were weird, tough, but she knew she'd get through it with Uzochi having her back.

But then.

Then, she'd made a terrible realization.

Vriana, her best friend, was gone, taken by a vile, sneaky St. John Soldier.

Zuberi still remembered the scream that burst from her body when she realized what had happened, when everyone was running to and fro in the Swamp after Uzochi had saved them from the flood. How she couldn't get ahold of Vriana no matter how frantically she tried to reach the girl via mobile, how she was consumed by nausea when she realized that she'd witnessed Vriana's abduction in one of her precognitive visions hours earlier, not comprehending what she was seeing. Zuberi had dropped to her knees right in the middle of the Swamp, right into a pool of water that had gathered from the flooding, and had begun to wail, her fists at her side.

It was a type of pain she hadn't known lived inside her, a pain she didn't think she'd ever get past, no matter how much Uzochi and her father tried to console her. Every night,

Zuberi was wracked by nightmares of what might be happening to Vriana. The elders tried to assure her that the girl was most likely alive, that there would be no reason for the militia to hurt her. But every day Zuberi woke up wondering if today was the day when it would be too late, when something irrevocably terrible had happened to her best friend.

The absolute worst was when Zuberi broke the news to Vriana's only living relative, her aunt Ekua. The woman had been fortunate that her shack-on-stilts home had survived the flooding, a small space that she shared with Vriana, from which she ran her T-shirt design business. Her possessions were intact, but after learning of the kidnapping, Ekua walked as if she was no longer human. She became a ghost who haunted the halls of her house in the Swamp and then her new makeshift home in the Jungle, one of many Nubians to move into the old, abandoned Divine HQ. Ekua would sit alone, her eyes glassy, speaking little to anyone except a couple of the elders. Sometimes Zuberi would go sit beside her, but she didn't offer the woman any empty words. Others might pat her shoulder and pull Ekua into a hug, saying it would be okay, but Zuberi knew how words could be knives that cut and twisted and pulled. The only thing that would guarantee Vriana's safety would be to get her from Krazen St. John's clutches.

And so, Zuberi had planned.

She'd first approached a group of elders on the street while they were in the middle of organizing Nubians to leave the Swamp, declaring that they needed to confront Krazen right away, that all able-bodied Nubians needed to march up to Central Park and the elevator towers and hold a demonstration.

They would let the world know exactly what Krazen had done, that he and his soldiers were in the business of kidnapping innocent children.

Beka, the elder who seemed to be everywhere, having clearly been chosen to run things with Adisa gone, had tilted her head and given Zuberi a pitying look. "I understand your pain, child," she'd said, her voice firm. "And I'm furious as well. But, really, what proof do we have? There's no recorded evidence showing that Vriana was taken by a soldier, as you claim."

"*CLAIM?*" Zuberi yelled. "Beka, no disrespect, but I know what I'm talking about. This isn't in my head, okay?"

The elder had raised her hands, trying to calm Zuberi down. "And I believe you, please know I do, Zuberi. But Krazen and his forces could easily assert that Vriana has gone missing as a result of the flood. Or that she's yet another Nubian who ran away from home or tragically succumbed to the ravages of Elevation. They will not simply return her because we've confronted them. We will get Vriana back, I assure you, but we must be strategic. We've all learned how much of a snake Krazen St. John truly is, and as we maneuver, we must take into account all possible repercussions for our community."

Zuberi had kept her fists by her side as Beka spoke, knowing that the elder was making sense, that she was right. But honestly it didn't matter. She wanted to scream again, a new scream that wasn't born of pain but of fury. And she might have let loose and railed at all of them if Uzochi hadn't taken her hand one afternoon and promised he would help her.

"We'll get Vriana back," he said as they stood together in the Jungle, surrounded by nonstop activity from other Nubians settling in. "I promise."

And so the two had pored over every blueprint, pamphlet, and holo ever made about the Up High that they could get their hands on. They'd visited the Sheep Meadow section of Central Park where the elevator towers to the sky city stood and created new maps, which they studied diligently.

Zuberi noted how Uzochi made sure to carve out time to be with her and work on this every day, no matter how many Nubians he helped awaken to their gifts, no matter how many elders wanted him to telepathically scan the floor of a building to make sure it was safe for habitation, no matter how distracted he was becoming with Adisa's memories floating in his head. She'd begun to notice how handsome he was as they sat in a foyer that had become their meeting space and studied the information they'd gathered on the Up High. Back at school, Uzochi had been fastidious about maintaining his cornrows and cultivating a preppy schoolboy style, favoring neutral colors. But now he often wore his hair out in a wavy afro, the clothes he wore much baggier and eclectic, more colorful and unrefined. His arms were sometimes bare in sleeveless tees he would put on when the day was particularly hot. In fact, she wondered, where exactly was he getting these clothes? Maybe borrowing them from his friend Sekou.

Uzochi had become looser, edgier, not caring anymore about being the perfect preceptor's pet, an insult some of their schoolmates used to throw at him that she thought was cruel.

Even as she fretted about Vriana day and night, Zuberi had found herself turned on by this suddenly sexy boy who was sitting by her side, sending her waves of encouragement and admiration with his empathy.

As the two studied the Up High, Sekou helped them out as well. Thanks to Uzochi, he'd come into his ability to astral-project, to send his soul from his body as an invisible, incorporeal entity. At first, he could only project for around ten to fifteen minutes, his spirit getting a woozy feeling that signaled it was time for him to return to his body. But gradually, with practice and more practice, Sekou was able to send his soul forth for two to three hours, with his corporeal body lying in the Jungle, usually watched over by his brother, Abdul. As Sekou had gained proficiency with his gift, the boy had soared to the Up High in his spirit form, getting the lay of the land and seeing what information he could gather. He'd come back with reports of the magnificent buildings that existed there along with the cars that flew high above the streets and the masses of people who were practically cyborgs with their implants that opened doors and projected holos. He still hadn't been able to figure out exactly where Krazen lived and worked. But, as his spirit form was undetectable, he would hover around St. John Soldiers as often as he could, trying to catch pieces of information that could provide clues as to Vriana's whereabouts.

And did you find out anything? Did they mention her? Zuberi would ask. And always Sekou would shake his head no, sadness in his eyes.

But Zuberi and Uzochi wouldn't give up. They'd pitched a different version of a plan to the elders, and each time, they'd been shot down and told to refine. When Zuberi revealed the plan that she and Uzochi were most proud of, infiltrating the Up High as St. John Soldiers and tracking down Vriana using Uzochi's telepathy, Beka had frowned at her and sighed.

"Realistically, how will you avoid detection?" the elder asked. "St. John Soldiers are so regulated. Surely they have standard codes and procedures that dictate their movements, how they speak to each other, effectively mobilize, that sort of thing. Even with Sekou's observations and Uzochi's ability to read minds, you have nowhere near enough information to convincingly imitate their protocols. And to be practical, what are you going to do, steal their uniforms?"

Zuberi had wanted to reply that she had no problem with stealing uniforms. She would be fine with sneaking up on one of the nighttime militia lower-city patrols, pulling aside a couple of St. John Soldiers, knocking their asses out with her staff or fists or feet (hopefully taking out some teeth), stripping them down to their undies, and voilà—uniforms. But perhaps sensing what was about to come out of her mouth, Uzochi had gently touched Zuberi's arm and said, "I have an idea."

He had vanished for about ten minutes as Zuberi left the elders and waited in another room, lost in thought, wondering how they could tweak their plan. When he reappeared in the doorway, he was holding something in his hand, an article of clothing. A black jumpsuit, Zuberi realized as she inspected the garment. She arched an eyebrow.

"You're trying to make me feel better about everything by giving me a . . . catsuit?" Zuberi asked. "I mean, is this really the best time?"

Uzochi laughed. "Not quite," he said. "But could you put it on? I have a point, I promise."

She was suspicious, even a little annoyed, but the earnestness in Uzochi's eyes got her every time. So she sighed as she took the jumpsuit in her hands. And then, because it was Uzochi, he placed his arms behind his back and turned around. Zuberi couldn't help but smile.

They had kissed plenty of times now—and boy could he kiss, a surprise considering that Uzochi had limited dating experience—but he was still thoughtful when it came to her body, always giving her space, never making assumptions. He knew what she'd been through and constantly respected her boundaries. And she appreciated that, most of the time, but sometimes . . .

Sometimes she wanted him to get as lost in their kisses as she did and then they could just give themselves over to passion, enjoying each other. But that was a thought for another time.

She stood in the corner, took off the tee and jeans she wore, and pulled on the jumpsuit. It was a decent fit—though, like everything that Nubians had to piece together, it wasn't perfect. It was tight on her calves but loose on her shoulders. Good enough, though.

"Well," she said, "here it is." She felt a little silly, like perhaps she should turn around to show off the outfit. She imagined Vriana's voice in her head. *Mmm-mmm-mmm, girl, you better twirl. You need to show your man what you're working with.* And with that voice, the ache in Zuberi's heart returned.

Uzochi had turned around, taking her in, nodding thoughtfully. Then, when she was about to snap at him and ask what the hell was going on, he spoke.

"I'm going to try something," he said. "With my gift. Just . . . bear with me, okay? It may not totally work."

She stared at him. Part of her wanted more of an explanation, but the other part was curious. His eyes slid closed and his face took on the expression that she knew well at that point. He was connecting to the kinetic in a way he wasn't used to, same as he had when he'd saved their schoolmate Zaire during his awakening and when, weeks later, he'd connected to every awoken Nubian in New York with his mind. Lately it was the same face he made when he was grappling with Adisa's memories.

"Uzochi," Zuberi said after a moment, "what, exactly, am I supposed to be—"

She stopped speaking and gasped as she felt a slight tingle around her body and looked down. She was no longer wearing the suit. She was now clad in one of the uniforms worn by St. John Soldiers, down to the exact threading of their crewneck sweaters and vests and trousers. She reached out her arms, examining how comfortable the clothing felt, how the fabric moved seamlessly.

"Wow, electric! It totally worked," Uzochi said, smiling a slightly weary smile. "Well, almost."

"How'd you do this?" Zuberi asked. "And . . . when?"

"I've been working on this for a little while now, but the

technique's not perfect," he said, then nodded at her feet. The sneakers she wore were still the same. "It's a very precise form of telekinesis. I'm going deep and analyzing items like clothing on a microscopic structural level, and then I'm creating the appropriate molecular shift to create something new. It works best if the original article of clothing is as simple as possible, like a jumpsuit." He winked and gave a tiny grin. "I'm not sure if I'm supposed to use my gifts like this, like if this is a betrayal of the Nubian way when it comes to spiritual powers of the mind, but hey, I figured I should put my science classes to use. Shoes are a problem, way beyond me for now, but I think we can easily find some boots to match what St. John Soldiers stomp around in. As long as I have a clean canvas to project onto, I can create our uniforms."

"For how many people?" Zuberi asked, hope building in her chest. One problem, solved.

He scratched his head. "Only like two or three at a time, I think, and then I need to rest. When I've practiced this on myself, things start getting fuzzy after three transformations—at least, if I'm doing other things. And when we go Up High, I'll need to be actively scanning guards and different people, right?"

"Waitaminnit here, you've been doing this on yourself." She put two and two together. "Is that where you've been getting your new threads?"

Uzochi said nothing and just looked up at her bashfully, batting his eyes.

Zuberi had gotten up bright and early the next day, eager to see how they could finesse their plans just a bit more to convince Beka and the other elders. But then a miracle had occurred. Another Nubian had awoken, one of the quietest of them all.

Zuberi had barely known the shy girl Tasha who used to hang around the Carter-Combs Theater, who Uzochi also knew from his early-morning special elective class. Tasha had displayed no gifts for some time, comfortable with observing the other kids and being a nurturing, mostly silent presence. She seemed content to draw on her little sketch pad, creating different portraits of the Children. Apparently she was quite the artist, which even Uzochi hadn't realized. And then that morning, less than twelve hours after Zuberi had donned the catsuit, Tasha had stood in the middle of the main floor of the Jungle, spread her arms, and released a sparkling three-dimensional portrait of Uzochi that floated in the air.

"I think I've awoken to my gift," Tasha said, blinking with a stunned expression at what floated in front of her.

Though she was momentarily taken aback to see that Tasha had created a portrait of Uzochi (was something going on between them?), Zuberi shook it off and quickly grasped the larger picture. Tasha had the power to create images made from light. Wholly convincing images. Illusions.

And so Zuberi and Uzochi had immediately amended their plan to rescue Vriana, incorporating Tasha into the mix. The three of them would only need to appear as St. John Soldiers for the elevator ride Up High. Once they reached their destination, Tasha could use illusions to help them blend in as regular sky city kids until they found Vriana. For the most part, they wouldn't need to worry about St. John Soldier protocols.

"I'm not sure I can allow this to happen," Beka said to Zuberi and Uzochi, even after she had begrudgingly admitted that the plan had merit. "Tasha has just awoken, her gifts still foreign to her. And Uzochi is our catalyst. You and he are the most powerful of the Children, so valuable to the community. What if you're hurt? Captured?"

Uzochi stepped forward. "I've sat with Tasha, Beka, and she'd actually awoken some time ago, her connection to the kinetic waiting to be expressed until she felt brave enough to do so openly." He raised his chin as he spoke, standing a bit straighter. "I know this mission is dangerous, but as your catalyst, that's a chance I'm willing to take. Vriana's our friend. And as your catalyst, I say this is what we've decided to do. And we won't be stopped."

With those words, Zuberi thought she might lose it completely then and there, she wanted to hug and kiss Uzochi so much. With those words, Beka had simply bowed her head, as she often did in his presence.

And then the real preparations had begun, with Thato relying on his security-business connections to provide the trio with Tasers and batons similar in make and look to what St. John Soldiers routinely carried. (Zuberi had known how her father would feel about the plan, and for the first time in her life she threatened him: If he didn't let her go on this mission, she wouldn't speak to him or deal with him in any way ever again, proclaiming that with everything that had gone down, she had options and didn't need to live in his house. Thato knew his daughter well and completely believed her.) Uzochi sat with Tasha for days, going over again and again how to create illusions that seemed real and lifelike, that had depth and folds, that mirrored how people moved. Meanwhile, Zuberi practiced the forms in a makeshift training area in the basement of the Jungle, focusing on key defensive and offensive maneuvers in case they were confronted Up High. She even took Tasha aside and taught her basic sparring moves designed for hurting your opponent and fleeing.

And now they were here. The elevators waited for them just a couple hundred feet away. And Vriana waited for them Up High.

"Let's do this," Uzochi said in a low voice as they approached Sheep Meadow, the looming elevator shafts right in front of them. She noticed a couple of clusters of real St. John Soldiers standing on the side while a few people exited elevator cars to make their way into the park. Zuberi knew that Uzochi was using his telepathy to scan minds left and right, quietly and quickly, just as she was using her precognition to pay close attention to the phantoms that floated above the militiamen's heads, preparing for any sudden moves that indicated that they'd been detected.

Thankfully, the coast was clear.

Zuberi inhaled, exhaled. She was ready.

Together, the trio started for the elevators.

Chapter 3

Lencho

Energy and opportunity, those were the words that now defined Lencho's world.

Lencho loved living Up High. He loved the clean gray walls of the training center he got to spar in, the glistening rows of stainless-steel polymer weights and machines that waited for him along the edges of the room. He loved the feeling of the slightly padded floor that allowed him to bounce on his heels as he charged around the state-of-the-art track at speeds of up to fifty miles per hour. (The gym sensors that tracked his every move never lied, and he knew if he really wanted to, he could run faster.) But most of all, he loved that all he needed to do was make a gesture and someone was there to tend to him.

Just now, as he raised his hand and a St. John servant scurried over to hand him a bottle of water, a grin spread across Lencho's face. He smiled all the time now, the attitudinal grumpiness he'd become known for back in high school gone. And why shouldn't he smile? He was finally being treated the way he deserved. Before his ascension, how had he ever thought he could have lived in the Rotting Jungle, with its nauseating odors of trash and filth and vermin? How had he ever put up with his tiny, plain bedroom at his parents' apartment down in Old Chelsea, feeling like his father was holding him prisoner whenever the entire family was home? Just the thought of those spaces, of that sickening, oppressive *life,* made Lencho's entire body tense up. Thankfully, he'd found ways to ease the stress.

His days were now defined by how much and how often he could drain. Since ascending more than two months ago along with the rest of his gang, the Divine, he'd figured out ways in which to leech the life essence of others in ways big and small, whether during training or casual touching during conversations or at night during parties. Among the waves of awakenings that had happened in the lower city, he was the only Nubian who possessed the power to lay his hands upon others and take portions of their life energy to use in whatever way he saw fit. This was what gave him the superhuman strength, speed, and agility he'd become renowned for on the news and social media holos, with broadcasters constantly replaying in slo-mo how he'd rushed into the flooding Swamp to get bystanders to safety. This was what gave him the magnificently muscular physique he hadn't possessed before awakening, what gave his skin a shimmering luster unrivaled even by the contouring tech used by sky city dwellers. His gift was what made him wondrously unique, the standout leader among Krazen's new specialized militia. As Lencho's estimation of himself and his abilities grew by leaps and bounds, his new inner voice would speak to him, egging him on, encouraging him to embrace his greatness.

Sure, there'd been setbacks. Two of the Divine had gotten into a nasty argument just weeks earlier. Lara, the only telepath among the gang, and Nneka, their teleporter, had never liked 'each other back in the lower city, and tempers flared when the two girls locked horns in the training center over Krazen's recruiting process. Sick of being labeled an annoying know-it-all, Lara had tore into Nneka's mind, causing the other girl's teleportation gifts to go awry. Nneka had started to port all over the place, shrieking in pain, and swept Lara up in her arms right before vanishing completely. The two girls hadn't been heard from since.

The rest of the Divine had been devastated for days, and Krazen's spirits had flagged upon losing a pair of such valuable assets. And so Lencho had done everything he could to be the soldier the sky king needed, continuing to get his gang into shape, reminding them that their skanky lower-city days were over. That their future path as St. John Soldiers 2.0 was bright.

He took a long pull from the water bottle before grabbing a pair of dumbbells—250 pounds each, specially made for him—and then started his reps. He watched other awoken Nubians train in the gym, manifesting an assortment of gifts that Krazen St. John had deduced would appear if one was pushed to the limit in just the right way, at just the right moment. Regular observers would find their gifts magnificent: Look at that one there in the corner, straining to levitate an exercise ball with her mind, and another one over there by the mirror, shooting sparks of yellow-and-blue electricity from his fingertips. Yes, it was spectacular, something that normal residents of the Up High still couldn't quite believe when they witnessed the Divine in action, even though they were pretty extraordinary themselves with their cybernetic implants.

But Lencho's observations of kinetic gifts at play meant nothing to him when compared to seeing each of his peers as a body of bristling energy, their aura catching his eye. It was how he saw everyone, Nubian and non-Nubian alike. But when it came to Nubians with kinetic gifts, for almost a month now their auras had beckoned to him in a way he couldn't explain. The energy gleaming off their bodies was rich, thick, a cornucopia of color and visceral sensation that he could practically taste. Lencho had become so attuned to the energy of his fellow Divine that he had slowly begun to realize that he could practically track their location, whether they were hanging in the nearby dormitory that they all shared or wandering around another section of the Up High, though Krazen mostly kept his gifted Nubians on a tight leash. It was a weird sixth sense that he chalked up to his powers morphing and changing over time.

It was a no-brainer why Krazen had selected him to run the Divine, to be in charge of all Nubians with gifts, who would make up the most spectacular militia Tri-State East and the Up High had ever seen. In fact, Krazen had declared that any Nubian families that wished to ascend and move to the Up High could do so. Their needs would be fully taken care of, with the caveat that all teenagers would be examined. But hardly any families had taken him up on the offer;

Krazen had more luck with Nubian kids who were orphaned or estranged from their relatives in some way. The registration act he'd helped create would put an end to the nonsense, with gifted Nubians having no choice but to be observed and trained for his militia.

The newest addition to Krazen's army of "special" Nubians was working a punching bag with one of the Divine, a kid who went by the name Sajah. Aren was showing the boy how to hold his fists so that the strike wouldn't injure his thumb. But it was apparent to anyone watching—and that included Lencho and the ever-present St. John Soldiers and employees scattered throughout the gigantic space—that the boy was no fighter. He moved hesitantly, barely extending his thin arms forward and lurching back after each tentative stab at the bag.

"You're wasting your time," Lencho said, dropping the weights he'd been holding so that they slammed on the floor, causing the boy to yelp.

"Ey, leave it alone, bruh," Aren said as Lencho strode up. "Sajah's just getting used to this."

"There's no time for 'getting used to this,'" Lencho said, putting a whine in his voice to taunt Aren. He crossed his arms over his chest. "Krazen needs us to be top-notch, and this dude clearly doesn't have what it takes."

"I'm not a dude, and you need to quit calling me 'he,'" Sajah said. "My correct pronouns are 'they' and 'them.' It's 2098, fool. I shouldn't have to tell you that." Sajah's dark eyes dipped to Lencho's crossed arms and back up again, a scowl overtaking their pinched features.

"Man, just go back to your weight lifting," Aren said, voice full of the authority that had bossed Lencho around for too long. Lencho shifted his gaze, narrowing his eyes at the former head of their gang.

Lencho guessed that, technically, the older boy was still the official leader of the Divine. There had been no formal stripping of his title, but everyone Up High knew that Aren was no longer in charge. Not after he'd gone off the deep end and tried to divorce himself from Krazen when he'd realized that the sky king was responsible for distributing Elevation across the lower city. Aren, who saw drug dealing as a necessary evil that the Divine only participated in for currency, who tried his best to avoid hooking young Nubians, was working with a kingpin who'd destroyed countless lives for the sake of profit.

After a few days of moping around Manhattan, Aren was confronted by a couple of the Divine who'd gone down to the lower city to beg his ass to come back Up High. And surprisingly, Aren had indeed returned to the sky, apologizing to Krazen in front of everyone, mumbling something about wanting to be there for his crew no matter what. But Lencho knew the truth. Just like the rest of the gang, Aren had devoured the oh-so-sweet fruit of ascension. Living poor and broke back in lower New York, even as a gifted Nubian, wasn't going to cut it.

No, Aren's time as Divine leader was over. The gang had only one leader now, Krazen St. John, which meant that every time Aren tried to throw his weight around, it pissed Lencho the hell off.

Lencho's lips curved into a smirk as he turned his attention back to Sajah.

"What's your power, anyway?" Lencho demanded. "Ain't that what you should be working on? Your ass obviously can't fight."

Sajah blinked at Lencho, their scowl deepening, a flash of something smoky and gray passing across their eyes. So something was already happening with their gifts after all. Krazen had maintained that Nubians would theoretically awaken when faced with stress of some kind, and that seemed to be the case for most recruits. After weeks of having different Nubians trotted into the training center, Lencho wasn't disturbed by the types of kids who wound up here, usually scraggly and way too scrappy, down and out without a penny to their name or any family to rely on. None of them were as powerful as he was. He could ignore this loser. A crazy eye trick wasn't going to unsettle him.

"Lencho," Aren warned in a low voice, stepping forward. "Leave Sajah alone. You need to go back to your own training."

Now Lencho met his former leader's gaze head-on. Whereas the Up High clearly agreed with Lencho, he could see the grayish tint to Aren's skin, the sunken quality of his cheeks. He'd lost weight, too, which didn't make any sense when one considered the bounty of the sky. Aren had become a shadow of his former self.

"Yeah, who are you anyway?" Sajah said to Lencho, defiance in their voice. "Who put you in charge?"

Now, this made Lencho jump. Everyone knew him. Or

they knew of him from his exploits with Krazen St. John, from the demonstrations of Lencho's powers constantly featured throughout the city as part of the sky king's mayoral campaign. Lencho powerlifting an aerial cycle over his head. Lencho completing a specially designed quarter-mile outdoor obstacle course in less than a minute. Lencho leaping high in the air past corporate holos as he held a glittering KRAZEN ST. JOHN FOR MAYOR banner, with Aren using his light powers to create fireworks. There was no way this kid didn't know that Lencho was a star. Sajah was pretending, trying to make Lencho feel small, just like his dad used to, just like some of those assholes back in high school.

Lencho refused to ever feel small again.

"I'm Lencho, Lencho Will, but I think you know that," he said. "And I think you're fucking with me."

Lencho sent his foot out before Sajah had time to react, sweeping behind their ankles and toppling them to the ground. As Sajah fell, splayed on their back, Lencho brought his elbow up and sank it into their midsection. Sajah grunted, squirming under the weight. Lencho knew that if he wanted to, he could rip out the kid's stomach, wondering if he should to teach the numbskull a lesson.

"Always prepare for the unexpected," Lencho said, his voice a hard growl as he yanked Sajah back up to stand. "Don't think your opponent's gonna wait for you to be ready just because you're talking junk. That was a standard rule to be part of the Divine."

"I didn't—" they croaked, but Lencho was already moving,

volleying his fists toward Sajah's chest, purposely tapping them lightly, though if he wanted to he could punch the kid clear across the gym.

"Lencho!" Aren's voice called through the thrum of blood that was crowding Lencho's mind. "Take it down a notch, bruh."

But what purpose would that serve? Krazen demanded excellence, perfection. Lencho was used to the sky king coming to the training center, watching the recruits, assessing how they could be useful to his larger plans. These new kids weren't good enough. Not yet. And that was because Aren wasn't willing to push.

None of it made any sense. No one had ever taken it easy on Lencho, who'd learned to toughen up when he was seven after his father, Kefle, started whupping his ass for no damn reason. And years later, when he took up with the Divine? He'd had to fight his way in. They all did. This kid Sajah was, what, fifteen maybe? They should've learned how to handle their shit a long time ago. How had they survived?

"Stop being on the defensive, kid," Lencho snapped. "Fight back."

But Sajah refused to follow orders. They slowly backed away from Lencho, who continued to stalk forward, undeterred.

"You a real Nubian or not?" Lencho snarled, fists snapping out. "What's going on with those eyes of yours? Use your fuckin' power."

"Enough, Lencho."

A hand caught Lencho's shoulder, and he whirled around, ready to crush Aren's fingers.

Only the hand wasn't Aren's. It was too big, too rough and unearthly. The hand on Lencho's shoulder belonged to Zaire, and he'd transformed.

Lencho realized that all eyes were on the group of boys as Zaire towered above them, his eight-foot rock form a huge, imposing mass of moving earth that shouldn't have been possible. Even after several weeks of seeing the Nubian boy use his gift during training, everybody stared at Zaire whenever he morphed. His ability to transform into walking, talking stone was practically unbelievable, with the usual reactions ranging from astonishment to abject horror. Krazen had decreed that Zaire should never use his gift in public outside of emergencies, that he was simply too frightening. Thus Zaire's primary objectives were to learn how to move in rock form, endure the constant tests that Krazen's people subjected him to, and practice combat techniques.

Lencho's chest heaved as he breathed hard, glaring up at Zaire, into the stony cracks that he knew passed for eyes. In truth, the boy was the only one who rivaled Lencho among the Divine for the amount of time spent in the training center. Zaire was ever-present there, a quiet, steady force lifting weights or running laps or following the direction of the scientists who sought to understand the contours of his gift. Though he was the gentlest of the Divine, Zaire was the only one of the crew who had a type of power that actually made him a contender with Lencho. This truth tugged at Lencho again as Zaire loomed over everyone, even as his inner voice reminded him that he was still the strongest, the fiercest.

"You can't push Sajah too hard," Zaire said, his voice low and scratchy, a weird distortion that got on Lencho's nerves. "They won't stay if you do."

Zaire's eyes flitted back to Sajah, and when Lencho looked over his shoulder, he saw that Aren was beside them, talking quickly, helping the frightened kid steady themself. Shame momentarily coursed through Lencho when he saw how Sajah was shaking, but that feeling was swiftly replaced by rage.

"I'm the only one here doing what Krazen asked," Lencho said, ripping his shoulder away from Zaire. "He needs us to be on top of our game, to be perfect soldiers, to show that his path for the awoken is the only way. You're all too fuck-ing soft."

"Lencho," Zaire said, his voice measured, as if he was talk-ing to a tempestuous child. "We're all doing what we can. But pushing the recruits like this . . . it'll only send them to the Children. Which is the last thing Krazen wants. I mean, you gotta know that."

At Zaire's words, Lencho's rage multiplied, a sharp, al-most painful burst of energy. Fiery, red-hot. Sweat formed on his brow as he glowered at the other boy.

Why would they leave when you're the most powerful? When you deserve to lead?

It was an errant thought, but an infectious one. Lencho, after all, was the one who could absorb power and let it fill him like a battery. Lencho was the one who had helped save those pathetic "Children" in the Swamp who Uzochi had aligned himself with, and a host of other Nubians for that matter. And Uzochi . . . who cared that he could read someone's thoughts, or create force fields when he was stressed out? His cousin didn't have the spine to use his gifts properly, to be tough when necessary. But Lencho, he could rip someone apart with his bare hands if he wanted to or take their life away with the slightest touch. The thought settled in him as he looked back at Zaire and Aren, the two having stepped in front of Sajah. Others in the gym had stopped what they were doing to stare at the confrontation.

"If you're just going to coddle this kid, then you're leaving them to get eaten up by what's out there, to be mediocre!" Lencho shouted at Aren, letting his voice ring out, not caring who heard what he had to say. "You never did that with me, did you? No. Your ass was always telling me how a real member of the Divine wasn't afraid of shit, that we had to keep it real and rough all the damn time."

Lencho spat on the floor. A few onlookers gasped and grimaced, like he was an uncouth barbarian. Finally, Lencho saw something akin to his old gang leader's fury flicker in his eyes. As much as Aren had his ethics when it came to dealing drugs, he could readily whup ass when necessary. Aren's hands glowed faintly, displaying his power to wield light. Lencho knew that Aren had been diligently training in the center, working hard to go beyond just bedazzling folks out of their minds, striving to create actual lasers. Something dangerous, deadly, becoming a real asset to Krazen. But he was nowhere close to perfecting the technique.

"How dare you, *bruh*," Lencho said, taunting Aren. "Krazen

has given us everything, and your ass can't even hold up your end of the bargain."

Aren shook his head, a pitying look taking over his face. "Lencho, like I told you when we were back at the Jungle, you need to learn some self-control. I'm tired of your attitude. You think just 'cause you kiss Krazen's ass all the time, we're supposed to bow to *you* now?"

A roar in his inner ear, that was all Lencho could hear. Red took over his vision. Fire filled his bones. Lencho strode straight for Aren, readying his fists. This had been a long time coming. Draining him of energy would be too good for Aren. He would totally pound his head and nuts into the floor, break his arms and legs. Who was this fucker talking to? He could—

In a flash, Sajah was standing in front of Lencho, their skinny arms thrown up. For a second, the action caught Lencho off guard as he stared into the kid's terrified face. All right, didn't matter. He'd take care of Sajah first then.

Lencho seized them by the wrist, his first instinct being to drain.

Take it, now, said a voice in Lencho's head. *Take it all.*

Lencho hadn't realized that he'd shut his eyes, but they flew open then when he heard the voice, clearer and more distinct than ever. He dropped Sajah's arm, and the kid quickly skittered back. A flash of smoky blackness began to spew forth from Sajah's eyes, like a thick, nebulous cloud. The blackness swirled and spiraled and grew larger behind Sajah, startling Aren and Zaire, causing both boys to back away even as Lencho stood completely still, a coldness creeping across his skin.

Sajah looked around the room, at the flabbergasted faces

that gawked at them, and said, "Fuck you people up here. Y'all too crazy." And with that they turned around, ran, and leapt into the orb of black smoke that they'd just created. In seconds, the smoke dissipated and the cloud disappeared, taking Sajah with it.

Lencho stood slack-jawed, not sure what to do, only aware that after a collective pause the team of scientists and trainers who'd witnessed the event all started to make a hubbub, immediately getting on their internal comms or making holo-calls via their implants. Lencho felt a mixture of emotions—surprise, anxiety, embarrassment—realizing that he'd just done the thing Zaire had warned of, that he'd just run off one of Krazen's recruits. Someone who might've been a standout addition to the team.

He still wanted to fight somebody, but something in Lencho's spirit said he needed to take a break, to get out of the training center and clear his head and not cause more chaos. All too much.

Lencho walked down the steps of the center, eyes to the ground. The scent of hyacinths laced the air from one of the many floral groves found throughout Up High streets. He breathed in and out, trying to gather himself, even though red still lined his vision and a roar still filled his ears. Even though part of him wanted to run back into the gym and smash Aren's face in and drain Zaire and anyone else who had something nasty to say.

You're better than all of them, his inner voice said again. *Never forget that.*

Lencho nodded and ran his fingers through his hair,

mumbling to himself, "Damn right . . . I won't." He didn't care that passersby looked at him confusedly, wondering if he was talking to himself or having a conversation via personal comm on a tech implant. Dread started to fill his body as he realized he'd just made a grave mistake and let Krazen down. He'd lost control of his temper, gone too far. What would be the repercussions? Would he no longer be in charge?

As he sat with this, as he wondered if he should go to the sky king right away and try to explain what had happened, asking for forgiveness, a tingling moved throughout his body, followed by slight discomfort and an intense craving. The telltale sensations he had of late whenever he was interacting with the Divine, somehow sensing their gifts.

His sixth sense kicked in, telling him that more gifted Nubians were close besides those he'd just left in the gym. These other Nubians, they were powerful, within easy reach, though he wasn't sure exactly where they were. And there was one whose energy he knew far too well.

Noooo.

Was he imagining things? Was it because he was still so angry?

No. He knew that sensation from anywhere, would never forget it after what had happened at the Swamp, after he'd let a telepath enter his mind.

His cousin . . . it couldn't be, but Uzochi was nearby.

Somehow, Uzochi had reached the Up High.

Chapter 4

Sandra

"MAKE THE RIGHT CHOICE FOR AN EMPOWERED FUTURE . . . KRAZEN ST. JOHN, FOR A FUTURE NEW YORK . . ."

Sandra peered down at her father from a glass-encased private balcony among the stands of Selene Hall, her face lit up by one of the hologram billboards that circled the auditorium. She was surrounded by a small retinue of militiamen, having recently decided that it was in her best interests to appear more often in public with armed guards. Krazen spoke forcefully from an illuminated podium on the main stage, gesturing grandly as a humongous holo of his body was projected live above him for all to see.

"With the mayoral election a mere two weeks away, I call upon all denizens of New York to gather, to speak as one with your collective voice and make the best choice for all corners of our grand city," Krazen said, his voice reverberating through the hall. The space had become standing room only, a testament to the popularity of her father's rallies. Though

Sandra knew his voice was amplified by personal implants, she imagined that he required no assistance to be heard by the thousands who'd gathered. He spoke as if he could sway voters and win the election by force of will alone.

"As the warden of this city," he said, "as someone who for years has run a premier security force to keep New York and the rest of Tri-State East safe, you have my word that I will do everything in my power to protect the lifestyle in the sky you so richly deserve. These are dangerous times, as you know, with Nubians awakening to abilities that most of us would have deemed the stuff of fairy tales and myth. But I assure you, my friends, that what you have seen on the holos, what has been reported on the news and social media, is very, very true."

Faint murmurs made their way through the crowd. Sandra knew that most Up High residents had accepted the notion that there were now mystical individuals inhabiting their city. Yet quite a few still exhibited a healthy dose of skepticism, wondering if this was all some sort of involved ploy to manipulate citizens and their votes. She couldn't blame the skeptics. If just months ago someone had told Sandra how radically her world would change, that her days would come to sound like a superhero holo, she would have laughed and scoffed.

"This is why, with great pride," Krazen continued, "I'm happy to announce that our city council has just passed the Paranormal Registration Act of 2098 after holding an emergency session. This means that, in a matter of days, all Nubians in New York, along with anyone else who might exhibit strange abilities, will be required to register with government check-in centers scattered throughout both levels of the city. These centers will be manned and supervised by St. John Soldiers, ensuring that the processing of paranormals will be handled in an orderly, secure manner. Order, stability, ascension . . . the hallmarks of our culture. This I promise you, always!"

The audience broke into thunderous applause, Sandra taken aback by the emotion that erupted. She slowly clapped along with the others, being one of the few people in the hall with any real idea of just how instrumental her father had been in pushing the act, even though he wasn't an elected official yet. It was his way of ensuring that all gifted Nubians would be brought to him, would fall under his jurisdiction for him to handle as he saw fit.

She homed in on Krazen once again as the applause subsided, creating a close-up of his frame with one of her eye implants. He had come to the rally wearing a bright embroidered blue-and-yellow caftan that matched the palette of the holo-billboard floating above his head. Sandra thought he'd made a poor choice. Matching the ethnic attire you'd wrongheadedly appropriated with the ads for your mayoral campaign was the epitome of tackiness. So undignified. It just was *not* something that anyone in their right mind would do, especially when running for New York City mayor. But who said Krazen was in his right mind? It was only of late that Sandra St. John had become aware of just how much of a clown her father could be. A fool. An extremely dangerous, manipulative fool to be sure, but a fool nonetheless.

He was barefoot, as usual, always having his team make

sure that the surface of whatever platform he would be standing on was shiny and spotless, not that it was necessary. New York's Up High had been voted the cleanest sky city dwelling for the seventh year straight as decreed by the judges at *Time Out TSE*. People could literally eat their lunch off sky streets if they so chose, but Krazen liked everything super clean, all the time. So extra, but Sandra supposed she should have been thankful that he wasn't trotting out his usual troupe of Divine Nubians with their assortment of powers to put on a show. Like how at one earlier rally he had that poor telekinetic girl juggling lollipops with no hands and floating them over to a few of the children in the audience. Or how at the same rally Aren had set forth cascades of light behind Krazen as he strutted across a stage. The sight had left Sandra with a queasy feeling, to see this rugged former gang leader reduced to being a jester, a living light show for her father.

Right after Krazen wrapped up his speech, Sandra watched him shake hands with several Up High corporate execs, their faces beaming. Then he padded over to the throng of citizens who wanted to take part in a quick meet-and-greet. An unusual sight to be sure, to see the mighty Krazen St. John paw and pander to other residents of the sky. She was used to seeing him associate with the grungy people of the lower city so that they would agree to his construction projects or economic initiatives, things that would supposedly improve their miserable lives. But to become mayor of New York, he needed the votes of people who dwelled in the lower city along with those who lived in the sky. Even though his two mayoral challengers were trailing in the polls by a significant margin, Krazen wanted Up High residents to feel like he was fully qualified and in their corner. He shouldn't be voted in because he was the head of St. John Enterprises and the richest man in the city. His future constituents needed to believe he truly cared.

Sandra also knew the other reason why her father held these rallies: He adored the attention, sucking in the adulation of the crowd as he strutted around in one of his outfits. Onstage, he could be grand, the showman he believed New Yorkers and the rest of Tri-State East craved. She took in her father's caftan again and then looked down at her own outfit, realizing how subdued her style had become. Gone were the sparkly neon-colored blouses and skirts and shimmering jackets sometimes embedded with holos. She'd taken to wearing simple sweaters, trousers, and long skirts in black, gray, or navy, with an accent of color via earrings or a special pin. Her striking crimson hair was color enough for most of her outfits. Maybe she'd top it off with a dark denim jacket now and then, everything exquisitely tailored, of course. The need to constantly play and be flashy with fashion had left her practically overnight. She'd told herself the change in style was the result of turning eighteen three weeks ago, that she was entering adulthood now and a new level of maturity was called for. But was that really it? Or was she simply trying to be less like her father?

For all of her life, she had watched him punish those who, in his words, made his life "unnecessarily difficult" due to their incompetence. She knew that for all his charm at public events, Krazen was happy to mercilessly cut down anyone who stepped in his path, ever ready to subdue anything he deemed too much of a threat. And the young Nubians who'd awoken to their gifts were the latest asset he had to possess.

But ever since the Children and Krazen's little army of "Divine" Nubians had been revealed, Sandra had noticed something else about her father: His ever-present ambition was overburdened. Between running St. John Enterprises, his militia units, his lower-city human scanners, his mayoral campaign, and the training of the Divine, he was spread too thin. And he was too stubborn to trust others and ask for help. He was also deeply worried that the Children in the lower city were starting to get good press, that he was no longer in control of how the public should view gifted Nubians.

Still, she embraced the news he'd just announced. With the registration act, Nubians would automatically be subject to governmental authority and funneled into his militias. There'd be no more need for bullying and theatrics, her father's trademark. These Nubians would be part of the St. John empire, or else. Sandra made a point to study as many of them as possible, having several moles who worked for her at the training center with the Divine and conducting her own surveillance of the Children. When and how did their powers appear? What was the range of powers that surfaced? And always, always, what was the lineage of the Nubians she studied?

Sandra was proud of herself, having been able to glean the necessary information on as many of the Children as possible, whose gifts seemed to be more varied than what she saw with the Divine. There were a handful of Children that Sandra had been keeping a particularly close tab on for weeks now. Sekou, for example, who was able to harness the power of astral projection. He was another Nubian who Sandra believed her father underestimated. His gift might not have been as flashy as, say, Lencho's or Zaire's, but it was one that allowed the Children to access information they otherwise wouldn't be privy to.

Sekou was also half Italian, which meant his lineage wasn't purely Nubian. If Sekou could still awaken to his gift as someone of mixed heritage, then so could Sandra. After learning she was half Nubian in typically callous fashion from her father, she had taken the revelation in stride. She pushed down all thoughts of learning more about her mother and cultural history and centered a more pressing concern—how she could activate her own potential powers. She knew what her father would say: If forced to endure the right amount of stress, most Nubian teens would manifest their gifts. An oversimplification in Sandra's mind.

She rose from her seat, a signal to her guards that it was time to make their way to meet her father. With numerous KRAZEN ST. JOHN FOR MAYOR banners floating above her head, she found herself reflecting on his motivations. Why did her father need to control these beings? Why not leave them alone to live as they wanted to, or nurture them in their abilities, allow them to be a real asset to the city and all of TSE? She knew the answer. Krazen was terrified of being found out for the foul being he really was and losing everything, of being usurped by something more powerful than he was. And letting a league of poor Black children who could read minds or throw fire or shake the earth with a snap of their fingers run around however they wanted? Well, that wouldn't do. In a few years, what type of rivals could they become if left unchecked?

After walking down several flights of steps, Sandra and her cadre of guards maneuvered through an intricate pathway of corridors that led them to the backstage area of the hall. There, her father was surround by several staffers, a holo beaming from his eye as he had a conversation with his campaign manager about his schedule. To his left stood Tilly, his personal assistant, ever by his side. Sandra thought at least the young woman had the good sense to be subdued in her style with her beige-and-cream-colored business suits, but she still couldn't stand her. Krazen St. John had entrusted Tilly with more information about his business and personal life than he'd ever shared with his own daughter. A repulsive fact that Sandra couldn't let go of.

"Father," Sandra said as she walked to Krazen just as he ended his holo-call, giving him a light peck on both cheeks. She knew that even backstage they were being watched, that it was her duty to play the doting daughter no matter how she truly felt. "Wonderful speech, as always. The crowd was totally amped, all because of you."

He nodded. "We expected nothing less." He frowned and made a dismissive gesture toward her group of guards. "Come now, is this necessary? No one's coming after you, daughter. And even if they were, I have soldiers in covert locations at all of my events. Our digital security sweeps are flawless. You know that. My militia can be put to better use."

Sandra nodded. "I get it, Krazen, really, I do, but you're about to become an elected official. And I want the presence of our guards to be an acknowledgment of the lofty position you're about to attain. I take all of what's happening very seriously."

She was lying, something she did more routinely with her father of late. She had in fact begun to pay her personal squad of guards a huge additional salary on top of their standard wages to ensure that their loyalty would be to her above all else.

Krazen squinted. The sky king was finding his daughter increasingly inscrutable, something she relished. Abruptly, Tilly walked over and placed her hand gently on Krazen's forearm, her manicured fingers lingering on his sleeve for just a moment. A small gesture. One that was brief yet a tad too tender. Sandra knew what was going on between Tilly and her father, and it filled her with fury.

"Sir, we have a situation at the training center," Tilly said. "Lencho and a new recruit are involved. Thought you'd want to know."

Krazen's eyebrows rose. "Tilly, thank you. Sandra, be on your way. I presume you'll be spending more time with our special asset?"

"Yes, of course. Be well, Krazen, and congratulations." Sandra swiveled, heading toward the exit as her squad of militiamen followed. She was relieved that she didn't have to stand in front of her father for another moment, that she didn't have to train her face to be calm and affirming when she really wanted to roll her eyes and sneer at him and his gold-digging assistant. But she was also thankful for the tiny morsel of intel they'd given her.

She quickly tapped behind her ear to activate her personal

comm. "Vincent," she whispered, "heard something happened at the gym. Get back to me, now." Sandra tapped behind her ear again to shut down the line. Vincent was one of several contacts she had at the training center watching how things were developing with the Divine. She'd learn shortly what had gone down.

Sandra and her guards entered the shuttle van that would take them several avenues over to the greenhouse. The van rose high into the air, the tinted windows blocking the glare of sunlight bouncing off the silver-and-glass buildings that were ubiquitous in the Up High. She thought about Lencho and how unsettling his behavior had become, how Vincent had reported that the boy often lost his temper for no discernible reason during trainings. Something had changed about the mysterious Nubian who Sandra had initially found magnetizing, even with his coarseness. She'd understood the disgruntled, broken boy who felt so unseen, who yearned for attention and affirmation. Sandra thought he could be an important ally. An ally . . . and possibly more.

But now? There was nothing left between them. Lencho had stashed all of his allegiance with her father. A huge mistake. He didn't know Krazen the way she did, how deeply manipulative he could be, how he saw people as tools unless they shared his bed, and even then . . . But Lencho saw Krazen as the type of father he'd never had, and Krazen saw Lencho as the son he wished he'd had. To her father, it didn't matter how competent and shrewd Sandra could be—Lencho took precedence. Krazen seemed all too content to put up with the gang member's moods, trotting the Nubian out for all the holos to see as the prototype of the new St. John Soldier who'd protect the city, a symbol of the "empowered future" Krazen would create.

As per usual, amid all of this, Sandra had been pushed to the side. Didn't matter, not anymore. She'd been disappointed by boys and men before, but she was resilient. She'd persevere. And she had a Nubian on her side who could take down Lencho if push came to shove.

Sandra's van descended and touched down at one of several greenhouses that could be found throughout the Up High, preserving all manner of plants and flowers that had otherwise gone extinct in the lower world. As she exited the vehicle, her eyes zeroed in on the person she'd come to meet.

Vriana sat on an outside bench in a billowy navy denim patchwork dress. Her multicolored braids were trussed up in a bun as she sat with her legs crossed in front of her. She was reading from a tablet, an odd sight for most of the Up High, who relied on holos beaming from their implants when it came to reading practically anything. The girl looked up and saw Sandra approaching. Her face lit up.

"Hey, sexy Sand-aaaaayyyyy," Vriana sang with a bright smile as she jumped up to give the other young woman a hug. "Lookin' all grown, all fabu, as usual. How was your pop's rally?"

As Vriana wrapped her arms tight, Sandra tried to lean into the embrace. She wasn't used to physical affection. And for days, every time she'd heard herself referred to as Sandy, she'd had to remind herself that she was a person of refinement and refrain from slapping Vriana square in the face. No one, absolutely *no one* had ever been allowed to call her Sandy, a nickname she detested, much less Sand-aaaaayyyyy. But she knew she had a role to play, that of a nurturing, caring friend.

"Vriana, hey there . . . uhm, girl," Sandra replied. She still struggled when it came to wrapping her tongue around Vriana's modes of speech, trying to mirror some of what she said. "The rally went really well. Electric, you know? If the excitement levels of the crowd are any indication, the polls are correct. Krazen's going to win this election easily, especially with you on his side." She paused. "How were classes?"

"Great. I mean, the tutors keep on emphasizing that I need to get my sequential math scores in order, but I just want to do my psych and English coursework 24/7. But you know that boring shit. So, were there any cuties at the rally?" Vriana gave Sandra a devious grin.

"Uhm, yeah, I mean . . ." Why did Sandra so often find herself at a loss for words with this girl? "No, not really. Well, I suppose, there's this guy Jermaine who's easy on the eyes. I see him from time to time at these sort of events."

"OMG, Jermaine Pendergast?" Vriana squealed, and clasped her hands in front of her. "The son of that art collector who lives on the North Side? Sandy, you and I, same page, sis, same paaaaa-aaaage, as usual. I mean he's always impeccable with what he wears and has some nice, tight buns. Mmmmm, I'm getting energized just thinking about it, though I do wish he had a sibling or two my age . . ."

Sandra nodded uncertainly, her cheeks flushed, not used to this type of frivolous banter, not quite believing how their relationship had radically changed since Vriana had first been brought Up High as a prisoner. For days, whenever Sandra had visited Vriana, she generally found the Nubian girl in the same place: sitting in the center of her cell, her eyes closed, her hands folded in her lap. She mostly ignored the meals that were given to her through an automated server, barely drinking her water, refusing to talk. Sandra hated the way Vriana's cheeks soon became slightly sunken. How she spent so much of her time curled up on her bed, crying. How her once-lustrous braids had become dirty and matted even though Vriana had been provided with everything she needed and then some to be the effervescent, stylish person she'd been in the lower city.

Once Sandra had attempted to communicate with the girl through speakers installed in the walls of her cell. "This doesn't have to be so difficult, Vriana, please," Sandra had said, the microphone of her implants capturing her words and broadcasting them into the room. "You can have a great life up here. We could help you develop your gifts. It'll be wonderful."

Vriana had been practically motionless on her bed all day. She'd turned her head toward Sandra, who was standing behind a glass barrier, adjusted her position a bit, looked up at the ceiling, and then closed her eyes. Sandra knew she wasn't sleeping, but that Vriana had essentially dismissed her. The prisoner had dismissed her.

Though she was one of the wealthiest people in the world, problems seemed to follow Sandra like a plague. After all, how did you deal with a person who, if you got too close and inhabited the same space, would instantly persuade you to do whatever she asked? Doctors and scientists who monitored Vriana were routinely told to keep their distance, to not enter her room no matter how gentle and benign the girl seemed.

Sandra hadn't posed as a militiawoman and kidnapped the girl just for her to wither away in a cell. And her father certainly wouldn't approve of a Nubian with such a powerful gift going to waste.

But then she'd hatched a new potential plan, one that would certainly be controversial but might do the trick of solving the issues Sandra and her team were having with Vriana. It was risky, yes, but this unacceptable conundrum had to end. Sandra was fair in ways that her father wasn't, and she had given Vriana a chance to cooperate.

"Flood the cell," Sandra said one day to the staffers monitoring the room when all was in place. She once again buried whatever conscience she had when gas filled Vriana's space, knocking her out in seconds. Doctors placed the girl on a stretcher and carried her off to the type of clinic that most Up High residents knew all too well.

Vriana had needed a few days to recover but was soon back to her normal self. Well, really the ebullient self that Sandra had observed in the Swamp, the vivacious girl who seemed to attract everyone's eye. Sandra had also realized that they now had to let Vriana out of her cell to adjust to her new life in the sky, so she'd begun to schedule regular afternoon hangout times. It was interesting to Sandra to observe the effect the Nubian girl had on others. Up High sensibilities favored those who were sveltely muscular or slender, but whenever Vriana strutted by in some outfit that showcased her buxom, voluptuous curves, eyes followed. Lots of teens and even some pervy adults would've stridden right up to Vriana and introduced themselves if the girl hadn't been constantly surrounded by militiamen supplied by Sandra. As far as Sandra knew, no one in the lower city was aware that Vriana now lived Up High, as she highly doubted she was recognized in that awful soldiers' getup she wore when she took the girl away. But it never hurt to be careful.

And so this was what was on Sandra's mind as she, Vriana, and their guards walked into the Starlight Greenhouse, the largest of its type Up High, renowned for being perched at the very edge of the sky city. Anyone who stood by its east-side windows or made their way to the observation deck would feel like their body was completely suspended in the sky, with no other buildings in sight. A lovely little excursion for Vriana to feel like she belonged.

Sandra knew what she was doing and had faith in herself, even if no one else did. Someday, she wouldn't have to listen to anyone else. Someday, they'd all realize she was the boss, the true visionary.

And that day would come sooner than any of them thought.

Chapter 5

Uzochi

Uzochi realized it was one thing to see short glimpses of the sky city in holos, or to see images of the Up High when Sekou gave him permission to explore his memories and review his astral trips there. It was another thing entirely to step into the Up High and be astounded by the opulence surrounding him.

Getting entry into the elevators was child's play. Because most St. John Soldiers traveled in packs, they only relied on one member of the group to input the access code for the elevators. Some preferred to use retinal scans, at least from what Uzochi could discern as he skimmed the memories of the group. Either way, Uzochi, Zuberi, and Tasha had just cozied up behind a random squad and walked right in behind them. He'd kept his cool as the elevator rose, waiting for some sort of body scan to be implemented that would indicate there were intruders in the car, but nothing happened. He was grateful that almost all militia folk wore black visors. His eyes being hidden gave him a sense of protection. He could feel Tasha's nervousness radiating from her body in waves, though she managed to keep it together, maintaining a stoic face. In contrast, Zuberi could have won an acting award for her performance, standing in military formation with her hands tucked into her vest, looking more like a St. John Soldier than real St. John Soldiers.

And then the elevators had opened, and the car's inhabitants had filed out. Uzochi had to catch himself, had to gently nudge both Zuberi and Tasha with his mind to stop gawking, as they were supposed to be soldiers who were used to the sky city. But to see the rows upon rows of glistening buildings of steel and glass, and the hyacinth trees and bushes planted in pristine sidewalks, and the cars and vans and bikes that swished and swerved high overhead, and the people who seemed to be beaming holos from their bodies . . . it was something else.

Relax, y'all, he sent to the two girls, using his telepathy. *Remember, play it cool, stick to the plan.*

Uzochi had become increasingly adept at sending his thoughts to others in the form of language, an act that they'd all agreed he should resort to as necessary as they sought Vriana. In fact, Uzochi would have to open his consciousness in a way he had never done before, scanning as many random minds as he could to locate his friend.

He glanced down quickly at the battered boots he'd borrowed from Thato, with their worn leather scratches and nicks and old laces. And just like that, he knew he didn't belong in this place. It was strange to think that, not so long ago, he'd thought he could belong, that his loneliness and sadness would magically dissipate if he could make it to the sky. He remembered sitting at his high school desk, listening to one of his preceptors prattle on about the glories of the Up High, imagining himself surrounded by equals, by people who lived in the sky because they were worthy, who wouldn't care that he was Nubian. And even without his gift, he instinctively knew he was very, very wrong.

How did Lencho live here, Uzochi wondered. Sure, there were clearly wealth and resources to spare, and Lencho grew up poor, but shouldn't that have made his cousin angry? To see how Nubians lived? Maybe it was after months of listening to Zuberi rightfully rant about what those Up High had access to and what those "below" did not, but Uzochi knew now that he'd been fed a lie growing up. Uzochi had always been special, more so than the people who tittered around him now with their implants and lustrous clothes. And still, he would've been deemed worthy of ascension only if he'd worked his ass off as a student or joined Krazen's army and lived under that maniac's thumb.

The specter of the registration act continued to haunt him as he beckoned to the girls. The trio quietly took in their surroundings, keeping their heads low as they casually moved away from the real militiamen. Tasha grabbed Uzochi and pointed to their left. There, attached to the rear of an eight-story building, was an alcove completely covered by a small canopy of gardenias, the fragrance reaching Uzochi's nose. The trio hustled over to the alcove and crouched down, scanning their surroundings to make sure no one was paying attention to the small group of St. John Soldiers taking a little break.

"Are you ready, Tasha?" Zuberi said, the tension palpable in her voice.

The other girl nodded. Tasha gave their immediate sur-roundings a quick review and then crafted the primary illu-sion she'd been practicing for the past few days. Suddenly she, Zuberi, and Uzochi were no longer clad in militia black but wore an assortment of purple-and-silver tunics, slacks, and sneakers that seemed to be all the rage among kids Up High, at least from what they'd been able to determine from the recent holos they'd studied. She'd also woven her illusion so that all three of the kids sported funky sport visors that covered half of their faces. It was important to conceal their identity as best they could, as Uzochi and Zuberi believed that they'd been watched for some time by Krazen and his people.

"Great work, Tasha," Uzochi whispered, looking down at his clothes, still amazed at what he was seeing even though they'd practiced this move countless times. He could almost swear that he was really wearing the outfit that had just ma-terialized around his body, the colors of the fabric rich and bright.

Zuberi gave a curt nod and rose, Uzochi recognizing the emotions coming off her body. *We need to move, like now.* The trio made their way out of the alcove and into the larger Up High. According to the schematics they'd studied, the sky city was roughly 1.75 square miles, just a bit larger than Central Park, which explained why parts of Manhattan were com-pletely covered in Up High shadow. Uzochi began to lightly skim minds, grateful that he'd been given permission by so many Nubians down below to practice with them. He felt odd, probing people's psyches without their permission, being privy to thoughts they believed were private. But he told himself that he was doing it for a greater purpose. That Vriana was worth this breach of ethics.

Uzochi surveyed the metallic sidewalks that covered the city. He couldn't help but think about how the streets, even with all of these people, were far cleaner than any space he'd inhabited down below, even indoor spaces. No matter how often he and his mother had scrubbed and dusted their home, it was never like this. Sterile. Immaculate to the point of creepiness. Not a smudge or speck of dust found anywhere.

He continued to jump from mind to mind as he and the girls slowly made their way north, with Uzochi paying close attention to any St. John Soldiers they passed. Out of all the sky people they would encounter, he thought militiamen would most likely have information about Vriana's whereabouts. But Uzochi still scanned the minds of ordinary residents, just to be on the safe side. Unfortunately, after almost fifteen minutes of scanning, many fragmented thoughts seemed to circle around the same frivolous topics.

How're people proclaiming her holo feeds to be better than mine? Disgusting skank!

Does he know I'm sleeping with his husband? Oh, so nice and tasty ... Tonight ... again ...

What an insulting offer ... my diamonds are far superior to most of what's out there on the market ...

Krazen St. John will make a fine mayor. Keeping those lower-city rats where they belong. And those detestable Nubians ...

Uzochi grimaced at the last thought, turning his head to

find the source, a statuesque woman with hot-pink nails that glittered. She threw her head back and laughed loudly at her companion's vulgar joke about Nubians being able to perform bushland voodoo witchcraft practiced by apes. The sound was like a screech in Uzochi's head.

He winced. Had the people Up High also altered their voice boxes? That sound didn't seem human. But as the woman started to laugh even more loudly, something else tumbled through Uzochi's mind.

. . . Nubian asset so important to Ms. St. John. Gotta make her proud considering all the extra currency that girl's paying me. Gotta prove myself to her dad, too. Wouldn't have ascended, not for him. Maybe grab a wrap before rendezvousing with squad later at Starlight Greenhouse. Shouldn't be late . . .

Nubian asset. Ms. St. John. The words were like a campfire suddenly bursting to life in dark woods, a guiding light for Uzochi to focus on. The soldier had to be talking about Sandra St. John.

Uzochi rushed toward the stray thought, ignoring the chatter of different minds as he hunted for its source. He found it easily in the psyche of a St. John Soldier positioned several feet away from him and the girls. The militiaman was walking east.

Gotta prove myself to stay up here, the militiaman thought. *Krazen won't accept any flaws. We gotta be perfect. Already he wants to replace us with some of those fuckin' Nubian freaks. Maybe Sandra will have my back . . .*

Uzochi didn't hesitate as he moved his feet in the direction of the voice.

Hey, he sent to the two girls. *I think I might have something. That St. John Soldier who's to our far left, walking down the street. Follow him.*

Okay, Zuberi thought back, Uzochi feeling her eagerness. She was slowly getting used to communicating with him via sending.

Uzochi and the girls began to trail the St. John Soldier, making sure they were significantly behind him so as not to attract attention. As they walked, Uzochi started to scan minds more rapidly, looking for information about Starlight Greenhouse. It would've been easy enough for him and the girls to stop and take out their phones to figure out the greenhouse's location, but doing so would've been far too conspicuous. Almost everyone they'd observed used implants and holos for their tech needs. He hadn't spotted one phone. So more mind scanning would have to do.

Luckily, Starlight Greenhouse was a popular Up High attraction that Uzochi remembered being called out on social and the holo-news for its rare plant life and spectacular sights. Thus a couple of passersby had its exact location on the surface of their mind, right at Kennedy and Branson by the easternmost edge of the sky city.

The St. John Soldier they were following entered a cafe.

"Should we go inside as well?" Tasha whispered. Zuberi lifted her head slightly and discreetly surveyed the area. Uzochi knew she was checking out people's phantoms.

"All clear," she said quietly. "No one's paying us any attention, at least from what I can tell."

Uzochi nodded and turned to Tasha. "I don't think we

need to follow the militia guy any longer. I think . . . I think we should go straight to this greenhouse, Starlight," he said, trying to maintain his composure, not wanting to get the girls' hopes up. "I think Sandra is already there, maybe with Vriana, if my hunch is correct."

That's all I need to hear, Zuberi sent to Uzochi. *Let's move.*

Uzochi touched Zuberi's hand, wanting so much to hold her close, to let her know it would be okay. "Tasha, how are you doing with the illusions for our clothes?" he asked.

She gave a thumbs-up. "I'm okay. It's not so bad, to keep it going. I'm a little tired, but nowhere close to my limit . . . I think. I'll manage."

With that, the trio walked east, both Uzochi and Zuberi having sufficiently studied maps of the sky city to make their way to Starlight with no additional guidance. Within twenty minutes, moving briskly, they arrived. There was an open-air space outside the greenhouse, full of fluffy pillows and chairs for Up High residents to lounge on as they chatted or played with droid dogs at their feet or read their holos. Nearby, a pair of St. John soldiers stood guard over the area, their gazes steady as they swept the space. Uzochi moved so that his back was to them, his own gaze facing the entrance just ahead of them.

He turned in place, looking around. Just as planned, Zuberi and Tasha began to talk a bit more loudly, acting the parts of distracted, self-obsessed teenagers so that he could more easily use his powers around them without appearing suspicious. He had to be still and focus, so he closed his eyes and sent a wave of his telepathy into the greenhouse, scanning as many minds as he could, finding dozens of random thoughts to comb through. It was overwhelming. Frightening. But he couldn't stop. Not if his hunch was correct about Sandra St. John's so-called asset.

And then he heard a voice in his head. A beautiful, earnest voice whose sweetness made him want to cry.

... it's soooo pretty here ... like super serene but also electric ...

Uzochi abruptly stopped scanning. He knew that voice that was chirping and singing in his head. Vriana. Uzochi saw Zuberi turn toward him, the question obvious in her gaze even under her visor.

Did you find her?

Uzochi shook his head slightly as he sent back to Zuberi, *I think so.* He lifted his chin as he once again scanned the space around them with his eyes and mind. People seemed to be walking in and out of the greenhouse freely, so he imagined that he and the girls wouldn't be stopped when they strolled in, that they could pass as regular Up High kids who wanted to gaze at some exotic flora for the afternoon.

They entered Starlight, only to be greeted by a variety of trees and plants and flowers that even studious Uzochi would've had a hard time identifying. The smells were incredible, a bouquet of floral scents that made him feel like he should stop and sprawl out on a nearby bench to take it all in. *Act like you're having a conversation about a reality holo or something,* he telepathically sent to the girls, and Zuberi and Tasha immediately started to chatter. Zuberi gave a carefree, tinkly laugh, so close in its affectation to the other Up High girls that Uzochi once again thought she could take the acting world by storm. He hadn't realized just how convincingly she could pull off different moods. He also noticed, even as the two girls were conversing in bubblegum voices, that Tasha was studying the ceiling of the greenhouse.

Uzochi sent his thoughts out once again to swim around the space, and then almost started to jump for joy. There was no mistaking it. He could sense her, just around the corner. He beckoned for the girls to follow him. Zuberi looked at Uzochi, who nodded slightly.

She's here, he sent. *She's really here. But we have to be careful. There're guards, though I don't sense any fear from Vriana.*

Uzochi could sense Zuberi having to restrain herself. She was instantly awash with new emotion, rolling off her like thick smoke. Relief. Joy. Determination. Want. As she moved forward as casually as possible, her thoughts bounced into the space between her and Uzochi, fast and frenzied.

I'm coming, Vri. I promise. Just hang on a little longer. I'm on my way.

Just be ready, he sent back. *Remember the plan, remember all the contingencies we've prepared for. Please.*

And then Uzochi turned the corner and there indeed was Vriana flanked by a small cadre of St. John Soldiers. They had prepared for an array of contingencies, yes, but Uzochi wasn't expecting to see Vriana sitting next to the young woman he knew from the holos to be Sandra St. John, the pair talking and laughing as if they were the best of friends.

Chapter 6

Zuberi

As Zuberi had made her way through glistening Up High streets with Tasha and Uzochi, trying to hold back her disgust at all that she observed, she wasn't visualizing a fighting form for the umpteenth time that she'd already mastered. Instead, she was visualizing Vriana's face and the way it would light up at the sight of her. She was imagining how her friend would sound, how she would smile and shriek, "Giiiiiiirrrrrl, what took your ass so damn long?!?" and tell Zuberi that everything would be okay now that they were together again.

Zuberi knew it shouldn't be up to Vriana to say those words. She knew that her friend must've been going through hell living Up High, a prisoner of a cause she hadn't even wanted to be a part of. But because Vriana cared about everyone, more than she cared about herself, she'd ended up in harm's way. No, correction . . . Zuberi had put her in harm's way. Zuberi should've been watching her. Just the thought of what had happened made Zuberi's anger burn brighter. She could still see Sandra St. John's face and wide eyes as she pretended to be a St. John Soldier, imploring Zuberi to handle the emergency at the theater because she and Vriana would take care of the unhoused man who'd collapsed. And Zuberi had believed her. A sucker.

It wasn't like Zuberi to be so easily fooled. She'd learned, long ago, not to trust strangers. She should've known better, regardless of all that was going on with the awakenings and the Divine. Even if Vriana had urged her to go, Zuberi should've known better. And because of her mistake, one of the most beautiful souls on this planet had been taken. Most days, Zuberi's guilt seemed to be on the verge of eating her alive. The plan had been the only thing pressing her forward, and her heart had lit up as Uzochi led them to Starlight, the end of her nightmare about to be reached.

As they entered the greenhouse, Zuberi thought the floor was made of a plush green carpet. But then, as her eyes adjusted to what was around her, she realized it wasn't carpet at all. It was grass, so thick, so green that Zuberi had never seen anything like it, flanked by trees that reached the heavens with shiny leaves hanging from interlocking branches. Her eyes tracked the branches higher and higher, noticing that a few actually touched the ceiling. The glass walls curved down around them in a dome, its translucence having a sheen that Zuberi thought seemed somehow off. An assortment of butterflies fluttered near the edges of the dome along with small green birds that sported bright yellow chests, zipping in and around tree branches, occasionally pausing to peck at the glass that surrounded them.

Of course. Starlight was one of the Up High's most coveted

spaces, one that Zuberi had seen in every scrap of propaganda that flooded her old school and the streets down below. On the holo-news, anchors would trot around domes just like this as one of the St. John mouthpieces chattered on, inviting those with enough wealth to "experience rare nature sights, preserved exclusively by Up High scientists." Then they would inevitably point out the golden-breasted birds and grin as they said, "You'll even see extinct avian species like these bee-eaters, brought back to life through the power of sky city tech."

The sight of it all filled Zuberi with rage, the idea that nature was something only the elite were entitled to making her skin prickle. She was frozen in place momentarily, but quickly remembered the mission and schooled her face into a sunny gaze, letting her eyes roam over the rest of the space as she followed Uzochi and Tasha around the edge of the dome. White stone paths ran in a circle around the greenhouse, and every few feet, the path would split and turn toward the middle of the room. These trails were bracketed by thick, lush plants and trees, making it impossible to see far beyond the path you were on.

She'd taken all of this in for just a few seconds while remembering to play the part of an airhead teen with Tasha. And then Uzochi had confirmed what they were waiting for. They'd found her. Vriana was here, just around the corner, just around a bundle of bushes and flowers.

Now, as what she'd dreamed of for weeks stood right before her, Zuberi found herself grappling with reality. There was Vriana . . . surrounded by guards . . . having an easy-breezy conversation with Sandra St. John. The very person who'd kidnapped her.

Zuberi tried to put two and two together. Right, of course. Vriana was playing a role, being her vivacious, friendly-to-everybody-and-their-mama self to psych out her kidnappers so that they'd believe she was now on their side. A survival strategy. Had to be it.

Something feels . . . weird, Uzochi sent to Zuberi. *I don't know. Maybe we need to . . .*

No, Zuberi sent back. *We're getting her, now.* Zuberi turned to Tasha. "Now," she whispered. "Do it now."

Tasha, whose eyes had lit up when she saw Vriana, whispered, "All right." She turned her gaze upward again.

Large shards of glass began to rain down from the ceiling. People started to cry out and run, some making their way to the greenhouse exit while others dashed for cover under trees or benches. No one seemed to realize that there should've been some sort of explosion to accompany the ceiling caving in, that a wave of raining glass should've made crinkling and crashing sounds. That the surrounding silence was odd.

Their guesswork had paid off, that people would be too concerned about protecting themselves from injury to notice that something was off. Tasha had studied holos of Up High buildings day and night and worked on a number of illusions that would be informed by the sky city's aesthetic. They'd correctly surmised they would need a major distraction or two.

Zuberi looked down at her clothes. She was back in her St. John Soldier garb. Even though Tasha was amazing with her gift, she couldn't maintain so many illusions all at once.

Didn't matter. Zuberi rushed forward, knowing Uzochi and Tasha would have her back as she took care of the part of the plan that only she could handle. Amid the raining glass, two of the St. John Soldiers had fled, while another pair had covered Vriana and Sandra with their bodies.

How kind. How thoughtful. Too bad for them.

Zuberi rushed over and grabbed one of the militiamen by the shoulder, cuffing their face with the side of her hand and pinching a key nerve at the back of their neck. The soldier's body arched in pain and then slumped to the side. Before the other militiaperson could react, Zuberi bent low and kicked the soldier's legs out from underneath him. As the man toppled to the ground, she ran on top of him, cuffed him twice in the face, and applied the nerve pinch. Basic forms that she could've performed in her sleep. He was out like a light, just like his comrade. She hadn't even needed to pay attention to what their phantom selves were going to do, that was how easy it was to take these fools out.

Both Vriana and Sandra looked up at Zuberi, completely stunned. Zuberi grabbed Sandra by the arm and forcefully pulled her up so that she and the foul rich girl were standing eye to eye.

"You!" Zuberi snarled.

Sandra blinked, her eyes consumed with fear. "Wait, I—"

Before Sandra could say anything else, Zuberi acted on instinct, doing what she'd dreamed of doing ever since she'd realized Vriana had been abducted. She pulled her fist far back and walloped Sandra St. John in the face.

Sandra crumpled to the ground, joining her militia. Zuberi

turned to Vriana, who seemed completely bewildered. She looked at her friend with a terror that froze Zuberi's insides, guilt and regret coursing through her yet again. Goddess, Vriana was obviously terrified, what with all the falling glass and the ensuing commotion and the fighting. They had to get her out of here immediately. Zuberi wouldn't let her endure this for another minute. She—

Zuberi stared at her friend, concern in her gaze, and held out her hand.

"Vri, it's okay," she said. "It's me. It's Zuberi."

Zuberi moved forward, hand still out in front of her, confusion rattling through her body. She saw Vriana's phantoms moving above her, all of them recoiling or fleeing.

Which didn't make sense.

"Who? Zu . . . Zuberi? Who are you?" Vriana said, starting to cry. "Oh God, please don't hurt me. Don't touch me!"

"Vri, what? Wait . . . what's happening?"

Zuberi remembered that she was part of a team and turned to find Uzochi and Tasha behind her. Tasha was still looking up, maintaining the illusion of falling glass even as she quickly glanced over at Vriana.

"Zuberi," Uzochi said haltingly. "Something's wrong. Vriana's memories, they're . . . they're not right. They're not making sense to me."

"WHAT?" Zuberi shouted, turning back to look at her best friend, her jaw dropping open.

"Oh no," Uzochi said as he pointed meekly at Vriana. "Oh, Zuberi . . . look. Right there."

Zuberi blinked, and then there it was, plain for her to see, something that would've been far too easy to miss unless you were looking for it. A small piece of metal embedded in Vriana's left temple.

OhmiGoddess. She's gotten . . . she has a tech implant.

A sick realization hit Zuberi. These people had done something to Vriana. The implant had to explain her odd behavior, why all her phantoms continued to recoil from Zuberi. "What'd they do to you?" Zuberi shouted, her hands around Vriana's shoulders, realizing she was losing it but too upset to care. They'd changed Vriana. They'd mutilated her friend. "What did they do?!?"

The rain of broken glass stopped. "I can't anymore," Tasha mumbled, huffing and puffing and letting out a deep breath. "Have to take a break."

"Get offa me!!!" Vriana shouted at Zuberi between her sobs. "Let me go. You don't want to do this. You . . . actually want us to be friends, don't you?"

And that was when Zuberi felt it, a tug on her consciousness, a pull and a light push, like her spirit was being tickled and soothed, like she'd do anything to make Vriana happy. Give anything, give up anything, the yearning so intense, so frothy and delicious.

No.

She realized what was happening. Vriana was starting to use her gift. On her.

Zuberi shook her head. She couldn't let this happen. No, this wasn't happening . . .

"What the fuck are y'all doing here?"

As Zuberi tried to push through the sweet murkiness that was Vriana's gift, she looked over to see Uzochi and Tasha swivel toward an all-too-familiar voice.

Lencho Will stood just a few feet away in the greenhouse staring at them, his fists coiled at his side, ready to pounce.

Chapter 7

Lencho

Lencho had thought he might be losing his mind when he sensed Uzochi earlier, that the stress of the afternoon had simply pushed him over the edge. But the boy's presence called to him like a beacon, pulling Lencho forward. He and his cousin had never been particularly close. But ever since Uzochi had entered Lencho's consciousness back at the Swamp seawall, helping Lencho better understand the potential of his kinetic gift, he'd had to admit that there was some sort of connection he felt every day. And there was no mistaking it, he could sense that Uzochi was close, could sense his energy in the same way he could sense the energy of other gifted Nubians he trained and lived with.

For all the fuss people created around the Up High, the sky city was small and could be traversed by foot quickly, especially by someone with Lencho's speed. So he'd allowed his newfound sixth sense to take over and draw him closer to wherever Uzochi was. Sometimes he had to stop in a crowded street to zero in on what he was feeling, to figure out if he needed to make a left or right or go down a particular avenue. Some pedestrians stopped and stared, wondering what was going on with the mumbling Nubian boy, a few recognizing Lencho from the holos where he appeared as the mighty, charismatic leader of Krazen's future militia. Why was a St. John star on the street, apparently lost and befuddled?

Find him. Find Uzochi, Lencho's inner voice said, impatient, furious. *Take what you need.*

Lencho ignored the stares and followed his senses, getting affirmation that he was headed in the right direction as Uzochi's presence felt stronger in his head and heart and limbs. He soon found himself at the easternmost corner of the city, which housed one of the largest greenhouses in the world, Starlight. He'd arrived only to find scores of people running out of the building, screaming in terror. Lencho couldn't see what was happening inside, but the pull of Uzochi's energy was irresistible. Regardless of the fleeing people, he couldn't turn away. He wouldn't turn away.

Lencho opened the door to the building, only to be greeted by the sight of cascading glass, large shards falling from the ceiling. He flinched, realizing he needed to get away—and then the falling glass vanished. The Starlight dome was still intact, with glass nowhere to be found among the trees and bushes or on the ground. Which was impossible.

Something very weird was going on, but weird was a fundamental part of Lencho's life now. He'd just witnessed a kid vanish in a swirling black cloud, and so with the vanishing glass, he deduced, *This gotta be some more Nubian shit.*

Lencho made his way through the greenhouse, his inner

voice still egging him on even as he felt uncertainty, even as the pull of Uzochi's energy drew him closer. The building was mostly deserted, with a few people hiding under benches or thick tree branches, timidly peeking out to see if the coast was clear. Lencho followed his instinct and sure enough was greeted by the sight of Uzochi with two girls as they stood next to Vriana, who was crying big-time. Sandra and a couple of guards were knocked out on the floor.

He tried to make sense of what he was seeing. He remembered Vriana from the hallways of their high school. She seemed like a sweet enough kid and he thought maybe she had a crush on him at one point, but what the hell was she doing up here? And what had happened to Sandra?

After a moment, Lencho realized that he knew everyone he was staring at. Both girls, Zuberi and Tasha, were from school as well. He wished Zuberi wasn't here. He hated to admit it, but something about this girl creeped him out. Maybe it was because, besides seeing the potential in how Nubian gifts could interact, she had another mysterious power. But even with all the intel Krazen and his team had gathered about her, no one could quite figure out what her Nubian gift was. Regardless, he wouldn't let himself be distracted.

"I'm not sure what's going on," Lencho said, "but I'm going to take this as a sign that maybe y'all have come to your senses and want to ascend and live Up High. I hear the Children are living in my old HQ. Hard to downgrade from the Swamp, Uzochi, but leave it to you to get people to take my sloppy seconds."

Lencho saw anger flash in his cousin's eyes.

"We don't want trouble," Uzochi said. "We just came for Vriana. Maybe you didn't realize, but she was taken up here against her will. We just want to bring her home. I have no beef with you today, cuz."

Lencho cocked his head. "I'm not sure what's going down here, but y'all ain't going nowhere except to a jail cell where Krazen can deal with you. You've broken all sorts of laws. Trespassing on Up High territory, assaulting militia, assaulting his *daughter* . . ." He readied his body to fight. "Wait till the press hears all about this shit. This is over."

"Lencho," Uzochi said. "It doesn't have to be this way. We worked together before and—"

"No, Uzochi," Lencho snarled. "Don't bring up that day at the seawall. I did what I had to do for myself and other Nubians. That's why I bolstered your power so you could hold back the waters. I've never, *ever* given a fuck about you."

Take what should be yours, the inner voice said. *Take Uzochi's power. Take it all.*

"I mean, when have you ever given a fuck about me?" Lencho yelled at his cousin, even as he saw Zuberi take out three small wooden staffs, which she put together, even as he saw Tasha back away, frightened.

Take Uzochi's power.

Operating by pure instinct, before anyone could move, Lencho zipped toward Uzochi, grasping his cousin by the neck. Vriana and Tasha shrieked while Zuberi went into fighting-form mode, punching Lencho's head and torso and whacking

87

away at him with her staff, rapid-fire. With his toughened endurance from all his draining, her strikes felt like little bites from an annoying horsefly.

Uzochi peered up at him, his eyes bulging.

Lencho, why . . . what . . . what are you doing? Stop!

Another voice. Uzochi, his words in Lencho's mind. Fuckin' telepathic shit. Lencho could feel his cousin probing, trying to get deeper into his thoughts, his memories. He would never let that happen again.

Zuberi placed her staff between herself and Lencho's chest, trying with all her might to drag him off Uzochi. A futile effort.

Uzochi gasped, and Lencho began to drain.

"Lencho, stop!"

The ground rumbled and shook, and everyone was almost thrown to the ground. There was a hand on Lencho's shoulder, the same heavy, amorphous hand that had appeared on his shoulder earlier in the day.

Zaire stood above them all, a miniature mountain of rock as he roughly grabbed Lencho and dragged him to the side, Zuberi and Uzochi falling away. The greenhouse shook with every step the huge Nubian boy took. Vriana shot up from where she'd been sitting and ran, heading straight for a side exit, while Tasha just stared up at Zaire, jaw on the floor.

"Lencho, relax, leave Uzochi alone," Zaire said. "Thought you were acting super weird. Good thing I followed you from the gym."

Lencho could hardly believe his ears. Zaire had followed him? How was that possible? Even when he wasn't in his stone form, Zaire was huge, instantly recognizable in a crowd. Was Lencho so distracted that he hadn't noticed the other boy?

Lashing out with little thought, Lencho twisted his body, clasped his fists together, and pounded them into Zaire's rocky arm. Zaire let out a scraggly grunt and threw Lencho forward. He sailed through the air until he landed hard, upside down, legs over head on a pile of white stones surrounding a palm tree.

This was impossible. It was . . . shameful. Unforgivable.

With a roar, Lencho reoriented himself and shot back toward Zaire, fury guiding his steps. Even though, logically, he knew he was no physical match for the boy made of stone, he threw himself forward anyway. The impact was like running into a wall at full speed, stunning even Lencho's fortified body. He was too blinded by anger to care. He pounded at Zaire, chipping away at his rocky hide, holding on tight to the boy's bicep. And as he did, the instinct to drain rose to the surface.

Take it, I say. Take it all!

Lencho didn't think twice. With Zaire in his hands, he drained, the feeling akin to having a ravenous thirst and taking a long drink of water. The power surged into him at once. Instantly, he closed his eyes and felt exquisite strength fortifying his frame. Distantly, he heard Zaire groaning in pain. Sometimes Lencho took his time when leeching, was gentle, subtle. But not now.

Now, he wanted Zaire to pay.

Lencho's eyes flew open as he let go of the other boy. He didn't just feel stronger. He felt . . . heavier. He looked at his arms, finding they had a grayish-brown tint. He turned them over, astonished.

He'd just taken a portion of Zaire's power of transformation for himself, even though he'd never absorbed Nubian gifts before.

Lencho looked up and saw Zaire stumbling backward, still in his earthen form, clearly confused as well.

LENCHO! A voice, howling in his head. *STOP THIS NOW!!!*

His cousin's voice. Yes, Uzochi was still here. His original target.

Lencho was charging at Uzochi, ready to drain again, when the greenhouse shook. Lencho whirled around. Behind him, Zaire had slammed his fist into the ground. A fissure streaked from where he stood, snaking toward Lencho.

Lencho narrowed his eyes. It would take more than that to bring him down. He leapt above the large, jagged crack in the ground, landing on plush grass at the far end of a narrow trail.

"You'll never be forgiven for this, you idiot!" he shouted. "You hear me, Zaire? You've fucked up, siding with these assholes."

Zaire regarded Lencho, his eyes full of an emotion Lencho had never seen in Zaire before. Abject horror.

And then Zaire swept Tasha, Uzochi, and Zuberi up into

his enormous arms. He bolted, racing past Lencho through trees and grass and plants right before he crashed straight through the glass of the dome with an ear-shattering *crack*. Lencho watched in horror as the four of them soared from Starlight, hurtling to the ground below, completely out of his reach.

Chapter 8

Uzochi

The air rushed past Uzochi's cheeks as a sense of shock and déjà vu overcame his body. He was used to falling in his dreams. How many times before major exams had he spent experiencing the same old nightmare? He would routinely experience free fall through a gray, overcast sky, anxious over his ability to maintain perfect grades.

But this wasn't a dream, the sensations of his real-world descent unfamiliar. Uzochi was thousands of feet in the sky, plunging faster than he could think. He knew Zaire had been scared, had done what he thought he had to do to save them from Lencho's rage, but now . . . ?

Swiveling and swirling as he fell, Uzochi frantically assessed the situation, realizing that Zaire had passed out in the air, his great arms locked around the three Children. Uzochi's heart stammered as the glass-and-steel buildings of the Up High became nothing but a silvery blur.

They were really falling from the Up High. Had Zaire meant for them to jump *completely* off the sky city?

My breath . . . Oh Goddess, please, Goddess help me. I can't catch my fuckin' breath.

Thoughts weaved frantically through Uzochi's mind. Lencho . . . being in Lencho's mind again, his red rage that overwhelmed, the feeling that he wanted to destroy Uzochi.

What had happened?

He'd failed everyone. They'd failed to rescue Vriana and now they were falling to their death.

His gaze flew to the girls. Terror in her eyes, Tasha shrieked as she clutched Zaire's rocky frame. Uzochi couldn't hear her cries, the wind consuming all other noise. Zuberi stared at Uzochi as they fell, her emotions a mix of fear and bewilderment and determination. Yes, he could feel it, Zuberi's determination, clear as rain, along with her defiance and bravery even as they plummeted.

He stopped thinking, tried to operate from instinct, tried to find a way to breathe even though his stomach still felt like it was Up High and his hands and feet were numb and his body was a cold, frigid thing as the beating of his heart clogged his ears.

Frantic, he threw out his powers of telekinesis, imagining there was a gigantic hand below them that was pushing back up, that could stop their fall.

No . . . no, that wouldn't work.

At their current velocity, Uzochi realized they would be crushed by the impact. He had to slow their descent, had to use telekinesis to instead create a field of levitation.

Uzochi now saw nothing but blue, the silvery blur of the sky city gone . . .

He wrapped a field around their bodies, remembering how he'd prevented the flood that had almost swept away the Swamp. He wrapped the field around the girls and Zaire, sweat breaking out on his brow, his nose starting to bleed.

And still they fell.

Zuberi was yelling something, but he couldn't hear her words. *Zaire!* she screamed out in his mind, sending her thoughts. *It's Zaire.*

Zaire?

Yes, yes, Uzochi understood.

Zaire was too heavy, and Uzochi couldn't stop their fall as long as the boy was in his stone form.

And so Uzochi entered the other boy's mind and screamed, *WAKE UP!!!! TRANSFORM!!!! ZAIRE . . . PLEASE . . .*

And still they fell, Uzochi trying to slow their descent. Was it his imagination? They had slowed down . . . yes, he had slowed their descent, he was sure of it . . . but they were still moving too fast.

They wouldn't survive.

Zaire, Uzochi sent once again. *WAKE UP!!!*

The gargantuan boy began to stir.

Uzochi began to see the green of the trees that lined Central Park.

He began to hear Tasha's shrieks over the pounding of his heart.

Zaire, please, please, transform!!! he sent again. *TRANS-FORM!!!*

Uzochi shut his eyes as Zuberi reached for him, squeezing

his hand tight. He threw out more kinetic energy than he'd held before, pushing them up with a final, huge thrust—

He blinked. He opened his eyes. The ground was there, inches from his face. And then he tumbled forward a few inches and hit the ground face-first, his face becoming buried in a mound of grass. The smack of the hardened earth hurt bad, but he thought, mind racing, that feeling some amount of pain might be good.

Had he saved them?

He tried to get his bearings. They were surrounded by grass and trees, which meant they must have landed somewhere in the park. Right next to him, Zuberi was already on her feet though she was bent over, hand on her knees as she shook her head. Uzochi noticed she was bleeding. Zaire rolled over in the grass, coughed, and threw up, his rock form gone, the boy flesh and blood once again. Tasha lay next to him, her body flat on the ground as she made wheezing sounds, gasping for air.

Uzochi tried to stand. He had to make sure Zuberi and the others weren't hurt too badly, knowing that they needed to move soon, that Lencho and the militia would make their way down the elevator towers and soon be on their tails.

But as he rose, Uzochi stumbled, his body woozy.

No. He couldn't afford to pass out, not when St. John Soldiers would be on their way to cart them off. He willed his legs to stand, but they buckled.

No, no, no. He refused to give up. He would do this, for Zuberi, for his friends. Uzochi closed his eyes, trying to call forth his powers again, but he was completely spent. And dizzy.

"Easy now," said a deep voice. "I've got you."

Uzochi blinked. He felt himself lifted off the ground. He tried to focus on the image in front of him, but it was fuzzy.

"I said I've got you now. Don't worry."

The voice . . . slightly familiar and strange all at once. Uzochi knew he should fight and hold on, but the last of his strength left him.

"Who . . . Who are . . ."

Uzochi didn't finish his question. The world spun around him as if he was still falling, the wide blueness of the sky becoming gray, heavy.

And then he saw nothing.

Chapter 9

Zuberi

Zuberi didn't know who the man was who'd lifted Uzochi up as easily as if he was clay, but the fact that he didn't seem particularly surprised that four teenagers had just fallen from the sky—only to hover in the air right before they went splat—told her that this was no regular human. He had to be a fellow Nubian.

There hadn't been time to decide if he could be trusted, even though she found the man unsettling, with his imposing height and tattered, layered robes that made him look like a Jedi from one of those ancient sci-fi holos. All of his phantoms were focused on tending to Uzochi, and that had to be enough, at least for now. Tasha was frazzled and could barely move, Zaire was still woozy and looked like he was going to puke his guts out yet again, and Uzochi was plain knocked out. That left only Zuberi to take charge. Zuberi and her, at the moment, borderline useless gift of precognition.

Okay, stop that shit, girl, she said to herself. *No time for moping around. Not now.*

Zuberi could feel that she had some sort of cut on her forehead, but it barely hurt, something to ignore. She looked at Zaire, who'd regained his footing, moving slowly as he managed to help Tasha to her feet. Zuberi could tell that the big guy was hurt. His transformations, the fight, the fall . . . that was a lot, even for Zaire. He wasn't meeting her eyes as the group trudged forward, trying to find an exit from the park, Zuberi all too aware that quite a few people had probably witnessed their fall from the sky. She wished for Uzochi's powers to sift through someone else's mind, to figure out who knew what around them. And another question arose: Why had Zaire helped them?

"So, what the hell was that all about?" she asked, turning to the large boy. "You almost killed us with that stunt. There had to be a better way to escape . . ."

Zaire shook his head, his face consumed with shame. "I didn't mean to do that, okay? I didn't fully realize where we were. I wouldn't have jumped from the window if I'd known."

"Oh, give me a break," Zuberi said, raising her voice. "Everyone knows that Starlight is right at the sky city's edge. The greenhouse gets featured on social every freakin' minute . . ."

"Well, I didn't know, okay?" Zaire shouted back. "In case you haven't figured it out, I barely know anything about the sky. It's not like I've had a lot of free time to explore, 'cause of my training."

"Exactamundo. You hit it right on the head, mister—your freakin' training!" Zuberi yelled. "You're in cahoots with the St. Johns, who've done all sorts of horrible shit to our people. Why in Goddess's name should I trust you?"

Zaire hung his head low, his body scrunching up. Zuberi remembered seeing that pose in their high school corridors, when Zaire occasionally looked like he wanted nothing more than to fold into his gargantuan frame and disappear. Tasha said nothing as the two bickered, holding her side as she walked. The stranger was silent as well, moving swiftly just behind them, carrying Uzochi.

"Listen," Zaire said, "I joined the militia because I . . . I felt like I needed to back up my gang and Lencho. And when we were given the opportunity to ascend, it was like a miracle, considering how Nubians live. It wasn't so bad being up there, having nice things, getting to practice my gift. But then we had to go and clash with y'all at the theater, which I wasn't cool with. And on top of that, seeing Lencho attack Uzochi just now?" Zaire frowned and shook his head, looking directly at Zuberi. "I'm sorry, but it wasn't right. Uzochi helped me out when I first transformed. I thought I was gonna die, but he stayed by my side, got me through my awakening. I couldn't just stand by and let him be hurt, not like before when we were kids, not by Lencho."

A look of fear crossed Zaire's face. "Something's up . . . with Lencho, I mean. Something ain't right with how he's been acting lately. Always mad for no reason, and there's . . . I don't know, a gloominess around him all the time. When he started to drain me, I sure 'nuff couldn't stay up there. I mean, I had to get away. Couldn't just leave y'all with him." Tears began to stream down Zaire's face as he walked, his words strained and ragged. "Listen, Zuberi, I know you have no reason to believe me after all the shit with the Divine, but I ain't trying to mess with you. Like I said, I was just trying to help out, to be there for Uzochi, like he was there for me. I fucked up with the escape, I know that, but you can trust me. Really."

Zuberi observed Zaire closely as he spoke, none of his phantoms indicating that he posed an immediate threat. In fact, they all showed Zaire hobbling forward, just as he was now, with one faint image showing him on the ground holding himself as he wept. A scared boy needing to be comforted.

She tried to think everything through, tried not to let either his real-world or phantom tears get to her. Yes, he'd saved them, but he'd also been one of Vriana's captors. The girl who'd always been kind to him, who'd even had a misplaced crush on him. How had he lived with himself, knowing she was a prisoner with those slimeballs?

But then Zuberi's heart sank again. She had more than failed to get Vriana back. She'd been too late. Her best friend hadn't recognized her. With those horrible implants, they'd done something to Vriana's mind. Maybe permanently.

No. Zuberi had to believe that it could be changed. As soon as they got back to the Jungle, she'd speak to the elders. She'd find folks in the lower city who specialized in implants, who knew how those things worked for Up High folk. They'd find a way to restore Vriana. They had to.

Except, how were they going to get back home? As they used one of the East Side pathways to exit the park, she noticed that the streets were crawling with St. John Soldiers. She had no idea how or when word would get out about what had just happened in the Up High, but her group was way too conspicuous. Zuberi had the good sense to take off her vest and instructed Tasha to do the same so they'd look less like militiamen. The last thing she wanted was for them to be questioned by others who thought they were actual militia, but was the switch sufficient? She peered behind her shoulder at the stranger, feeling unease in her bones. She knew she couldn't blindly lead this person to the Children, not without answers. But then again . . . she could barely keep her own feet moving. She had to get home.

Zuberi led them into an alley, then looked up and scanned for cameras. There was one, at the far end of the alley, but she saw that it was shattered. For that, Zuberi was grateful, though she kept her eyes peeled for any video drones that might've been sent their way, swift and hard to spot. Under cover of the alley's limited darkness, she held up her hand, indicating for Zaire and the stranger to stop. The man gently laid Uzochi on the ground while Zaire and Tasha both leaned against the side of a building.

"We're a pretty good distance from the elevator towers now," Zuberi said. "Zaire, you have the most experience with Krazen's militia. You think they'll try and come for us?"

His eyes stayed low as he answered Zuberi's question. "Probably. I mean, they're probably regrouping and comparing notes and trying to figure out who to send after us. It'll be St. John Soldiers for sure. Maybe a lot of 'em."

Shit. Zuberi tried to run through all that had just happened. She didn't think any one of them was immediately identifiable, though once Lencho spilled the beans, Krazen and his forces would know that a trio of Children had managed to enter the Up High without proper accreditation, destroy public property, and knock out his oh-so-pretentious daughter. And Lencho would be able to identify Uzochi and her as the culprits. Even though it had felt wonderful to do so at the time, Zuberi now regretted her decision to lay hands on Sandra St. John. What would be the repercussions for the Children and Nubians in general? They'd already passed that horrible registration act. What else would come their way?

Zuberi paced the alley, forcing herself to breathe but feeling her anxiety ratchet up with every moment. She was at a loss for how she was supposed to get from here back to the Jungle. They could just take a hover cab or public transportation, but that seemed way too conspicuous. Maybe Tasha could summon up a few more illusions to help disguise them and they could head downtown by foot.

And she had another, more immediate issue to consider. Zuberi turned to the stranger. "So who are you and why were you following us?"

The man seemed genuinely taken aback. Zaire and Tasha stared at him accusingly as well.

"Let's not BS," she said, trying her best not to curse at an adult. "You ran up to us right after we landed. That can't be coincidence. You had to be watching our movements, right? You knew we were up there."

The man continued to struggle to find his words. "I . . . well, yes, I was following you once I became aware of what you were trying to do. I purposely lingered in the park after you took the elevator towers to ascend. It was only through divine fortune that I happened to be close when you fell from the sky. But please, my intentions are not nefarious. I simply wanted to be there for my boy. For Uzochi."

What? His boy?!?!

And then Zuberi heard a slight crunch, the sound of footsteps on garbage and pavement.

Even in her weakened state, Zuberi whipped around toward the passageway behind the group. She was fighting-form ready to defend them against whoever had followed. She refused to go down without a fight, inhaling as she prepared to face St. John Soldiers.

But instead of militiamen, she saw nothing but darkness. An empty alley.

A kid slowly crept out of the shadows.

A mix of emotions spiked inside Zuberi at the sight of the youth. Confusion. Distrust. Anger. But Zaire moved forward at once, surprisingly undeterred. Zuberi quickly looked down at the stranger next to her, who'd crouched beside Uzochi.

"Watch him closely," she told the man.

The stranger's eyes narrowed as he glanced up at her. She got the sense that he didn't like being bossed around, but frankly she didn't care. She strode forward after Zaire, coming to stand alongside him.

"Sajah?" Zaire said. "That you?"

The slim youth nodded as they took in the group. "Yeah, it's me. What are you doing down here?"

"I should be asking you the same thing," Zaire said. "Up in the sky, at training, you just . . . vanished. It was kinda sick. I mean, I'm not one to talk with my gift . . . so that's your power? You some sort of teleporter?"

Sajah said nothing, their eyes continuing to scan the group, clearly distrustful of Zaire. "I guess you could say that," they finally said. "I create portals, but my gift's different from that nutty Divine teleporter girl I once heard about who liked to pop around like she was Elevated. But you didn't answer my question." Sajah crossed their arms. "What're you doing here?"

Zuberi scanned Sajah's phantoms, seeing no indication that they were about to harm the group in any way, only seeing a couple of figures running for safety. One version of Sajah, the version that Zuberi discerned would be the likeliest future, continued to talk to them, albeit warily.

She didn't know this kid, but she was going to trust her gut, trust her gift, just as her father had advised.

"Sajah, my name is Zuberi Ragee," she said, extending her hand. "We're here because we just tried to save a friend who was taken to the sky against her will by Krazen St. John. We had to run to save ourselves."

Sajah's eyes widened. They took Zuberi's hand, giving it a light shake. "That place, the Up High, it's nuts." They looked accusingly at Zaire once again, like the Divine was to blame for whatever madness had gone down. "Life's been hard, you know," Sajah continued. "I used to live in the Swamp with my pops, but when he died, I didn't have anybody, didn't have anywhere to go. Those militia guys have been making their rounds with those holos, saying how good life is once you ascend, that if you're a gifted Nubian, there'll be all sorts of opportunities." Sajah looked at the ground. "I took out the street camera and camped out here, super close to the park just so I could more easily get to the Up High"—they paused—"with my gift."

"Wait, you got to the Up High just by using your power?" Zaire asked.

"Only a couple of times," Sajah said. "I mean, I needed to see for myself if everything they said about the sky city was true. Honestly, I didn't think I fit in, but what choice did I have?"

"Why didn't you come down to SoHo to the Jungle, where the Children are?" Zuberi asked. "The Up High wasn't your only option."

Sajah looked at Zuberi as if she was the dumbest person on Earth. "Listen here, lady, do you know that I've lived in the Swamp for my entire life in a freakin' one-room shack with my pops? After he died, I had to bust my ass working odd jobs every day to come up with currency to pay rent, and then after alla that my place tumbled into the floodwaters when the seawall collapsed. I mean, no offense, but y'all Children and all those other Nubians look like you're living in a shithole." Sajah crossed their arms, peering at Zuberi and Zaire defiantly. "I shouldn't have to live like that. Not anymore, not with what I can do. So I went up to one of those militia dudes and let them know I was Nubian and gifted, to sign me up, that I was ready to ascend. It was all solid. Got nice clothes, a real nice place to live with everything provided for. I mean, I never experienced anything like the sky. I just didn't think that the dude they have in charge of training gifted Nubians was loco."

"That's . . . that's Lencho," Zaire said, his body shuddering at the mere mention of the name. "Something's wrong. Something's changed. He wasn't always like that."

Sajah gave a big shrug, glowering. "That's not my fuckin' problem. I didn't sign up for training and a better life just for some loony guy who looks like he's on steroids to take my head off. I mean, that bozo looked like he was really gonna hurt me. To hurt *you*." Sajah pointed their index finger at Zaire. "I needed to get the hell up out of there."

"And so you returned here, to where you're camped out," Zuberi said, fully grasping Sajah's situation.

They nodded. "I just needed a moment, to try and figure things out. I mean, with my gift, I could technically go wherever I want in the city, maybe even all of Tri-State East in general, but I still need to support myself. So I was trying to come up with a—"

"Uhm, Zuberi," Tasha said as she crept forward, clearly not wanting to interrupt. "I think you might want to see this."

Tasha led the other girl to the alleyway entrance and pointed to a holo-billboard a few buildings south on the same street.

**LOWER-CITY NUBIANS BREAK INTO
UP HIGH PROPERTY, ASSAULT SANDRA ST. JOHN
AND MILITIA . . . STORY IN 5 . . .**

"You've got to be kidding me," Zuberi said under her breath. How had reporters gotten ahold of the story that quickly? She turned back to the group, trying to assess their options. "All right, y'all, we've gotta move. Tasha, I'm sorry, I know you're probably not feeling so great, but I must ask you to create your illusions again. Create a disguise. We're gonna have to take a hover bus or cab or . . ."

"I . . . I can get you where you need to go," Sajah said, their voice cracking just a little. "I didn't exactly mean what I just said about y'all living in a shithole. Sometimes I say things without thinking." They looked down. "What I should've said is, I can help . . ."

"You mean by using your portals?" Zuberi replied. She took a moment to reflect. It would be the perfect solution, freeing them from worry about being recognized or about Tasha burning out from using her gift.

Zuberi focused, taking in once again the phantoms floating above Sajah's head, seeing them walking into a mist by themself, walking into a mist with the group, returning to the little shelter they'd constructed in the alley . . . There was nothing that indicated danger, and Zaire seemed like he was vouching for the kid, even though Zuberi still wasn't sure she trusted Zaire.

"All right," she said. "Is everyone okay with this?"

Sajah stepped off to the side, their eyes dispelling a blackish-gray mist that filled much of the alleyway. In an instant, the mist became a shadowy circle, smoke rolling off the sides.

"This is my portal," Sajah explained. "I've only traveled with additional people a couple of times, so I suggest everybody hold hands, and then I'll be able to get us to the Jungle. I know where it is, so it's easy for me to visualize."

"It's that easy?" Zaire asked, mirroring Zuberi's skepticism.

"This is a trick!" the stranger said behind them, finally speaking up after being silent for so long. "No Nubian gift has ever worked this way. We don't parlay with shadow. I don't know what this child is trying to prove, but such abilities have nothing to do with the kinetic."

Zuberi shifted on her feet, the stranger's outburst confirming the assumption she'd made upon meeting him. He was definitely Nubian, or at least considered himself an expert on their lore, and he was claiming that Sajah's gift wasn't authentically Nubian.

Zuberi looked back at Sajah, using her precognition once again.

She had to trust herself.

"Sir, I don't know who you are, but I believe Sajah is telling the truth. And we need to get home safely, with as little drama as possible. We need to get to my people. Who knows what's coming." *Because of me,* she wanted to add.

"Everyone, let's join hands," Zuberi said to the group. The stranger managed to take her left hand even as he balanced Uzochi on one shoulder. His strength was amazing.

The others warily joined hands as well, forming a short chain that Sajah soon led through the darkness.

Chapter 10

Uzochi

Uzochi first heard the sound of water. He became aware of his fingers next, flexing and stretching them. But when he opened his eyes, he didn't see the grass he'd blacked out on. Nor did he see the walls of his room at the old Divine headquarters that he now regarded as home. Instead, where he was standing . . . he'd been here before, somehow.

Sand whipped in the air. Uzochi tasted salt on the wind. He looked around, finding an ocean lapping at his bare feet. Above him, the sun melted into the horizon, tinging the world with rose and golden hues.

"Please, don't do this. There must be another way."

Adisa's voice.

Uzochi realized he'd once again fallen into the elder's consciousness and been tugged into a random memory. He was in fact inhabiting the body of Adisa, his feet moving forward of their own volition, movements playing out in what had already come to pass.

"I'm begging you to reconsider," Adisa said to someone.

"What you speak of, it's dangerous. Incredibly dangerous, in fact. Though you are our revered catalyst, there's simply no need to use your gifts in this way. Consider the ramifications."

Uzochi blinked, focusing on a figure in front of him who was partially enclosed in shadow, the scene darkening with the setting sun. Adisa remained rooted to the spot, terror running through his veins. Uzochi's mind spun at what he was experiencing, finding such emotions bizarre coming from Adisa. He had never known the elder to show fear even when death had arrived.

"You have a responsibility," Adisa said again. "To your people. To your child."

The figure turned, revealing a flash of deep brown eyes, eyes that Uzochi had seen thousands of times in the mirror, for they looked exactly like his own.

All at once, the memory sharpened. A key clicking into a lock.

He was seeing his father, Siran. This encounter must've happened soon before he died. Adisa had begged Siran not to put himself in harm's way, for Uzochi knew the story of how his father had stood up to the storm that destroyed all of Nubia, how he'd done everything in his power as the catalyst to protect his people. Had Adisa detected the severity of the storm that would submerge their land? Was he begging Siran to abandon the idea of saving Nubia?

Something rippled in Uzochi's own memory . . . his uncle Kefle's words about how Siran's actions as catalyst had actually been selfish. But Uzochi knew that such an accusation could only be taken half seriously. Listening to a take on his father from Kefle, a bitter, violent man, would be like listening to Lencho's account of anything Uzochi had done. Colored by hatred that thrummed through his heart.

The memory abruptly shifted, like mist pouring into a room, and Uzochi was taken to another time and place. He wanted to reach out, to stop the change and stay with his father longer. But it was not to be. Now, in the new memory, he was Adisa as a ten-year-old child, sitting on a field of grass, his head tipped up to the sky.

"It's time for you to learn how Nubia began," said a voice that felt shimmery and incandescent. It was almost as if the voice carried a trilling melody, bounding through the memory like a song. Above little Adisa, an elder's face appeared, with milky eyes and flowing gray tresses. She was someone Uzochi didn't recognize, but the young Adisa knew her well, for he was filled with joy and anticipation upon seeing the woman.

The elder smiled at Adisa's eagerness. "Are you ready, child, to fully embrace our history?"

Uzochi as Adisa nodded, and then the elder touched his forehead with her finger. Instantly, a new landscape snapped into existence. A field of wildflowers bloomed as far as the eye could see, children racing up and down the terrain. One child dragged their hand along an empty patch of dirt. At their touch, flowers exploded from the ground. Another child leapt and spun and danced, sending forth platinum arcs of light that dazzled.

"In the days when our people first awoke to their heightened potential, Nubia was a utopian place," the elder said, her voice echoing over the memory. "Almost all Nubians saw their kinetic-based gifts as a natural extension of who they were, using their gifts to play or contribute to the betterment of society or exult in their beauty."

Uzochi through Adisa's eyes watched with wonder as more kids appeared, each of them wielding their powers. One child scrambled on all fours and in seconds had morphed into a sleek and swift leopard. Another Nubian dashed past the animal, running at breathtaking speed before leaping across a slim river to land on a sandy bank. Uzochi saw a third child wiggle his fingers before creating large hoops of kaleidoscopic light through which another Nubian glided, using their gift to fly with the winds.

It was all so wondrous.

What must it have been like, Uzochi thought, to grow up with the idea that your gift was something to be cherished? That it was intrinsically part of you? How would his life have been different if he'd known as a kid that what he could do now was as much a part of him as his eye color or the texture of his hair?

In the memory, one child burst forth from the others. They glowed almost as bright as the sun above them, then turned toward the sky and slowly rose, hovering above the rest.

"Catalysts were particularly honored for their ability to understand the potential uses of the kinetic," the elder continued. "It is our job, young Adisa, to guide the catalysts of our time and all the times to come, to help them use their abilities wisely, judiciously, as informed by the triumphs and tragedies of the past. As telepaths, as keepers of Nubian memory, we are their guides to the richness of our history, just as they are the key to our people honing and developing our gifts. Catalysts are the key to our evolution as Nubians."

The sight of kids exulting in their gifts faded away. Uzochi as Adisa continued to sit, enraptured by the elder's words.

"You, our young telepath," said the woman, smiling down at Adisa, "hold a great gift. Your ability to augment and manipulate memory is among our most powerful and essential treasures. Once you come of age, so long as you live, you will hold the memories that I and other elders bequeath to you. And when you are as old as I am, with hair just as white . . ."

The elder reached forward and tickled the young Adisa, who let out a laugh.

". . . then you will continue our tradition. You will pass down our history to future catalysts and whomever else you choose, making sure that Nubia never truly dies."

Uzochi felt the young Adisa's awe even through the decades that must've passed since the memory was fresh and new. Uzochi was overcome, starting to fully grasp the resilience of his people. Through their gifts, they'd created a sort of psychic oral history, one that could be explored through the ages even after previous generations had died. His heart swelled with pride at what his community had done. His heart swelled with pride . . . to be Nubian.

"But Auntie," said the young Adisa, "what if I can't remember all the memories? What if I forget?"

It was such an innocent question, so unlike the wise words of future Adisa, that Uzochi chuckled.

The elder only smiled. "You, little historian, cannot forget the memories that will be shared. They will be protected by the power of the kinetic, a power that surges through you. They will be protected by the strong, robust mind you already possess. So long as you continue to pass our memories on when the time comes, our history will be protected."

Uzochi's heart flipped. So this was why Adisa had transferred his subconscious to Uzochi at the time of his death. He tried to breathe, to grapple a bit with what this meant. All of Nubia's history, then, rested in his mind. The pressure of it felt heavy, overwhelming. In the real world, Uzochi sometimes felt like he was drowning in the responsibility he carried. Why had Adisa trusted him with something so precious when he knew Uzochi wasn't ready to be a leader?

He looked up, hoping that somehow young Adisa would ask a question that gave him the answers he sought, but the scene shifted again. The light was pulled from the room as Uzochi was yanked into a deeper memory. This, he knew instantly, was not a happy one. The memory was tinged with red, colored by anger, a furious, destructive rage.

Uzochi didn't understand what he was witnessing, the pounding of his heart almost unbearable. The idyllic scenes with Adisa were replaced by Nubians crying out in anguish, their mangled bodies intertwined in a great ravine that scarred the land. Humongous shards of rock flew through the air and smashed into already damaged golden towers, bringing them crashing down. Thick black smoke obscured a large outdoor market that burned.

Quite simply, it was hell.

A figure floated above it all, like the image of the catalyst that had just appeared before in Uzochi's consciousness. But this figure wasn't silent and serene. He laughed maniacally, gesturing wildly and shouting out harsh words in a language Uzochi couldn't understand.

He had to get away. The carnage. The death. This place wasn't safe.

He had to . . .

Uzochi gasped as he opened his eyes. He struggled to sit up, realizing he was in a bed somewhere. Zuberi's gaze appeared above him. At the sight of her warm eyes, Uzochi's breathing steadied, at least until he saw the thin line of blood on her forehead that reminded him of what had happened before he blacked out. He sat straight up, reaching forward, pulling Zuberi to his chest, holding her as tightly as he could.

"Uzochi," she said. "Thank Goddess you're okay."

He breathed, taking in the feel of her arms around him, taking in the waves of uncertainty that emanated from her body. Someone nearby cleared their throat.

Zuberi pulled back.

"What is it?" Uzochi asked her. "Is everything all right?"

She hesitated just a moment before nodding toward a spot behind Uzochi. Slowly, he turned, finding a man standing in front of the crumbling exposed brick walls that were common in the Jungle. A rather tall man, in fact, with thick, braided black hair and a long, unkempt beard and eyes that looked just like his.

The man's face cracked into a sad half smile as he said, "Hello, son."

Chapter 11

Sandra

As Sandra surveyed her reflection in her bedroom mirror, evening having descended on the Up High, she supposed she should have felt gratitude. She wouldn't need surgery or contour tech after that vicious Nubian she-beast had attacked her. There was a light bruise that could easily be covered by makeup and slight swelling on her right cheek, nothing that would be noticeable to the casual observer. But, with the news media having learned of the incident at Starlight, she was about to be subjected to tons of unwanted scrutiny unless she lived like a hermit. Or perhaps her father would make it clear through his media back channels that absolutely no one was allowed to harass his daughter. She highly doubted that.

Krazen had just sent Sandra the briefest of messages on her personal comm after learning of the attack. He was busy. He had a lower-city rally in the Bronx in the next hour and then had to travel over to Staten Island. He was sure she was fine. She knew what to do, how to deal with those circling vultures from the holo-news. Sure, his only child had just been assaulted . . . not a big deal. She could handle it. The election took precedence.

As Sandra looked at her face for the umpteenth time, she held back the tears, swearing to herself that she wouldn't cry. How long had she wished that her father could somehow transform into someone else? That *she* could be someone else? The indignity of it all, to be passed up for opportunities time and time again. To see his favor bestowed upon the likes of basic lower-city people like Tilly, and Lencho, and the Divine. A filthy *gang*. To be constantly dismissed like she was the help, not the daughter of the wealthiest man in Tri-State East. She was beautiful, intelligent, charismatic, immeasurably rich . . . and routinely demeaned.

Sandra closed the closet that held the mirror she gazed at and sat at her desk. Should she do as her father advised and activate one of her implants to record the holo that the press would be expecting, saying everything was fine? Give them that trademark vixen performance? "Oh, that Sandra St. John!" a popular Helios Network talk show host had once exclaimed. "That glittery girl can flash and sashay her way through anything."

She placed her hands flat on her desk, the coolness of the metal invigorating.

No.

There'd be no clip recorded for the press. Let those idiots conjecture to their hearts' content about how she'd responded to the attack. She needed time for herself.

Sandra looked down at her hand, noting the seams of circuitry glinting faintly underneath her skin. When she needed to shut out the world, her implants were always there for her, enabling her to call forth whatever distraction she desired in the form of classic films or fashion documentaries or secret files that her father thought were adequately encrypted. Sandra had been one with technology for as long as she could remember. As an infant, she'd had an exterior monitor installed on her scalp, a procedure considered relatively safe even for babies. This allowed her caretakers to monitor her every move, her brain activity, her heartbeat. It had been that tech monitor that had caught the slightest variation in her vital signs and alerted her family to a potentially life-threatening viral infection when she was a toddler. She'd promptly been given the proper medicine, but she'd heard the story growing up from enough nannies to know the truth: technology was life-saving, part of humanity's evolution, an essential tool for those who'd ascended.

Her father's work, of course, epitomized this philosophy, as over the decades he'd helped build a massive temple to advanced technology and cybernetics, literally woven into the fabric of how the Up High lived. Sandra's implants knew her bodily patterns intimately. Each morning, she was gently awakened by the vibrations they sent through her skull and her body. She needed only to utter the name of a favorite song— the singing group Complete's "Summer Kisses," for instance, which she listened to all the time—and it would play for her via the tiny comm embedded in her ear. Messages had historically been a mere tap of the wrist away, able to be projected as a holo from her eye and sent to anyone whose body address she knew. Thankfully, she could now take things to the next level with her implants . . . well, really with all of the devices that surrounded her. Sandra had always found fresh ways to manipulate the tech that existed in the sky, but her current understanding of the digital world . . . exquisite.

She had spent much of her young life quietly indulging in tech hobbies when she wasn't immersed in holo-shows or history books (her most hidden passion) or keeping track of her father's exploits. Her tutors had marveled when at fourteen she had created featherlight accessories that could be worn like lashes but would actually capture a picture with every blink, storing the image in the user's implant. The following year, she'd figured out a way to make articles of clothing shift color depending on someone's mood, becoming all the rage among Up High teens for months. By the time she'd turned seventeen, Sandra had several patents in her name for original tech, creating her own stream of revenue independent of her father. It was an accomplishment that she kept under wraps, having learned from Krazen long ago that it was to her advantage to be underestimated.

So using tech to get what she needed from a lower-city Nubian, to bend Vriana to her will? Elementary. Sandra had fully understood the Conway Protocols, named for a scientist who had once used experimental rehabilitation techniques on sky city convicts. Up High crime rates were low compared to the rest of New York, but there were still people here who didn't appreciate their good fortune, living far above the flooding that besieged the rest of the city. And so Travis R. Conway had endeavored to correct this flaw by creating implants that would provide convicts with artificial memories. Their new personalities were informed by the belief that they were happy, well-adjusted people minus the troubles thought to have shaped their criminal behavior. The trial program was declared successful, significantly lowering the recidivism rate among the Up High convicts who'd been given the Conway implants. There was even talk of eventually using the procedure among the incarcerated in the lower city. But everyone from civil rights attorneys to philosophers had deemed the Conway Protocols problematic, something akin to modern slavery. And there was concern that the device might cause unforeseen damage to the brain.

Sandra knew all of this when she okayed giving Vriana the implant that would realign her memories as established by the protocols. The procedure was illegal and taboo, so Sandra had bribed a team of doctors to complete the operation, paying them enough currency so that they'd be set for the rest of their days. And then she had to figure out how to configure a life for Vriana where she would only meet people who would never challenge the details of the memories created for her. When Sandra had explained to her father that it was the only way to ensure that their asset was under his control, considering the girl's powers of persuasion, he'd agreed, though of course he wanted the operation to be a secret. And so Vriana was given a fresh set of memories, one where she believed she was a Nubian orphan raised Up High and that the St. Johns had taken her in as a foster child. In this fabulous new life, Vriana and Sandra were something akin to sisters, Vriana having her own set of private tutors who worked around her schedule. And why didn't Vriana have implants placed throughout her body like so many other sky city dwellers? That was due to polymer allergies, an issue that legitimately affected some Up High residents. Vriana would thus only have one implant, a simple personal comm, with the girl not realizing the true nature of the device on her skull.

Other alterations had to be made to her backstory. Because of her heritage, Vriana had awoken to her gift of persuasion just like other Nubians had come into their powers. But above all else, her loyalties were to her family, to the older pseudo-sister who'd shared everything she could when they were growing up.

After the attack on the greenhouse, Vriana had holo-called Sandra several times, making sure she was okay, apologizing profusely for running away when the attack happened. "I was so scared," Vriana said. "And I tried to zap that crazy girl with my gift to get her to leave us alone. Sandy, I feel terrible about leaving you there."

Vriana was in fact the only person after the attack who'd actually called Sandra and talked to her at length to make sure she was okay. That was the thing about the Conway Protocols. The procedure didn't alter the core personalities of its subjects. If someone was subdued and stoic, they remained subdued and stoic. If someone was chipper and bouncy, they remained chipper and bouncy. Vriana's kindness and effervescence and ability to care for loved ones, unwavering. She was the first friend Sandra had ever had.

Sandra had reassured the other girl that everything was fine, that she was okay, that these were volatile times and weird attacks sometimes came with being a St. John. She reminded

Vriana that that was why they had to get these other Nubians under control, why Krazen needed to become mayor. That was why Vriana thought it was okay for her to use her powers on several of the city councilors who'd given Krazen their mayoral endorsements or backed the registration act at her oh-so-sweet behest. Sandra and her team were only just beginning to fully understand the scope of the Nubian's gift now that they could study her up close. How the girl could fully take over someone's emotions for short periods of time but could also give people more subtle suggestions whose effects lasted for days, if not weeks.

Sandra gave a grim sort of smile, her satisfaction tinged with bitterness. She was the one who saw value in Vriana's gift, something Krazen had ignored. She was the one who, all by herself, had gotten the girl to the sky. And had her father given her any credit for what she'd accomplished? More access to his projects and plots? Real responsibility now that she was legally an adult? No, of course not. Why should anything change? She was only his daughter.

Sandra felt a tear tumble down her cheek.

Damn it. She'd broken her promise to herself.

Sandra tried to hold back the tears to no avail and found herself sobbing, an ugly, wretched sound that filled the corners of her room. She would never have access to all the privileges that being a St. John promised, not while her father held the reins. It was clear as day to her now. The futility of the games she'd played for so many years, trying to earn his favor. To be the perfect little agreeable creature.

Fuck that.

No more.

She rose from her desk and walked to her window, taking in the nighttime lights that dotted the surrounding buildings. The sky and its wonders were her heritage, what she was owed. From this day forward, Sandra swore she would never laugh or giggle or play coy ever again in order to appease others, much less her wretch of a father.

Her life had changed . . . radically so, in such a short time. She had real power, secret power, unimaginable power, and she would use what she had to change the world.

Chapter 12

Uzochi

Uzochi floated, his body light and airy as he drifted in and out of memories. He saw Adisa at different points of his life as a young man, learning about his powers of telepathy and carefully sifting through Nubian history in some sort of temple with gilded walls and ceilings. But he also saw Adisa as a boy, running across his native land. Through his eyes, Uzochi saw a stunningly clear turquoise ocean and more fields full of wildflowers. He saw people who laughed and sang, who would lift individual petals with their minds to create fanciful portraits of each other before scattering the flowers to the wind. Smiles and frolicking and communion with nature . . . unending warmth, everywhere he looked. Nubia was the heaven that his mother, Com'pa, had recently begun to describe in detail, and Uzochi's heart swelled with every sight he took in.

At some point, Adisa's memories gave way to Uzochi's, a switch he had increasingly grown used to, almost as if exploring Adisa's past encouraged Uzochi to revisit his own. Uzochi was now a child, no more than ten years old. His mother was showing him how to season his favorite dish, baked salmon, a rare treat considering their tight budget, but one Com'pa thought Uzochi deserved after getting almost straight As on his latest report card. (Uzochi had sworn that he would never get a B+ in math class again. Such a lowly grade.) He took in the apartment, the one they'd just moved to after years of living in the Swamp among other Nubians. There were still plenty of boxes left unpacked. A pair of pants that he tore during school recess was lying on the couch, waiting for Com'pa to mend. That was his mother, always working nonstop for herself and her son.

After the two had eaten dinner, with Com'pa sitting on the couch watching a reality dating holo, Uzochi had wandered to where the illustration of his father was perched on one of the living room bookshelves. *Siran, My Dear Heart,* his mom had written under the portrait of her husband that she'd drawn. The same term of endearment she called Uzochi. He'd stared at the image, wondering why the world had taken his father away. *Things would be different,* Uzochi had thought, *if my dad was alive.* His mom wouldn't have to work so hard all the time at her nursing job, taking all the shifts she could to earn currency and get them out of the Swamp. He'd imagined Siran as the kind of person who, through hard work and leadership, would have managed to find an excellent job, even in the rough lower city. Maybe his dad would even have found a way to get the family Up High.

Sometimes during his middle school years, his mother's portrait of Siran would appear to Uzochi as he slept, especially when he dreamed of ascension and having an easier life. But Uzochi was wise enough to know that all the yearning in the world couldn't bring someone back from the dead. And so he'd let go of his father and pressed forward for his mother. He'd worked hard enough and become an academic star so that *he* could be the one to get them Up High.

A misplaced dream.

Uzochi became vaguely aware that something was calling him to leave his memories. He tuned into reality, leaving the depths of his unconsciousness behind as the deep timbre of a voice rumbled in his head. The voice of the man who'd picked him up once he'd plummeted from Up High.

His father's voice.

Uzochi forced himself to focus. He flexed his fingers and his toes, positioning himself in the real world rather than the world of the mind. He vaguely remembered that after he had briefly awoken in the Jungle, drifting in and out of sleep, his parents had brought him back to the apartment he shared with his mother on the East Side in Manhattan's Kips Bay neighborhood. Uzochi was almost never at the apartment nowadays, spending far more time at the Jungle downtown. He remembered groggily walking up the steps of his building and then quickly falling asleep on the couch.

Parents. Uzochi had never used that word before when referring to his family.

He kept his eyes closed, breathed in the air around him, finding it full of the smell of spiced chicken and couscous with herbs, one of the standard meals of his household. His mother was cooking, and he could hear her pacing around their tiny kitchen, utensils clanking, water running in the sink, dishes being moved around.

Uzochi listened a tad more closely. She wasn't alone.

"I know you have many questions, my love," someone said. His father's voice. "And I will answer them all. But for now, please tell me more about our son?"

"*Our* son?" Com'pa said, her words coming out high and strained, nearing hysterics. "Our son. The son I've been raising alone in this Goddess-forsaken city because I thought you'd drowned."

Uzochi didn't dare open his eyes, didn't dare move. He knew that type of voice from Com'pa as well as he knew her cooking. It screamed danger, to not even think about trying to put anything over on her.

"Com'pa," Siran said, his voice a low rumble. "I assure you, I did not stay away with the intention of relinquishing my duties to my family. It was not until the children began to awaken to their powers that I had the strength to—"

"Our son is *mighty*," Com'pa said. Uzochi could tell she was speaking through gritted teeth. "A catalyst, like you, Siran. Just like you always dreamed of. He's a boy who's spent his entire life wondering about his father. And I had to be brave and tell him how his father died—"

She was sobbing. Something clattered to the floor. Maybe a cup or big spoon? Uzochi dared to open his eyes, crooking his gaze toward the kitchen. He saw his father's hands on his mother's.

"I thought I lost you," she said. "And now, all these years later . . ."

"I thought I lost *you*," Siran said, taking her hands, interlacing their fingers. "All of you. When I felt the power leave me, that was my only explanation. All of my people must have perished. I woke up in a place I didn't know. And when I dared to charter a boat to where I knew Nubia should be, I found nothing. My loss . . . it ate me alive, Com'pa. It was as if I was a dead man."

Uzochi's father paused, placing his hands against Com'pa's cheek. She recoiled, stepping back from her husband.

"My son," Siran pressed again. "Please, Com'pa. You might not accept me back into your heart. That, I can understand. But my son . . ."

"He will decide for himself," Com'pa answered. "Another time, when he's fully recovered. He is—"

"Awake," Uzochi managed, sitting up on the couch, trying his best to appear lucid and strong. "I'm awake, Ma."

Instantly, Com'pa was at Uzochi's side, pressing the back of her hand to his forehead.

"Uzochi," she said, uttering his name like a prayer. "I was so worried. I—"

"I'm fine," he said, trying not to sound petulant but also not wanting his father to see him as a child who needed to be babied. After all, hadn't his mother just said he was mighty? That was how Uzochi wanted to be treated. He was supposed to be catalyst, and he needed his father to see him that way.

Uzochi sat up, and Siran came around to stand before him. Uzochi wondered whether he should bow or kneel, having remembered that his father was technically royalty according to older Nubians. Wasn't that what you were supposed to do when greeting a king or queen? Or wait, was his father technically a prince according to the ancestral traditions? But before he could decide, Siran had pulled up one of the chairs and plopped himself down.

"He has your good looks, Com'pa," Siran said with a smile.

"Pah," Com'pa dismissed him, but Uzochi swore he saw a slight smile on his mother's tear-streaked face.

"Uzochi," Siran said, his voice light, yet laden with awe. "I am astonished to find myself sitting here across from you."

Uzochi swallowed. He wasn't sure what to say. He was so nervous that he was fighting to keep his legs from jiggling. He needed to exude strength. Calm and confidence.

"And I'm . . . I, uh, feel the same way," Uzochi managed, sounding like a pathetic copy of his father's bravado.

Still, Siran grinned. "I was even more shocked to see you falling hundreds of feet through the air."

Com'pa let out a gasp. "You did *what*? Zuberi and Beka didn't tell me—"

"—and even *more* shocked to see you slow to a stop just before you hit the ground," Siran continued, holding up a hand, turning toward Com'pa. Uzochi felt what he was trying to tell her, *It's okay.*

Siran turned back toward his son. "You did that with your kinetic gift, correct?"

Uzochi glanced at his mother, the warring emotions she was grappling with radiating from her skin—gratitude, anger, resentment, anxiety . . .

"Yes," Uzochi said, responding to his father. "I'm learning how to better use telekinesis, which is what saved us, but I consider myself to be more of an empath and telepath." And then, because Uzochi remembered his recent dreams, he added, "Like Adisa."

Siran regarded him quietly. He leaned back, running a hand through his thick beard.

"And you are catalyst, correct?" the man said. "I am not surprised, sitting here looking at you. But remember, Uzochi, as catalyst you could have drawn upon your friends' connection to the kinetic at any time to bolster your own power, to make your telekinesis mighty, as I have been told you have done before. You have every right to do this, whenever you choose."

Uzochi felt Siran's energy fill the apartment, a cozy heaviness that matched the man's raw power. It reminded Uzochi of the way Adisa could command a room. He wondered what the pair of them had been like when they interacted back in Nubia. Surely, the two would've been formidable.

"My son," Siran said in a quiet, pride-filled voice. "The catalyst."

Instantly, Uzochi's heart lifted. This was what he'd been waiting for all these years. Siran's appearances in his dreams weren't just the result of immature yearning, he decided. They were a promise of what was to come.

Without thinking, Uzochi jumped up and threw his arms around his father. For a moment, the room was quiet and everyone was still. And then his father embraced him in return.

"My son," Siran repeated yet again. "My *son*. How very good it is to be here."

Chapter 13

Zuberi

After almost falling to her death from the sky, Zuberi had reentered the Jungle with her spirit crushed, trying to come to terms with the fact that her mission to get Vriana back had failed. That she in fact might have made life insurmountably worse for her community.

Her group had managed to arrive at the Jungle safe and sound through Sajah's shadow portal, even though the experience was disconcerting. Zuberi wasn't afraid of the darkness, but something about the shadows felt unusual, as if pinpricks were passing over every inch of her skin with each step she took. After people had gotten over their surprise at her disheveled group's appearing out of thin air, Zuberi had been greeted by Beka and a couple of other elders, who quickly tried to piece together why Zuberi and Tasha had returned with a member of the Divine, a gangly kid with an attitude, and a rough-looking man who held Uzochi in his arms. And then she watched as Beka's face transformed when she took in the man's face.

"It . . . it isn't possible," said the elder. "This simply isn't—"

"I shall give you the explanation you need and deserve," said Siran, his voice low. "But first, we must tend to my son."

Yes, Uzochi's father was alive. Zuberi had realized this right outside Central Park as she and the others hid in the alleyway. It wasn't just that he'd called Uzochi "my boy," it was his features. Or rather his eyes. When Siran had met Zuberi's gaze, his dark brown eyes had flashed at her with a strength she recognized.

Those were Uzochi's eyes. Or, she realized with a start, Uzochi's eyes were this man's. Com'pa was a pretty good artist, though nowhere close to Tasha, and Zuberi remembered seeing random illustrations of people the few times she'd visited Uzochi's apartment. Among the images, she'd seen portraits of a man who looked like this one, though he'd been younger, stronger. More whole.

And so she'd traveled through a shadow portal with the last great Nubian catalyst alive and intact, clearly happy to be reunited with his son. At first, Zuberi worried that it would be full-out war between the adults, demanding to know how Siran had survived. But thankfully Beka kept the peace, merely giving a curt nod and saying, "Let's get Uzochi to a room," gesturing for Siran and Zuberi to follow.

Uzochi will be okay, she told herself as they disappeared around a corner. *This would happen to any of us who just exerted themselves the way he did. Uzochi's sensitive, but he's also tough.*

And thankfully he *was* okay. After Siran had lain Uzochi down on a mat, that girl with the shiny hair, the healer Veronique, sprayed his body with mist from her fingertips for several minutes. Zuberi hoped with all her might that they wouldn't need to take him to a med center. And then Uzochi had woken up, meeting the father he thought was dead.

It was an awkward moment, and Zuberi had enough sense to know that she probably needed to give father and son time to themselves. Com'pa had been alerted about what had happened and was on her way downtown. Zuberi had left the small room that held Uzochi and returned to the Jungle's main hall, lost in thought, trying to understand her emotions, something she found herself doing constantly now that she had a boyfriend who was an empath.

She stopped herself. Boyfriend. Was that who Uzochi was to her?

Zuberi scanned the space, trying to spot where Sajah and Zaire had gone. Then she saw the small, communal holo-unit that had been placed in the hall, the broadcaster reporting on the developing story of the Nubian attack on Starlight Greenhouse that had occurred not even an hour ago. Zuberi turned away from the holo. She didn't have the strength to deal with the news right now, not when it meant she'd have to accept the fact that they didn't have Vriana back. She just couldn't do it.

Zuberi noticed a cluster of adults walking toward her, probably wanting to get intel about what exactly had happened Up High. Suddenly Thato appeared in front of her, blocking Zuberi from their path.

"I'll be taking my daughter home now," he told the group, the dismissal in his voice clear.

At that, Zuberi's heart swelled with gratitude. No one . . . absolutely no one fucked with Thato. Father and daughter hurriedly walked back to their newly established "home," which was really an old Divine apartment several floors up.

After taking a long shower, Zuberi gazed upon the cracked mirror in the bathroom, running her hand across her forehead. She'd had a bad gash from broken glass at the greenhouse, but Veronique, after helping out Uzochi, had quickly swiveled to Zuberi and placed her fingers over the cut. That was just a few minutes ago. The gash was completely gone. Zuberi instead traced the silver scar on her chin, still her most prominent injury. A reminder to keep going.

After some time, when she walked into the makeshift living room, she saw that her father had brewed them tea. He poured her a cup and gestured toward their makeshift wooden table for her to sit down. She grabbed the drink and took a seat. He sat across from her, hands steepled, and waited for her explanation.

Where was she supposed to begin? Zuberi inhaled a breath, letting the scent of the tea steady her.

"She was up there, Dad," Zuberi said, her voice failing her and breaking. "But they did something to her. Something horrible."

Thato only watched her, his silence urging her on.

"They've given her a tech implant, and I think it's done something to her mind," Zuberi said. "Like maybe it's made her forget who she really is. She didn't remember me, and Uzochi said that something about her thoughts felt off."

Her hands shook slightly as she gripped the mug. It was so hot that she knew she must be burning her skin, but she held on just the same as she told Thato the rest of what had occurred, from the moment Lencho appeared to when they'd finally returned to the Jungle. "I failed Vriana," she said finally. "I failed all of us. You know Krazen's going to use this to his advantage to continue to turn public opinion against Nubians. To make sure the registration act is *truly* enforced."

"Daughter," Thato said, moving closer so that he could put his hand on her shoulder. "This wasn't your failure. You are in fact such an astounding success that it boggles the mind to think you've been on this earth a mere seventeen years."

Zuberi looked up at her father.

"Aw, Dad . . ."

"You are correct," Thato continued. "Krazen will use this to his advantage. I'm sure the measures to be put in place for enforcement of the registration act will be draconian, to say the least. I've long said we won't be safe in the city with the awakenings. But even I will admit, the situation has grown more . . . complicated."

"In what way?" Zuberi asked, wiping at her eyes with her sleeve, grateful she was able to hold it together.

"You haven't noticed the change because you've been consumed by your wish to get Vriana back. And you've been distracted by a certain young catalyst who's captured your attention." Thato arched his left brow and tilted his head, as if he was daring his daughter to disagree. Zuberi just sucked her teeth and rolled her eyes, pursing her lips in a tiny smile.

"Nubians in the lower city, even with the waves of paranoia and uncertainty directed toward us, we now have people who are on our side. Some of the holo-commentators have decreed that our collective awakening might be the dawn of a new age for society, that we might be a harbinger of what's to come. But more important, Beri, is that many of our neighbors here have welcomed us. Haven't you noticed, in the main hall of the Jungle and other buildings, how non-Nubians come now to sit and talk with us? Back in the Swamp, that was practically unheard of."

Zuberi blinked, sitting with what her father had just said. "I . . . yeah, okay. I haven't really been paying attention, I guess."

"You've been distracted. Some have brought us food and tools we might need after being displaced yet again from our homes. Ever since the fire broke out at that building a couple of blocks down and the elemental Abdul and a few of the others saved so many people, public opinion has shifted slightly. Those acts of bravery were caught on camera, daughter. And did you know that that Nubian boy with the strange haircut who can accelerate the growth of plants . . . what's his name again?"

"His name's Leonard, Dad."

"Yes, Leonard . . . such a bizarre, non-Nubian name . . . at any rate, this Leonard has started a community garden where all manner of fruits and vegetables are propagated. He gives them away for free to those who need food, Nubians and non-Nubians alike. Krazen has this story that all of the gifted must be under his control, that otherwise we're far too dangerous, but we're showing that when left alone, we're just as capable of helping others." Thato paused. "Even after the wickedness we've endured."

Zuberi let her father's words rush over her. "You . . . you think we might be safe here?"

"Not at all. My position hasn't changed. It's clearly in our best interests to leave the city, and I've been working to make it happen. With the registration act, who knows what terrible protocols they'll be coming up with for Nubians to live under. Considering the history of this land, our children could literally be enslaved, and I will not have that. I'm simply saying that we have allies, that not everyone believes we are inherently dangerous because of our gifts. Some commentators have even decried how Krazen is training minors for what are essentially future military operations. It harkens back to a time before Tri-State East existed, when some territories forced students to participate in recruitment programs."

"Huh . . . well, okay." Zuberi reflected momentarily on what her father had just said. "Dad, you just mentioned . . . you've been working on getting us out of the city. I mean, what are you saying? You've been speaking again to the elders?"

Thato took his daughter's hands in his own. Though Zuberi's father was considered one of the toughest Nubians around and had been a warrior in his native land, his palms were remarkably soft.

"Beri, perhaps I'm setting a bad example here," he said, "but do you really think I'd wait for the elders' permission to do what I know to be right? I have a plan."

Chapter 14

Lencho

"No, we have no immediate sign of their whereabouts, though they're probably back to hiding in their usual place at the Jungle in SoHo," Tilly said from a holo that beamed out of Krazen's right eye. "Some of our aerial footage managed to capture glimpses of Zaire and the others falling, but that's about it. Our cameras didn't manage to spot exactly where they fell, but some eyewitnesses commented on seeing a small group of people falling from the sky who somehow managed to slow their descent right before impact. They put their location somewhere around Seventy-Ninth Street on the East Side, near one of the park's exits."

"We're certain there were no casualties?" Krazen asked.

"None that we know of. Based on word of mouth, looks like they all survived. Should we press charges and send a team down to the Jungle?"

Krazen shook his head. "No, not yet. We've gotten the act passed, let's take a moment to weigh our next moves, especially considering the accusations they might throw back at us. Do we want to call this a Nubian terrorist attack? Do we want to wait to see what the public has to say, how that might influence registration protocol?" Krazen started to massage his left temple, a surefire sign he had a headache. "Still, make sure you loop that footage from the militia body cams of them attacking our forces in the greenhouse unprovoked. Place it on social. Edit out Sandra as much as you can, as she's sensitive about these things. The news holos will have a field day with the clip. We want the story to be clear."

Lencho wrung his hands as he waited for Krazen to finish his billionth call of the day. The waiting was agonizing, Lencho itching for something to do, to train or drain. Usually it would've been an honor to sit in Krazen's office as he went about his meetings, letting Lencho observe his dealings with the world as sky king. But right now, he didn't give a fuck. He knew what was coming once the calls were done.

Ever since Lencho had confronted Uzochi at Starlight yesterday, his entire body had been uneasy, his mind unsettled. He wasn't sure what had happened, when he'd started to drain Zaire, when he'd started to take a bit of Zaire's actual power of transformation. His gift, it must've been changing, evolving. It should've been something to celebrate, but everything was such a mess right now he barely had time to think about that.

Tilly had informed Lencho later that evening that Krazen wanted to meet with him the next afternoon. He'd found no peace, going over again and again what he would say to the sky king when they sat down together. He knew he'd fucked up royally. Once Lencho had confirmed that Uzochi and his friends were indeed Up High, why hadn't he alerted the proper authorities? Why the hell hadn't he called Krazen right away?

Lencho honestly wasn't sure how he'd answer those questions. He just knew that feeling Uzochi's presence sparked something within, something that said he had to get to his cousin no matter what, to confront him, to deal with him.

To take what is yours, his inner voice said again as Lencho lay in bed, a voice Lencho tried to ignore as he stared out the window, his vision consumed by the ghostly brilliance of sky city lights at night. The voice had intruded on his thoughts all evening, constantly reminding him that he was powerful, that he deserved all he'd fought for. Lencho was finding it harder and harder to tune those words out, to relax his mind. Was he that nervous about seeing Krazen? Was he going nutty?

When Lencho rose that morning after a deep sleep, he realized that resting had done him good. He felt like a rejuvenated man, speedily completing morning lessons with his tutor and taking on his standard exercises at the gym. He ignored the strained looks of the other members of the Divine, how the staff seemed to be going out of their way to avoid him, with no one wanting to spar or see how much he could push his strength or speed. Everyone was still spooked from the previous afternoon. *Fuck it,* Lencho told himself as he completed his training alone, figuring he needed to clear his head anyway before seeing Krazen. There was no one to touch, no one to drain as he worked out, but he'd be okay, no sweat.

Lencho tried to keep his eyes on the floor as Krazen continued his meeting with Tilly, who provided numerous updates about the election campaign before shepherding another stream of information about what was happening with St. John Enterprises. Lencho noticed that sometimes Tilly glanced over at him, her eyes full of reproach from the holo-projection.

To hell with you, Lencho wanted to say, a slight roar building in his ears. He didn't need her judgment, someone who'd only ascended based on how well she gave it to the boss. *You have no right to judge me.* Tilly's evil-eye stare reminded him of Sandra, how lately Krazen's daughter acted like she wasn't going to give Lencho the time of day even though she was so into him when he first got to the Up High. Seeing that she'd been knocked out by someone from Uzochi's crew, well, he didn't feel a thing.

"Lencho," Krazen said, pulling Lencho from his thoughts. The holo of Tilly blinked out. "Thank you for your patience. My time isn't what it once was ever since the campaign began." He continued massaging his temples as he gave a big sigh. "So, my boy, I believe we have a problem."

"Uhm, yeah, right," Lencho said, sitting up straighter at Krazen's words. He'd just realized that Krazen wasn't wearing one of his usual caftans but was instead in a loose cream suit and black turtleneck. Krazen occasionally wore the more standard suits sported by other Up High residents, usually when he was working at his office and had tons of stuff to do, which meant he probably wasn't hitting the campaign trail today. Lencho sucked in a breath, waiting for the sky king to start in on him.

"I know the election has consumed my time," Krazen said, "that we've had far fewer opportunities to connect, for me to show you the ropes of the business, but I've tried my best to be there for you. And I've certainly made my expectations clear."

Lencho didn't reply, his hands between his knees as the roar grew louder.

"It's been brought to my attention that you harassed a Nubian youngster who'd recently awoken to their gift. We'd been keeping an eye on them, this Sajah Osei, for a few days, as they'd started to intermittently appear in the Up High via some sort of shadow portal. It's certainly a bizarre Nubian gift, to be sure, but useful, especially as we've been unable to locate Nneka since she vanished some weeks ago."

Lencho gave a slight nod and mumbled, "Right."

"Do you know what an incredible asset it would be to have a teleporter for our future militia, someone who could transport scores of people and goods at a moment's notice? Nneka's power was useful, but she appeared to be limited in just how many people she transported at one time. This Sajah . . . well, I don't need to speak more on the possibilities here. Suffice to say, I wasn't expecting, on their first day at our training facilities, that Sajah would be publicly bullied by the very person responsible for nurturing their growth with our organization." Krazen placed his palms on his table and leaned closer to Lencho, his voice low. "Everyone at the training center has said your behavior was . . . abhorrent. Have . . . you . . . lost . . . your . . . mind? Have you lost any sense of control?"

Lencho looked into the sky king's eyes. The roar became louder.

Do not let him talk to you like that, a voice said over the noise.

Lencho swallowed. That was exactly what he wanted to tell Krazen. *Don't talk to me like that.* But he couldn't. He was too frightened.

Krazen reclined in his chair, steepling his hands in front of his face as he shook his head, seemingly gathering his thoughts. "And then, this stunt with your cousin. Lencho, I'm confident we can use this incident to our advantage, as we do, but do you understand what we've lost? Zaire is apparently gone as well, for no good reason I can discern, another treasured member of the organization. And apparently your cousin was coming for what could be our most powerful asset among the gifted."

Lencho's head shot up with that remark. *Someone more powerful than me?* he wanted to ask.

"Think of what we could have managed to accomplish if we'd captured your cousin on Up High premises, if we'd had the *legal* right to detain him, without worrying about enforcing the act? If you had followed protocol and called for immediate backup upon realizing he was here? The possibilities would've been endless. The negotiations that would've ensued. I'm sure the Up High holds a powerful allure for Uzochi. He was well on his way to ascension based solely on his drive and intellect."

"I . . . I know that," Lencho croaked out, barely keeping his composure, sick to death of hearing how remarkable Uzochi was at every damn thing he did.

"I know you do," Krazen said. He cocked his head slightly. Lencho knew this was an indication that the man had received another message on his personal comm, probably from Tilly again. "So, though it pains me to say this, I need for you to take a moment and think about the inappropriate decisions you're making, how they're starting to threaten everything we're building. Effective immediately, you're no longer in charge of training new recruits. Aren will resume leadership."

Lencho shot up from his chair. "No! You can't fuckin' . . . you can't do that."

Krazen stared at him wide-eyed, as if the boy had lost his mind, talking back to him in such a way. "Lencho, I suspect all of what's happened has been too much, too fast. Perhaps we can put you back in charge one day, but you need a break, and I simply don't have the time to supervise the trainings, run my business, run for mayor. Do you think I even have time for this conversation so close to the election? I should be among my future constituencies, getting things in order with the registration law."

"You can't demote me. I'm the one who got those kids to ascend!" Lencho shouted. "You woulda never gotten such quick access to the Divine and their gifts if it wasn't for me. *I'm* the one who got everyone on board. *I'm* the one who brought everyone up here . . . for you."

Krazen rose, Lencho's heart beating wildly as the huge man towered over him. Lencho could bench-press three hundred pounds when called upon to do so, a fact that mattered little to the sky king. "And *I'm* the one who gave you and your vile little gang opportunity when you had nothing," Krazen said, his voice a growling, ferocious thing, spittle flying from his mouth. "Who gave you the drugs to sell that allowed you to survive? Me. Who gave you the safety and wealth and access to the greatest sky city in the world? Me. Who gave you the clothes and tech and glory that you've been sucking up like a pig since you got up here? Me. All of that had nothin' to do with you, you fuckin' disrespectful, insignificant lower-city gutter rat. It . . . was . . . *me.* And don't you ever, *EVER* forget it, you hear?"

Scarlet filled Lencho's vision, Krazen's office becoming tinged with red. Unholy. The roar in Lencho's ear was deafening, and still he heard the voice again, an insidious whisper.

Take what is yours.

Krazen had never cursed at him, never tried to make Lencho feel small. If he wanted to experience that, he could've stayed with his dad, Kefle, in the lower city. He had worked his ass off, made all sorts of compromises for the sky king, had turned against his own people, and this was the thanks he was getting.

Take what is yours. Are you his dog to command as he sees fit? That should be you behind that desk. You are the one with power.

Lencho inhaled, exhaled, inhaled . . .

Take what is yours.

Krazen sat back down, believing he'd said all that needed to be said. "Now that we've cleared that up, you'll do as you're told, Lencho Will. We have big plans to tend to."

Lencho grabbed the chair in front of him and hurled it to the left side of the big man so that it slammed against the wall. He watched as Krazen's stern expression cracked for the briefest of moments. Lencho knew what he saw. Fear.

Good, he thought. *Be afraid, mofo.*

"I won't be told anything," Lencho snarled. "I'm the most powerful Nubian you have here. You need to respect that."

"Lencho, please," Krazen said. "Calm down, son. Calm—"

"Now I'm your son after you just called me a gutter rat?"

It was the word "son" that radiated through Lencho like a bomb. Two men now had called him that word. Neither had meant it. He was just something for them to pick up when they wanted to, when it was convenient. Lencho didn't need anyone. He realized that now.

Yesssss, you're better than him. You're better than all of them. Don't you feel the power you have?

His inner voice was right. Lencho did feel the power. It surged through him, all around him.

The lights flickered. He stared at Krazen, hatred and hurt pulsing through his veins. He would never be betrayed again. He would never be looked down on again.

"Lencho," Krazen said, glancing around wildly, trying to keep his sights on Lencho but befuddled by the failing lights. "Son—"

Lencho stalked ever closer. "Krazen St. John," he said. "I'm not your fuckin' son."

He leapt onto the desk and grabbed Krazen's wrist as the man let out a wheezing, strangled sound, almost as if he was choking on his words. Krazen stared straight at Lencho as the boy grabbed the sky king with his other free hand.

Lencho began to drain, more mercilessly than he ever had in his life.

A gurgling sound escaped from Krazen's lips.

A trickle of blood ran down his temple.

The man started to shake.

At first, Lencho didn't fully understand what he was seeing as Krazen fell to the floor and started to convulse, the most violent reaction anyone ever had to being drained. But then, as the office began to pulse with a dim light, Lencho realized what was happening.

All of the electronics in the room were reacting to him. His power.

He was sending the man into tech failure.

He was sending Krazen St. John to his death.

Yes, don't stop, the voice whispered.

Krazen's eyes rolled back into his head. He wheezed and gasped again. Lencho let his fists unfurl, coming to his senses. The most famous man in the Up High was lying on the floor, a gibbering, convulsing thing, fluids seeping from his body onto his immaculate white carpet.

The office went completely black.

He heard a sharp, piercing siren, an alarm, and then the room was illuminated once again. It wasn't the scarlet in his mind's eye that had colored his sight just seconds earlier. It was the emergency light coming from a backup power source.

Lencho began to tremble, looking at Krazen on the floor

one last time as he backed away, just as the door opened behind him and a squad of St. John Soldiers rushed in.

"What happened here?" the lead militiaperson said, placing their hand around Lencho's wrist. "What happened to Mr. St. John?"

Lencho grabbed the soldier by the torso, picked them up fully off the floor, and threw them against the wall. And then he streaked out the door, not looking back.

As Lencho ran at top speed, his body whizzing through corridors, the omnipresent voice returned.

He deserved to die. You'll see that in time. I'll show you the truth.

Chapter 15

Sandra

Krazen's body was still, his olive skin paler than Sandra would have thought possible against the crisp white sheets. Around him, machines beeped and clicked and whirred as they tracked his vital signs, a symphony to accompany the tubes that were shoved everywhere: his nose, his ears, his veins. Sandra's father had been his usual robust self only hours ago. Now, a mere husk.

Krazen St. John was in a coma, with doctors having no idea when he might recover.

Vriana stood beside her, a tear slipping down the girl's cheek as she clutched Sandra's hand. Sandra knew Vriana's devotion was due to the implant in her skull, essentially a thing of artifice, but she was still grateful for her presence. Having Vriana close made it easier to press forward, to face the path that now awaited her.

If his condition didn't improve miraculously, all of New York would soon know about her father, how he'd been struck down less than two weeks before a general election in which he was the front-runner. *Was it an assassination attempt?* the holo-newshounds would ask. *Or a major health emergency? Was he this medically unfit for office?* The types of questions that would be the stuff of Krazen's nightmares.

Sandra could barely digest what she'd been told by the guards closest to her father's office, that Lencho had been having a private meeting with Krazen when he collapsed. That they had cause to believe that Lencho had attacked her father. Which didn't make sense, as the two got along marvelously. There were no cameras to check what had really happened, as her father never allowed any of the spaces in which he worked or lived to be surveilled without his express permission.

And then there were the issues with his implants, which had all somehow failed simultaneously. Krazen's team of doctors were baffled, understandably so. Even if Lencho had attacked her father and drained him, the Nubian's powers worked on organic bodies, on human life energy. Her father's tech, the best in the world of course, should have been left unscathed.

Sandra once again heard muffled wailing outside the room and knew that it was Tilly, who'd been crying uncontrollably since she'd arrived at the hospital. Was she really grieving for Krazen or was she lamenting the end of her days of luxury, since her meal ticket was in a coma? Didn't matter. If the usually composed woman wanted to make a sobbing mess of herself outside, that was her business. Sandra had the right to insist on privacy when she was with her father, and she would send that gold digger back to the lower city first chance she got.

She would have to move fast to assert herself as the one in power. Her father had distant relatives, but as Krazen's only recognized heir, Sandra had uncontested claim to St. John Enterprises, especially with her great-aunt Myrtle gone. She just had to make sure she seized it all the right way. The coming days would be crucial. She would have to affect the look of a grieving daughter while also appearing strong. A tightrope for sure, but Sandra knew she could walk it—with the proper support.

She glanced at Vriana, realizing she would need to adjust her plans. Sandra pulled the Nubian girl close to her.

"We're going to be okay," Sandra whispered in Vriana's ear. "I promise. I'll make sure Father is taken care of and handle all the rest. Don't despair. I know what to do."

Chapter 16

Lencho

Lencho paced the unfamiliar room, threatening to flatten the carpet with his heavy tread. Sweat beaded his forehead, his shirt stuck to his chest. The room's climate was carefully modulated, as was everything in the Up High, but Lencho felt like he was in a desert. His whole body was on the verge of overheating, as if fire was circling through his veins. He thought back to when he'd touched Keera at the theater, the awoken girl who had become a molten, fiery thing. How it had felt when he'd grabbed and drained her. How he'd been sure he was going to burn himself up into nothingness. That was what he felt now.

He'd known he couldn't go back to the dormitory where he and the rest of the Divine lived. That would be the first place the authorities would look for him after what had happened with Krazen. And sure enough, when he'd gone back to the building, zipping over at high speed and hiding behind a bush, he'd found a full brigade of militia perched outside the dorm, waiting for him to appear. Lencho cursed under his breath, realizing that the bush was full of sharp branches and thorns that cut into his skin.

He had run again, looking for all the out-of-the-way, sparsely populated Up High spots he could find. They were mostly located in the northwestern quadrant of the city. He'd sat still for a moment and hatched a plan, thankful that his head felt relatively clear. Minutes later, Lencho hid behind a large cherry tree flanking a modest apartment complex, a place where the less wealthy lived, including people who'd recently ascended from the lower city.

Someone exited their parked car and entered the building. Lencho raced into the complex just before the door closed behind the young man, quietly following the occupant up two flights of stairs. Right when the man used eye identification to open the door to his home, Lencho streaked up to the stranger.

"I'm sorry," Lencho said, taking the stranger by the wrist before he could utter a word, draining him swiftly and dragging him inside.

Lencho placed the man on the floor, judging that he would be unconscious for hours, that he might need to drain him again afterward to keep him that way, though not wanting to kill him, not wanting to do to someone else what he'd just done to Krazen St. John.

He hurriedly explored the studio apartment, which was small and minimally furnished, though there was a good amount of food in the refrigerator. The space was clean, tidy. Lencho figured that items like the lights and shower fixtures had probably already been synced to the man's implants, if he had any, but it was easy enough to turn things on by hand when necessary. Lencho sat in a chair, feeling safe for the first time since he'd fled Krazen's office.

How had he lost control? Krazen had given Lencho everything he'd ever wanted. The sky king had pulled Lencho away from his miserable life below, had given him a safe place to live, had trusted Lencho. But it hadn't been enough. And now . . . Krazen might die.

He deserved what he got. He should be answering to you. Can you not see the might you wield?

The fuckin' voice was back.

As Lencho settled into the apartment, deciding that he would be as quiet as possible so no one would know he was there, the voice became relentless. A constant refrain of Lencho being all-powerful, holding the key to everything. The words, sometimes offered in the faintest of whispers, they were terrifying. What had happened to Krazen . . . could never happen again. Not that he'd get the opportunity. When word got out what he'd done, he'd be seeing the inside of a prison cell for a long time.

A cold laugh rattled in the air. Lencho whipped around, looking for the source, but nothing save for his own reflection looked back at him from a plain oblong mirror hung on the wall. Lencho saw himself there, the heaviness under his eyes, the scratches on his face and hands.

Take a good look. Yes, you're mighty. But look at you. Terrified of yourself. Don't you see? Your power will do nothing but amplify this body that's trying to resist. Give in to it, Lencho.

154

Give in to me.

Lencho's chest heaved. His breathing was labored, hitching higher and higher as he looked back at himself. In the mirror, the image changed, becoming a distorted blur. Lencho jumped back in alarm, nearly tripping as he ran into a heavy chair behind him. The furniture made a resounding thump as it toppled over.

For the first time, Lencho realized that something wasn't right, that this was no regular inner voice prompting him to be assertive and confident. This was . . . something else.

Had he really lost it? Was he going insane?

He looked at his reflection more closely.

The Lencho in the mirror tipped his head back and laughed. As his face became visible again, he noticed that the cuts and scratches had disappeared, his reflection now adorned with gold. A large, pointed crown sat on his head. Flowing links of jewelry covered his neck and chest. A pair of earrings dangled and a stud sat in his nose.

You were meant to be a king, Lencho. Celestial in design. You could have the power of a Nubian catalyst at your touch. Why do you lower yourself?

Lencho stared at himself in the mirror, fascinated. He'd never seen himself look so confident, so sure. So . . . Nubian. That version of himself he was witnessing . . . was it his future?

"Who are you?" Lencho managed, speaking to the empty room, even as he knew doing so meant he was crazy. "Why are you doing this to me?"

The rattling laugh in his head returned, echoed by the laugh of Lencho's reflection.

I'm showing you what's possible—no more, no less. But to seize it . . .

The voice stopped, Lencho only hearing his rattled breathing, the pounding of his heart.

And then within seconds the voice returned, a seductive whisper that reverberated through Lencho's body.

Give in to me.

Chapter 17

Uzochi

In the morning, Uzochi woke up on the couch where he'd slept the previous night, still not quite believing that he found himself in a world where he had two parents. The hope he felt in his gut spread through him like a beacon.

His father was alive. His father had his back.

His father . . .

And even though his mother was still furious over Siran's absence, this morning she seemed to have decided to forgive him, or at least a bit. She was moving through their kitchen and humming a song to herself that Uzochi had never heard before. He picked his head up and peered over the couch, watching as she busied herself at the stove, the apartment filled with the smells of cardamom and cloves.

Siran was already at the table with a pamphlet in his hands, his brow furrowed. (Uzochi wondered for a moment where exactly his father had slept if he spent the night, then brushed the thought aside.) Uzochi recognized it as one of Krazen St. John's propaganda pieces that he distributed in the streets, advertising his plans for his future militia and the various other changes he promised to make as mayor. He longed to know what his father thought about what he was reading, what he thought about so many things.

Uzochi leaned forward on his elbows as he contemplated sending out his telepathy just for a moment, just briefly to touch Siran's thoughts and see what he really believed about this new world where Nubians had landed. He could discover how much Siran had missed his wife and other Nubians, what he'd been through over the past sixteen years, living in Ghana as he said. How he'd dealt with the cataclysm and *survived.* And, most importantly, what he thought of the son he'd just met. He could—

"Are you curious about my thoughts, Uzochi?" Siran asked, never taking his eyes off the pamphlet.

Uzochi's cheeks heated as he ducked behind the back of the couch, immediately realizing that he was acting like a dopey three-year-old. He stood up, scratching his scalp, trying to appear confident.

"Of course not," he said. "I have a rule about . . ."

"You're a terrible liar," Siran said, looking up from his reading, flashing a grin. "Which is a good thing."

Uzochi stammered for a moment and then cleared his throat. "Okay, okay, I'll admit, I was thinking about it, all right? It's just . . . it's just I'm curious about you, you know. You can learn so much so quickly from someone's mind, but I wouldn't do that. I actually do have a policy about that with most people, especially family and, um, close friends."

"As in his girlfrieeeeend," Com'pa sang from the kitchen.

"He does his best not to read her mind. I taught him well. A good thing, too. She's a magnificent warrior, excellent with her staff and fists, and could knock his head off. But they do that bask-in-each-other's-emotion thing, just like we used to do back home."

"OhmiGoddess, Mom!" Uzochi yelled. "Cut that out, please."

Siran chuckled. "The girl I met, then. Zuberi, who also fell from the sky. She is quite fierce. And intelligent."

"Of course," Com'pa said, holding up the spoon she was using. "Uzochi knows I wouldn't let him date an empty-headed creature."

Uzochi didn't appreciate this turn in the conversation. Here he was, thinking of the ethical boundaries of his ability, and his parents—his *parents* . . . really?—were discussing his romantic life. "Mom, it's not up to you who I date. And furthermore . . ."

"Never mind, son," Siran continued, still grinning. "I like the girl. And more importantly, I would like to sit with you and learn more about your gift, to fully understand your abilities. Come, have your morning repast so afterward we can . . ."

At once, the sound of banging against the front door boomed through the space. Uzochi instantly threw up his hands, protecting his face as Zuberi had always taught him. His heart raced as he thought that maybe the authorities had come for them, that a squad of St. John Soldiers stood outside. He would need to protect his parents—again, *his parents*—and . . .

The announcer chirped in a modulated voice, "You have visitors," sending forth a desaturated, crinkly holo into the middle of the living room. The image showed an angry man banging nonstop at the door.

"Oh Goddess," Com'pa whispered. "Can't we just have a sliver of peace?"

Siran stared at the holo. "Please, let him in."

Com'pa pursed her lips and walked to the door midbang. There stood Kefle, Uzochi's uncle, Siran's brother, the pain in the ass who in the past three months had visited Com'pa's place far more frequently than he had in the past five years.

Kefle said nothing to Com'pa, offered no salutations, quickly adjusting his line of sight until he settled on Siran.

"So it's true," he said, placing his hands on his hips. "My brother has seen fit to come back from the dead."

Still seated, Siran stared back at Kefle, a glowering, huffing and puffing hulk of a man. Uzochi saw his father's jaw tense, imagining he might be grinding his teeth.

"Hello, Kefle," Siran said. "Brother, I am glad—"

"Don't fuck with me, Siran," Kefle snarled, stepping into the apartment. Uzochi saw over his shoulder that Kefle wasn't alone. There was a trio of elders hanging back nearby, no doubt having traveled with Kefle to see Siran, their revered Nubian catalyst back from the dead.

"Control yourself, Kefle," Com'pa said, her voice a low hiss as she, too, spotted the elders. "Have you no sense of decorum? Remember where you are."

"I know exactly where we are," Kefle replied. "In this shitstorm of a city because of one man, a fool who had the nerve to lug his sorry ass back into our lives."

"It is good to see you too, brother," Siran said. "Thank you for the warm, *delightful* welcome."

Kefle's eyes flashed before he scurried forward. Siran stood just as Kefle reached him, the brothers practically chest to chest. Uzochi held his breath, Kefle's rage pulsing through the room, a suffocating, stifling thing.

"You arrogant son of a bitch," Kefle said. "You think you can just waltz in here and take over? After what you've done?"

"I am not here for battle, little brother," Siran said, his tone remarkably placid. "Not when Nubians face such daunting challenges. Not when our very freedom is at stake with the laws of this land. I have returned to be of service to my community, to my family."

"Have you now?" Kefle snorted. "I don't remember you coming to see me, big *brother*."

Siran's face twisted into a slight scowl, the first time since Uzochi had met his father that he detected agitation. It was easy to see why. Kefle had a way of bringing out the worst in everyone. Even though Lencho had gone all weird and berserk, the more Uzochi experienced Kefle's biting rage, the more he understood why his cousin seemed to be in so much pain.

"As charming as this reunion is," Com'pa said, "this is my place, and the rules of my household will be obeyed." She turned to the doorway and the elders who were standing outside, launching into the traditional greetings she used whenever Nubians stopped by. "Exalted guests, please come in and make yourself comfortable. I'll prepare us some snacks and tea. Aunties, sit here. Baba, take this chair. Dear heart . . ."

Both Uzochi and Siran turned to Com'pa and said, "Yes?"

Com'pa was momentarily startled and then smiled. "Ah yes, I will have to be more specific with my language going forward. Dear heart *Uzochi,* please clear up your bedding and help me prepare snacks for our company, as you seem to be fully recovered. And Siran, sit with the others so you can . . ."

"Uzochi!"

He turned to the door and elation filled his soul.

There was Zuberi in a navy hoodie standing in the doorway, her eyes taking in Uzochi, who felt his stomach swoop. She darted inside the apartment just as Com'pa closed the door behind her.

"Hi, everybody," Zuberi said. "Auntie Com'pa, hi, and uhm, Siran . . . hello. I apologize for coming by unannounced." She looked over at Uzochi again, waving at him timidly. "Hey, buddy. I texted you, wanted to see if you were okay."

Uzochi placed his hand on his forehead, jaw dropping, realizing he'd forgotten to retrieve his phone from its usual spot between couch cushions and do his morning text ritual with Zuberi. "I'm so sorry," he said. "It's been way intense over here. I was sleeping like a baby for most of the day yesterday."

"Hey, no problem. I get it. You totally overtaxed yourself . . ." Zuberi's voice trailed off at the sight of Kefle and Siran standing close to each other, looking as if they were about to square off. "Don't mean to intrude, but is everything okay here?" She raised an eyebrow and looked back at Uzochi, who realized that she was using her gift to see Kefle's and Siran's phantoms. Perhaps she was witnessing a future where they had thrown restraint to the wind and were going at each other.

"We're all fine here," Com'pa said, glaring at her husband and brother-in-law, as if she could command them to knock it off with an I-will-kill-you stare. "Just having an unexpected family reunion right before breakfast. Zuberi, how're you feeling? How're the others?"

Zuberi worried her lip, looking from Com'pa to Uzochi.

"I'm fine," she said. "Tasha and Zaire, that new kid Sajah, we're all fine. Thanks to Uzochi."

She smiled at him with that I'm-tough-but-loving look that Uzochi adored. His heart swelled.

"It's good to see you, buddy, but we need to talk," she said, lowering her voice, taking the initiative and guiding him to an unoccupied corner of the living room. "It's important."

Uzochi felt conspicuous, realizing that he and Zuberi didn't have any real privacy in such a small space. But he also knew that now wasn't the time to take a casual walk down the street, not when they might already have been identified as the culprits behind the incident Up High. He hoped Zuberi had been careful making her way over to his place.

"It's about a plan my father has for Nubians," Zuberi said, talking quickly. "And Vriana. I don't think we should wait to go back after her, not if she's been implanted. The longer she stays up there, the more she's indoctrinated . . . it's just horrible, right?"

Uzochi blinked. He hadn't thought at all about Vriana and the botched mission, though he'd had the sense from the holos, between periods of sleep, that the world was aware of what had gone down at Starlight. He'd been far too preoccupied with having his father back, with having a family that was intact, whole, for the first time. He looked at Zuberi, trying to figure out how to make her understand.

"Uhm, can we talk about this later?" he asked. "I mean, I'm sort of dealing with a lot."

He nodded back to where the adults stood and sat, hoping she'd understand.

"I know," she said. "I know you are. But I just thought . . ."

"I'm sorry," Uzochi said. "I'm sorry, Beri, but I can't have this conversation right now, okay? I really need to be with my dad."

Instantly, he regretted his words as Zuberi slunk back, as he felt waves of disgust and irritation and embarrassment peel off her frame. She scanned the room.

"You know what?" she said. "You're right. Now's not a good time to talk. I'ma go."

Zuberi swiveled around, ran over to Com'pa and quickly pecked her on the cheek, and left the apartment as Uzochi stood there, slightly stunned.

She has to understand, he told himself over and over as he helped his mother with refreshments for their guests, as Siran spoke to the elders of how he'd managed to get to New York, as Kefle said nothing but sat quietly in a corner, fuming. *Zuberi has to understand, I've gotta focus on my dad.*

Yet no matter how often he repeated the words to himself, Uzochi remained unconvinced.

Chapter 18

Zuberi

Racing down the final flight of stairs, Zuberi left Uzochi's building, thankful to get out of there, ruing the day she'd decided to give her heart to a boy who could be so thoughtless and self-involved.

"Fuck you, Uzochi Will," she mumbled under her breath as she stomped down the street. She kept her head low and tightened the strings on her hoodie, hoping no one would see the sting of betrayal on her face, though there were more practical reasons for her getup—she had to make sure she wasn't recognized by any of the militia. The news holos hadn't identified the Nubians who were behind the attack at the greenhouse, but there was a chance they could do so at any time. And even if she hadn't been identified on the holos, her name and face might be floating among private St. John Soldier comms. It was all she could do to sneak away from her father, who was on the verge of placing her under house arrest, and convince Sajah to shadow-walk her over to the section of Manhattan where Uzochi lived with his mom. (Zuberi was proud of the name she came up with for traveling through Sajah's portals.) Still, she'd have to get back to the Jungle on her own. She'd been sure to strap her staff along her left side, covering it up with baggy clothes, but she'd need more than that if an entire squad descended upon her.

But Zuberi wasn't scared. In fact, she had so much pent-up anger that needed to be released that she thought she could jog all the way down to SoHo and not work up a sweat. What had happened up at Uzochi's apartment? How had their conversation spun out of control so quickly? She had thought she was bringing him urgent news, that he would be on her side about getting Vriana back, like he was before.

But he hadn't wanted to hear it.

. . . I can't have this conversation right now . . .

Those were the words that rang in her ears as she walked briskly southward. Zuberi decided that she wasn't going to jog, that a brisk walk was exactly what she needed. She took in the sights around her on Third Avenue, trying to lose herself in the city, only to spot one of Krazen's mayoral billboards floating overhead. The sky king looked as ridiculous as ever in a colorful caftan as he stood across from one of his campaign slogans.

The smell of street food filled Zuberi's nostrils, a cluster of vendors offering varieties of barbecued chicken, tofu, and crickets. New York pedestrians hustled to and fro, on their phones or lost in thought, flanked by nonstop traffic. She turned to spot a caravan of hover trucks hurtling down Twenty-Second Street, carrying neatly packed loads of brick and metal. She figured they were headed toward one of the

East River seawalls, probably to make repairs. With an election on the horizon, Krazen had become all about making sure the lower-city seawalls were in top-notch condition, especially with everyone scared that what had happened to the Swamp could happen to their neighborhood. If only they knew that their future mayor had purposely tried to destroy a seawall, potentially killing thousands, simply to make a point. Zuberi felt sick all over again whenever she thought about what that man was capable of.

Zuberi felt a chill, even though the sun beat down relentlessly on a warm early-autumn day. It was the same chill that had crept into her bones during the weeks after she'd first lost Vriana. Now that she'd failed to bring her back home, the cold was settling in yet again.

How desperately she wished she could talk to her friend. She could imagine them both sitting on a bench in the park, sharing a wrap, Vriana twirling a magenta braid over her finger with her legs crossed as she gave relationship advice.

Uzochi's just setting a boundary, you know, Vriana might've said to her if they were hanging now. *There's no way he was trying to hurt you. Think about it. He's just met his supposedly dead father for the first time in his life. You gotta look at intent over impact. So . . . how can we fix this?*

Vriana's classic mix of tough love and Psychology 101 jargon never failed to make Zuberi roll her eyes. But now that Zuberi only had echoes and fantasies of her friend, she would've given anything to hear Vriana's words. Because getting her back now seemed really, really tough. What if she was gone for good?

No. Zuberi told herself she was getting carried away, thinking the worst. That was also something Vriana loved to call her on. Another memory surfaced. Zuberi had been ranting after a mandatory Krazen St. John scholarship informational meeting at HS 104 about how they were forced to compete for scraps while the Up High kids were guaranteed to attend good schools. Vriana had sighed.

"Beri, it was just a meeting," she'd said. "I know you're annoyed but I think the scholarship reps are trying to help us. Can you please chill for two seconds?"

But Vriana had been wrong. It was all a game to the people Up High. A strategic game of chess set up in such a way that those in the lower city would be grateful for the smallest of handouts while those Up High hoarded society's advantages. She'd now seen it for herself. And the Elevation that had hobbled so many families . . . Aren had revealed that it was Krazen who'd flooded the streets with the drug, all while making street gangs look like the true culprits. Even now, in the old Divine HQ, after the thorough scrubdown they'd given the place, Zuberi still ran across the stuff. The pills were immediately tossed out or destroyed, but all it took was one hapless Nubian kid trying the stuff on a fluke and their life could become a mess. Another gift of desolation and despair for the masses, courtesy of St. John Enterprises.

What would Vriana say about all of that now? Zuberi almost didn't want to have that conversation with her friend. And after what they'd done to her . . . would they even be able to have it again?

Her chest tightened, her breathing becoming shallow. She

needed to get back to Vriana, set her free. There was no time to lose. But without Uzochi, would she be able to reach the Up High again? Sajah was probably her best hope of getting back to the sky, but the teleporter seemed so put off by their experiences up there that Zuberi thought they would flat-out refuse her request. Plus security would be doubled or tripled, of that she was certain. Going anywhere near Central Park would be asking for trouble. Sandra St. John might even put Vriana on some sort of lockdown, Goddess forbid. It could be a complete disaster, and now she'd lost Uzochi.

You're getting ahead of yourself again, Vriana's voice said, echoing in her mind. *You and Uzochi just had a misunderstanding. And these are particularly stressful times, okay, girl? Y'all will be chummy-chummy, all nasty and up in each other's stuff again in no time.*

Zuberi took a deep breath.

The Vriana Zuberi carried with her in her head and heart was right. She could give Uzochi time. He'd apologize to her. Maybe she'd apologize, too. They'd figure it out.

Zuberi reached SoHo in forty minutes, deciding after her initial outburst that she wanted to feel the air against her skin, that the risk of being outside was worth it. She slowed her brisk walk down to a leisurely stroll, unburdening herself of her troubles, just for a moment.

After entering the Jungle, she took a moment to observe what was happening in the main hall. Leonard had created a giant patchwork of flowering vines that framed the entranceway, filling the space with fragrances Zuberi wouldn't have thought possible considering the disarray they'd found the building in.

She looked over to her left and saw several Nubian kids practicing fighting-form poses. Then in an alcove to her right, she spotted Veronique, who was sitting with a little girl who appeared to have scraped a whole patch of skin off her knee. The child's tears eased as the healer dispensed her mist. And behind the alcove, she saw Sajah enter one of their shadow portals, carrying a large chest in their hands as a frail male elder made his way up the anterior lobby steps. The elder had clasped his hands together in thanks as Sajah carried his possessions to whatever room he was headed to. And then even farther back, she saw Abdul and Zaire whispering to each other animatedly, sitting close in the same way she often found herself sitting with Uzochi. The two boys were watching something together on a tablet, Zaire expressive in a way she'd never seen back in school. Zuberi quickly surmised that the pair were on a date, happily getting to know each other.

It dawned on her, perhaps for the first time, that the Children had really managed to build a community here. Something worth fighting for.

Her feet soon carried her to the communal kitchen that the elders had cobbled together. The Divine had clearly treated it as storage for their various stashes, but several kids had pitched in to scrub the space from top to bottom, Abdul taking special care with his elemental washing and rinsing even though he grimaced during the entire process. Food was being carefully rationed, secured behind locks that only the elders had access to, though their meal situation was becoming less dire with the fruits and veggies that Leonard produced in his community garden.

Someone had recently boiled a pot of water, which rested on a towel on one of the tables. Zuberi found herself gravitating toward the pot and its warmth, anything to alleviate the tumbling sensation in her stomach and the chill in her bones. She fished out a huge mug from the cupboard and turned back to the pot. Only, before she could grab it, there was a growl from a nearby table.

"You could at least ask before helping yourself to the water I prepared. Don't tell me, Thato taught you the cursed fighting forms day and night but forgot basic manners."

Zuberi turned to find Kefle seated in the shadows. Had he just been watching her stumble around in here? This miserable man . . .

"How . . . how are you here?" she asked. "I just left you at your nephew's apartment. Shouldn't you be with your brother?"

Kefle shrugged nonchalantly. "I needed to see for myself that he was alive, that he was okay. I left soon after you had your lovers' spat, got here by bus. I could see for myself that I was looking at the same old Siran. A bit haggard and gaunt, yes, it's sad how he's let himself go, to be honest, but that was still him. I saw what I needed to see."

"And you decided to make your way down here? Why?" Zuberi crossed her arms. Kefle would occasionally come down to the Jungle even though he still had his apartment in Old Chelsea with Lencho's mom. Maybe he felt guilty for his past behavior and the way he'd treated his son? Regardless, based on what Zuberi had observed of the man, she wasn't particularly inclined to trust him.

Kefle twisted his lips, annoyed. "Little girl, spare me your judgments. Just because you're the fierce warrior of the moment, that doesn't give you the right to question me. Don't forget, I'm Nubian royalty. I'll always have a place among my people whenever I choose."

Zuberi gaped right back at the annoying man. "I wasn't having a lovers' spat with Uzochi, not that it's any of your business. We were just talking."

Kefle blinked rapidly, gawking at Zuberi as if she thought him a naïve fool. "You don't need to lie to me, girl," Kefle pressed on. "Catalysts. Real assholes, aren't they?"

Zuberi stilled. She immediately touched the side of her pants, feeling for her staff, suddenly having the urge to whack Kefle across the face.

"At least Uzochi's carrying his burden," Zuberi said. "Some of us have to, seeing as others won't."

As she said the last syllable, she flipped her locs before helping herself to the hot water, pouring what remained out into the sink. She grabbed a tea bag from the cabinet and tossed it in the cup before sitting across from Kefle, hoping to piss him off with her blatant disregard. Judging by the way his eyes narrowed, she was successful.

"Ah yes," Kefle said, dark eyes gleaming in the light from the open window behind him. "The *burden* of being the catalyst. Siran loved to say that as well. How burdened he was in having to be responsible for the continual evolution of Nubians and our alignment with the kinetic. How understanding we all needed to be with his elemental experiments. Have you figured out what that understanding cost us?"

At the mention of Siran, Zuberi couldn't help but notice the curiosity that was piqued within her. Uzochi was clearly over the moon to have his father in his life. Even if it hurt for him to put his father first, she understood his elation. Zuberi couldn't fathom what she would do if her mother was to show up out of the blue, telling her daughter she'd somehow escaped death.

But there was something about Siran's reappearance that made Zuberi uneasy. She'd checked out his phantoms, hadn't seen anything that put her on edge, but so far his explanations about his whereabouts seemed . . . flimsy. Plus, she did notice that a handful of adult Nubians were keeping their distance from him. Sure, he was sometimes getting the whole "O wonderful, revered catalyst" treatment that Uzochi got, but a few folks looked like they didn't want to give Siran the time of day. Were they pissed that he hadn't returned earlier, like Uzochi's mom was?

"What do you think happened? What kept him away for so long?" Zuberi asked Kefle, the question flying out of her mouth before she could pull it back.

A smirk crossed Kefle's face.

"Doubting my dear brother's story?" Kefle asked. "At least one of you numbskull Children has sense. My time explaining the actions of catalysts is done. You and my doltish nephew will figure it out. But I'll tell you one thing, girl—"

"My name is Zuberi," she snapped, glaring at him. "I'm sick of you calling me 'girl' when I have a name. And I'm sick of you bad-mouthing Uzochi. You don't have to be so rude."

Just then, Zuberi saw how much alike he and Lencho looked. The same harsh edge to their eyes, the same sharp jawline. All hardness and strength, as if even the mere suggestion of softness was unwelcome. So unlike Uzochi's demeanor.

Kefle chuckled. "Okay, fair enough. But here's some parting advice from a rude old man. Cut your ties to the catalyst while you can." Kefle rose. "He'll never be on your side when he has all of Nubia relying on him as he learns more and more about his gifts. As he becomes *obsessed* with his gifts. Focus on yourself. Focus on what you want to do with your life."

Zuberi really didn't know how to respond to advice she hadn't asked for. She instinctively glanced above this ornery man, looking at his phantoms. They barely moved, all standing and staring her down just as Kefle was doing in the real world.

"Trying to read my next move?" Kefle asked. "Are they giving you the answers you seek?"

Zuberi said nothing, just taking in Kefle's seriousness, how he earnestly believed what he was telling her, not a laugh or a lie to be found among his future selves. Just as she opened her mouth, ready to give the man some sort of attitudinal retort, she heard the rapping of knuckles against the wall. Both she and Kefle turned to see Beka standing at the kitchen entrance. The youthful elder wore a mint-green blouse and blue jeans, her hair pulled back in her typical bun.

"Beka, hi," Zuberi said. "What's going on?"

"It's Krazen St. John," Beka said, her eyes widening as if she couldn't believe what she was about to say. "He's . . . he's had some sort of implant failure. Or he was attacked. No one's quite sure."

Zuberi's jaw scraped the floor. Behind her, Kefle let out a low whistle.

"I don't yet know if this is a blessing or curse," Beka continued, "but our sources are saying he might very well be dead."

Chapter 19

Lencho

His knuckles were bleeding again.

Lencho had been punching them raw in the apartment after having woken up and draining more essence from the man, his eyes glued to the news. He'd kept the holo on through the night, waiting for word that Krazen had been badly hurt, that the militia was looking for Lencho as a prime suspect. He ignored the way time kept slipping away from him, how he was only able to discern what part of the day it was by the position of the sun in the sky. Lencho couldn't find any sort of clock in the apartment and he'd ditched his mobile right after attacking Krazen, knowing he could be easily tracked through the device.

The holo-channel he had on showed old footage of Krazen leaving one of his rallies, Sandra standing on the side, as per usual. She looked different, more grown-up in her choice of clothes, more grown-up in attitude. Lencho looked at her a bit more closely and could've sworn she was scowling at her dad. Like she thought she was better than him, better than the sky king.

Her haughtiness made Lencho sick.

She is nothing in comparison to you.

Lencho drove his fist into the wall of the apartment again. The voice had kept him up throughout the night, Lencho so undone that he refused to look at his reflection in the mirror. He'd thought when he woke up that the voice had gone, that maybe he'd had a moment to clear his head. But then it had returned just as he walked to the kitchen to make himself breakfast. And that was when he had to hit something, had to act like he was at the gym, releasing energy, showing off his strength. He'd been concerned that neighbors would hear his pounding and think something was up, but he was surprised by the lack of sound associated with his punches, chalking it up to that funky steel polymer they used for everything Up High.

But there was blood smeared across the wall where he'd made significant dents. Lencho couldn't help it, not with how hard he was punching. He knew that because he healed fast, his hands would be good as new in no time. But the blood on the wall, he felt like he could smell it, taste it. In his dreams last night, there were rivers of blood, people screaming in a sea of crimson reflected by a storming, scarlet sky, a sky that seemed oddly familiar to Lencho. Across the waves, a large, fully rigged ship was tugged into the water's murky depths, the wails of despair piercing Lencho's ears before he jumped up from where he slept, a shivering, gasping mess.

Now he gazed at the blood on the wall, and then he heard laughing.

Lencho flitted across the room, looking bewildered, trying to tell himself once again that he wasn't hearing things. He turned and found himself in front of the mirror, spotting his reflection, once again adorned by a crazy crown and layers of jewelry.

This time, his face and chest were covered in blood.

"Shit!" Lencho shouted. "SHIT!!!" He started toward the door, but then realized that he'd gotten a bit of blood on his clothes, that his knuckles were still pulpy. To anyone he met, he would look a wreck. And where would he go?

The laughing resumed.

"Leave me the fuck alone!" Lencho yelled, staring beseechingly at the man on the floor, whom he'd drained, as if he could help him. "Please . . . please . . ."

The voice returned.

Give in to me.

Chapter 20

Uzochi

When Uzochi was with Siran, almost nothing else in the world mattered.

The two had been sitting on the floor of his apartment for two straight days doing nothing but talking and eating, Uzochi doing his best to listen closely to his father's words. He tried to offer thoughtful questions as often as possible, to modulate his emotions accordingly when Siran spoke about the tribulations he'd endured. Uzochi had become far wiser about the world of emotion than he could ever have imagined in such a short time. When he felt pangs of pain emanating from his father, he knew that the appropriate thing to do was to listen solemnly, to say he was sorry, to try to be supportive.

But in truth, Uzochi felt almost nonstop joy. He was elated that his father was here, alive, interested in who his son had grown up to be.

Siran had at first asked Uzochi and Com'pa lots of questions about New York City and Tri-State East, wanting to better understand their place in such a foreign land and how they'd managed to survive, even thrive, considering how Nubians were treated. And Siran wanted to know everything about Uzochi, from his childhood favorite toys to his experiences in school. Uzochi felt his father's earnest interest in his life as he spoke, the attention causing him to open up in a way he never had before with someone who was still essentially a stranger.

After some time, Siran launched into his own story, detailing how he had washed up on the shores of Ghana half dead days after the Nubian cataclysm. He'd been found by farmers and gradually nursed back to health at a hospital for the poor, though it would be years before he felt like he'd regained the strength and vitality he knew before the storm. "I was a man who lived like a wraith," he said, reaching for his wife's hand as he spoke, Com'pa tentatively taking his in return. "I had lost my wife, who was pregnant with you, Uzochi. I had lost my nation, my abilities. My *power*. I struggled with finding a reason to live, but something in my spirit persevered. I held on."

Uzochi simply nodded, his elation over being in his father's presence as strong as ever even as he felt Siran's sadness. He observed how Siran spoke as if he was an orator, kind of like Adisa in some ways but more formal. His father didn't really use slang or contractions and was super thorough when describing his thoughts or a particular locale. Uzochi recognized most of those traits in himself, wondering if he'd inherited them from his dad.

Siran went on to explain that he'd eventually left the

hospital and worked a number of odd jobs in the cities of Accra and Tema. No one knew his real identity as a Nubian who lived on an island that only existed in most people's minds as myth. It wasn't until five years after the destruction of his land that he turned on the local holo-news, watching a short clip about Nubians who'd settled in New York City as refugees. Siran had been stunned, not believing what he was seeing, with the Ghanaians around him mumbling that something wasn't adding up, that there was no such thing as an island called Nubia. Siran saw no reason to correct them, finding it more disturbing that other Nubians had apparently lost their gifts, just as he had.

"But I knew I had to come find you when the awakenings began," Siran said, looking at Uzochi as he spoke. "Though my elemental gifts were long gone, as catalyst of Nubia, my connection to the kinetic had not been entirely frayed. I could feel that a change had occurred, or rather a restoration, to be more precise. A vitality that I had known well. My connection to the kinetic was always a place of refuge and renewal for me. A place of safety. And thus I knew I had to return to our people immediately."

"But why didn't you return to us before?" Com'pa asked from her seat on the couch, her face tightening. This had been his mother's way since the reunion, emotions vacillating between glee, resentment, and rage. "The absence of your gifts had nothing to do with being here for your family, Siran. With being here for *me*."

Siran looked down, shaking his head. "My wife, you must

believe me, I was not myself. I was a man who had been responsible for the well-being of our people, who had made grave mistakes"—he looked at her pointedly then, just as she looked away—"who could not bear the thought of having you see me in my degraded condition. I . . . I am sorry, and I sincerely hope that one day you will find forgiveness in your heart, Com'pa, though I see you are not there now. I sincerely hope you will forgive me as well, Uzochi."

"Of course, Dad, I will . . . I mean, I do," Uzochi mumbled, seeing no reason why he shouldn't even if his mother refused to do the same. He looked at how they were interacting, suddenly curious about what their relationship was like back in Nubia. Which made Uzochi think about his own relationship.

He'd messed up. He knew that. As soon as Zuberi walked out of his place, the words he'd said circled his mind, pressing down on him with shame. How was he supposed to handle all of this? When Uzochi had been in school and felt overwhelmed by his classes, he'd always been able to make lists and portion out his time to better manage everything. But being the catalyst and dealing with awakenings and trying to rescue a good friend and falling hard for a girl and trying to be a good boyfriend and learning that his father had just come back from the dead . . . too much, too much. No matter how he parsed it out, every minute felt like he needed to give it to someone else. But what choice did he have? After all, hadn't he seen just months ago what could happen if he was too selfish?

But Zuberi wasn't asking for him to be selfish. She wasn't

asking him to steal away in the middle of the night and waste time. (Though truth be told, depending on her idea of wasting time, Uzochi might've been inclined to go along with the suggestion.) But no. Zuberi was asking him to help her save Vriana's life, to be there for her, especially after discovering she had an implant. He should've been able to say yes without thinking.

These thoughts weighed on him as he sat with his dad, dampening his spirits just a little as he looked over at his phone on the couch, hoping Zuberi had texted him back. He'd called and sent her several messages, but he realized that she was probably really, *really* mad at him and wanted space.

Eventually, after Com'pa went to bed, having to get up early for work in the morning, Siran encouraged Uzochi to speak more about his abilities, to present what he could do as an empath, telepath, and fledgling telekinetic. And of course, catalyst. "I appreciate the privacy you have afforded me, Uzochi, in respecting the boundaries of my mind," Siran said. "Your thoughtfulness is wonderful, my son, an elixir to my spirit. But perhaps I can help you learn more about who you are when it comes to the kinetic. As a catalyst of Nubia, I was responsible for understanding all manner of abilities, even though my gifts were tied to weather."

And so father and son sat with each other, speaking about their connection to the kinetic. Siran diligently took notes as Uzochi spoke about the feelings and sensations he regularly experienced as an empath and telepath, and how Adisa's memories seemed to be continually calling to him. He believed that maybe there was some big lesson he needed to learn about Nubian history that would help their people in the here and now.

Siran tapped his pen against the notebook he wrote in as he considered his son's words. "Perhaps. I agree with you, Uzochi, that a consciousness like Adisa's would not randomly pull at your mind for no reason. I suspect there's something there to ascertain, to discover. I, too, carry the history of Nubia within my spirit as bequeathed to me years ago by another elder, but these memories have long been integrated into my consciousness. I will help you make sense of your dreams however I can, son, though I believe you will have to be our primary guide."

It was difficult to read Siran's expression; he didn't let his emotions radiate off him like Com'pa would. Besides a few outbursts of joy around being close to Uzochi, he was an enigma. But for a moment Uzochi thought he saw the ghost of grief haunting his father. Was he missing Adisa, wishing he could've managed to see the elder one last time before his death? Was it guilt? But then Siran straightened, and the look was gone.

As father and son wrapped themselves in a cocoon of learning and exchange, Uzochi let go of his responsibilities as Nubian catalyst. He was relieved to be unburdened, at least for the time being. Still, the larger world continued to turn and change. The elders at the Jungle sent word that Krazen St. John had been seriously injured. The holo-news soon confirmed that the sky king lay in a coma after having experienced some form of tech failure, with no additional information being given. Uzochi immediately wondered if this meant that the attack at Starlight had become less of a priority? And would the registration act still be enforced if Krazen wasn't overseeing his militia? Would Nubians finally be safe?

Rumors swirled throughout the holos and social media channels about what had happened. Now that Uzochi knew far more about how the Up High operated, he met each bit of gossip with suspicion. He was particularly doubtful of the news that Krazen's daughter, Sandra, was slated to take over her father's business. Even if she had managed to get her clutches on Vriana, the flighty girl was mostly known for her fashion show socializing. Uzochi also wondered how Lencho might be faring with all of the news, still perplexed by his cousin's crazed attack in the greenhouse. But then he couldn't give that much thought, not with his father here.

As evening descended on the third day of Uzochi and Siran's communion, they continued to sit opposite each other on the floor, legs crossed, eating slices from Uzochi's favorite pizza shop down the block. (Siran had never tried pizza before, declaring that he found the taste of the dish mildly appetizing.) Adisa's journals were beside them, along with Siran's notebook and scraps of paper that they used to jot down major ideas. Upon hearing a light ping, Uzochi glanced down at his phone.

Zuberi had texted.

Hey, buddy . . . how are u? Wanna talk in the morning? she'd written.

He typed frantically, writing that he would call her first thing as he woke up and that he would be back at the Jungle tomorrow, for sure, for sure, that he could call her now if she wanted.

Tomorrow's fine. Talk then. Miss u.

Uzochi wrote *Okay . . . nighty night* and clutched his phone to his chest, so happy to have received Zuberi's message.

Siran smiled gently at his son. "You're worried that you've become distracted since I've arrived," he said. "You're worried about letting others down."

Uzochi's cheeks heated at how easily Siran picked up on what was happening.

"I feel like . . . like I haven't been able to check in with, um, everyone," Uzochi said.

Siran leaned back, running a hand through his voluminous beard.

"You're missing your girlfriend," Siran said.

Uzochi's first instinct was to shake his head and deny what was obvious. His father said it like it was something so basic, but it wasn't.

"Um," Uzochi began. "I mean, yeah. I mean, we haven't technically defined our relationship, but yeah, I consider Zuberi my girlfriend. For sure." Uzochi felt his heart sing, so happy that he'd finally admitted to someone what he'd felt for weeks now. "But I think I sort of . . . messed things up. She wanted to go back Up High right away for her friend, really our friend, an awesome person, and I kinda shut her down. But I didn't mean to." He folded his hands in his lap. "You've just arrived, Dad. You need to be my priority now."

Siran raised an eyebrow. "You made an informed decision,

son. Zuberi is smart, wise beyond her years from what I have observed, and extremely tenacious. I am sure she understands our need to spend time together, even if she felt rejection."

"I dunno," Uzochi admitted. "I . . . I could literally feel the betrayal with my gift, but you know that. Her friend, she's so important to her. And I feel like, maybe, I should've heard her out more . . . or something."

Siran nodded as if taking in every word. "It is difficult to have to figure out which parts of your life to prioritize in each moment," he said. "One moment, you are being called upon to be a friend, a brother . . . or a boyfriend, as people say in this land. In another, all of Nubia calls for your assistance. It is important to ask for help in those moments, to ask for understanding, patience. Talk to her, Uzochi. Apologize if she was hurt. But she must understand, as your mother did back on our homeland, that being a catalyst is not easy. Sacrifice is demanded. Costs are inherent. Forgiveness will be part of your world more often now, seeking it, expecting it."

Uzochi nodded, taking in words that he didn't fully grasp, slightly overwhelmed. He remembered how Adisa had told him something similar, that being the catalyst meant putting Nubians first above all else. But to Uzochi, such an idea still felt . . . off.

Later that evening, the expectations associated with being a catalyst swirled in Uzochi's mind as he lay on the couch. He found it hard to sleep, though Siran had easily fallen into slumber on a pallet he'd made on the floor, snoring lightly. (Uzochi hadn't realized at first that this was where his father had slept ever since entering their Kips Bay apartment. His mother, prone to speaking openly about sex, had declared one night that she would allow Siran to stay in their home but that after all these years her bed was her own.)

He'd turned on the apartment's holo-projector, making sure to keep the volume and picture brightness low so as not to wake his dad, hoping he could find an old movie or documentary to help him drift off. The projector was on a news channel, actually, with the *World Village Report* insignia floating at the top of the image. James Bradley, the show's host, was speaking again to Professor Cassandra Johnson, a lower-city scholar Uzochi really liked. He'd only heard her speak a few times on the show, but he was struck by how poised and fair-minded she generally appeared to be. And she always seemed to have Nubians' backs, even after the awakenings.

Unable to make out what she was saying without raising the volume, he turned on the captions.

". . . I mean, we really need to be wary of this registration act considering the periods of enslavement and internment that have existed in North America," she said. "How regressive are we going to become as a society considering we're actually about to make it to the twenty-second century? James, I know it's a frightening time for many considering the alleged abilities that Nubians possess, but mass subjugation is unacceptable. Why don't we take this moment to finally get to know the Nubian community? Long overdue, in my book . . ."

Uzochi smiled. Indeed, Cassandra always had their backs.

After watching the holo for a few minutes, Uzochi did feel more relaxed, less amped up. He closed his eyes, sitting with some of Siran's words from earlier in the evening.

. . . a consciousness like Adisa's would not randomly pull at your mind . . .

If that was the case, that meant Uzochi had a problem to solve, and as an academic, that was his specialty. Perhaps it was time for him to stop waiting for answers to randomly appear from the departed elder. Perhaps it was time for him to go to the source of his power.

For the first time since Uzochi had taken Adisa's consciousness into his own, he acted impulsively, following a hunch. He would tap directly into the kinetic without using his gifts, like his father had briefly mentioned earlier. Siran had described the kinetic as a place where he always felt safe, so maybe Adisa would have viewed the kinetic in the same way. Uzochi would visit the glistening turquoise sun that shone in his soul, a representation of his particular expressions of kinetic power. That was where his strongest self lay, he realized. Where, if he was someone like Adisa, he might seek to take refuge.

From this place of courage and confidence, Cassandra's voice in his ears, Uzochi drifted off to sleep.

Instantly, he was full of warmth, his sight limned with blue before the world opened up to him, the world of Nubia from long ago, full of glittering temples with spires of gold, something Uzochi remembered Adisa describing in his journals. The streets were sparkling, full of life, with an assortment of gigantic shea trees rooted in what looked to be large municipal gardens. Nubians sauntered by in lustrous robes, bodies lean or full or muscular or plump, hair cut and configured in intricate styles. These people were healthy, strong. A couple of Nubians flew high overhead, holding hands. Singing filled the air. Uzochi turned to see a bare-chested man in an ochre skirt standing on a small platform, crooning away, a legion of birds slowly bobbing and weaving overhead, as if they were dancing to his song.

What part of Nubian history was he witnessing? How long ago was this memory? He had the sense . . . that this was long ago.

Uzochi was suddenly yanked by an invisible thread and pulled into a misty swirl of images. He saw rugged landscapes and village huts and raging seas, the sky bright, blue, and then, abruptly, full of fire and smoke.

What was happening?

Uzochi breathed, trying to make sense of what he was seeing, centering himself even amid the madness.

I can figure this out . . . I'm not going to get lost . . . I won't get lost . . .

Uzochi stilled his spirit as the images continued to swirl around him. He occasionally recognized slivers of what he'd seen in his previous dreams with Adisa.

He began to understand.

Right . . .

He wasn't in the midst of just one crazy, cracked-up memory. He was in a trove of recollections that had been held within Adisa's mind, now transferred to Uzochi. He focused again, willing himself not to become distracted or anxious or overwhelmed, to impose order on chaos.

The churn of images gradually slowed. Uzochi found himself completely encircled by what he knew to be Nubia's history. He remembered the words of the kind female elder who had once guided young Adisa. These images . . . memories . . . they were a tapestry, woven together by previous historians to form the stories that passed before Uzochi's eyes. Solid and tangible at certain moments, misty and translucent at others.

Uzochi's heart was full. In his spirit form, could he cry? Here it was, the collected story of his people . . . a magnificent story . . .

But then his eyes were drawn to a memory that filled him with revulsion, one he recognized from before as well. He saw the city of Nubia, but not the shining beacon he had glimpsed repeatedly in his dreams. Instead, he saw smoldering ruins and scorched earth. Uzochi saw his people cowering in fear, the color of blood shining in the sky.

Such desolation happened ages before you were even born.

A chorus of voices echoed in Uzochi's mind, decades of historians telling one story. And he heard Adisa's voice above them all. Uzochi immediately visualized the elder's baritone as a luminous thread that pierced his form, something he could cling to as history hummed all around in all its glory and madness.

The chorus spoke again.

We are descended from those who left our ancestral nation

during a time of upheaval, trekking across the vast mother continent to a sacred, remote island.

Our people would later face a foe unlike anything we had ever known. This abomination created a wave of torment and death that nearly tore our adopted land apart.

In the deep memory of his people, the mist swirled, forming the image of a man. He was faceless, but Uzochi saw that the kinetic pulsed through him, the same deep crimson of the sky. A crimson that felt vaguely familiar to Uzochi.

He was called Liv'e, a Nubian born more than two thousand years ago. He was gifted, and the connection to the kinetic thrummed mightily in his veins, as it does for all Nubians.

Uzochi watched Liv'e, a misty figure, walking through a village, approaching a family, a mother cradling a young child in her arms. He placed his hands on the youth's brow, both starting to glow red.

Liv'e was a low-level telepath who could manipulate life energy. For his people, this was a boon, for he could mend wounds and serve other Nubians through the healing arts. Such was the custom of those born to his abilities, but for Liv'e, an ambitious, restless young man, such a vocation wasn't enough. As a child, he had always been inquisitive, questioning Nubian traditions, questioning why we held certain rituals so dear. He was reprimanded by elders of the day, told to accept and be grateful for what he had been given, told that his questions were narrow, foolhardy.

Around Uzochi, the chorus of historians hissed. Liv'e's smoky figure removed his hands from the brow of the child and threw up his arms before dissipating, sending streams of mist in Uzochi's direction.

As a healer who yearned for more, Liv'e declared that too much was asked of him. Too many came to him seeking his gifts. Too few understood his desire to move beyond the roles prescribed by our society. And so he declared that he was trapped by this place, that there was a greater world he yearned to explore. For most Nubians, his yearnings continued to be seen as bizarre, as heresy, for why would you seek more when you live in the garden?

Liv'e saw his island home as a prison he could tolerate no longer, and so he sailed away, leaving his people for territory forgotten or unknown . . .

Uzochi watched Liv'e throw himself into the wind, mist swirling wildly, only to solidify and coalesce in the shapes of different locales. Some of the ancient architecture he recognized from his history textbooks, like the pyramids of Egypt and the colosseums of Rome.

We do not know the full extent of Liv'e's travels or all that he discovered. We do know that he found himself fascinated with despotic rulers, with their need for order and control at any cost, that he immersed himself in the mystical arts and forms of witchcraft that fell far outside the kinetic. For Liv'e was obsessed with ways to augment his natural gift. The kinetic was an effortless connection to an exalted place. Liv'e's arcane manipulations . . . a perversion of the natural order, twisting expressions of power that were beautiful and rapturous into rotten, raging decadence.

Liv'e was no longer a man before Uzochi. He had become wisps of mist that spread far and wide, pulsing red, painting the sky. A scarlet storm loomed that shook Uzochi to his core as it solidified . . . bristling, pulsing. Cries of betrayal and disgust filled Uzochi's mind as the historians bemoaned Liv'e's fate.

And in that moment, Uzochi realized where he'd seen this raging storm before.

The chorus continued.

Unbeknownst to his people, Liv'e became an aberration, a Nubian who actively sought to use the kinetic for conquest. His power multiplied in ways no one could have imagined when he returned to his native island more than two decades later. He had manipulated his abilities through practice and study, and could now absorb the life essence and powers of other Nubians. A corruption of his natural gift, a forbidden practice that his people were forced to condemn. Liv'e's expression of the kinetic had become a raging, frightful thing that saw humans as mere vessels of energy to consume.

The chorus wailed and moaned.

Liv'e cared little about Nubian judgments and condemnations. He was fueled by vengeance, bitter toward the island folk he believed had rejected him, who had never understood the depths of his curiosity. Upon returning to Nubia, cloaked in the language of peace and conciliation, Liv'e sought a meeting with our revered catalyst Jalisa Somae, a fantastically gifted light wielder who could create works of art that illuminated our skies. She was the first he drained, taking her power, her life, and her ability to powerfully align herself with the kinetic, as was her right as catalyst.

With Jalisa gone, with Liv'e's power greatly bolstered by stealing her abilities, he demanded that Nubians bow to him as catalyst by conquest. He sought to have the traditional line of royal succession eradicated and be crowned ruler. A Nubian Augustus, claiming the title used by Roman emperors, his time abroad twisting his mind.

The crackling crimson mists swirled and thrashed, and Liv'e was a solidified figure once more. Only this time, he held up a pointed, golden crown, the echo of a laugh sweeping through a grand hall, a laugh countered by roars of anger and outrage. Other Nubians, refusing to bow to his rule.

As expected, violence ensued. Many Nubians perished while attempting to vanquish and destroy him. Villages burned. Our capital city, leveled in hours. For how did you kill a Nubian who by his mere touch could siphon your gifts, your very ability to live?

Cries and screams echoed within Uzochi's mind, and he watched as other figures approached Liv'e, only to have their existence snuffed out by his might. With each blow, he grew larger, more powerful, towering in the memory until, at last, a group of figures surrounded him, the gargantuan sorcerer howling in rage. And Uzochi felt fear as understanding settled into his spirit, as he began to realize that he had indeed encountered Liv'e before in the real world.

We were not used to conflict at such a scale. We had never fought a war. So many lives were lost until a valiant team strategized, studying ways in which they could take advantage of Liv'e's primary weakness . . . that he needed to lay hands on all of those he drained. And so a brave league of more than one thousand telepaths, telekinetics, energy wielders, elementals, and others managed to trap Liv'e in the palace he'd fashioned for himself. They attacked him with their abilities all at once, being sure to maintain distance so he couldn't drain their life and powers, even as he used his stolen gifts to kill so many of their number. But thank Goddess, our defenders succeeded.

With a final, harrowing cry, Liv'e evaporated into thin air, leaving wounded people and devastated terrain in his wake.

And the chorus continued.

Though destroyed, Liv'e succeeded in changing Nubia forever, as he wished. Our home became a place of sorrow, of grief transmitted through generations. Of an all-encompassing regret, for many asked themselves, if they had nurtured young Liv'e, if they had sat with his queries and guided him wisely, would he have become a monster?

Even with such reflection, there was also a growing militancy, a combativeness that overshadowed questions of responsibility. For the first time in our history, many of us began to train as warriors, learning how to use our gifts in martial ways, ever ready in case we were attacked again. For the first time in our history, we cultivated strict rules around how the kinetic could be used, barring the study of any form of mystical power foreign to our land. For the first time in our history, we created decrees that forbade Nubians from leaving our island home outside of the most severe emergencies. We would not leave paradise, no, never again, and we would not have our paradise sullied by outsiders.

New memories appeared in Uzochi's mind's eye. Brighter, more solid, less ancient. Uzochi saw images of African and European sailors alike caught in storms, attempting to reach the island for safety and succor before being pushed back to sea by winds that appeared out of the ether, winds controlled by the elemental who stood guard on Nubian shores. He saw shipwrecked people who'd actually managed to reach the shores of his ancestral land, only to be greeted by a telepath.

We would not have our paradise sullied, the chorus repeated.

Uzochi was yanked from his floating space and unceremoniously thrown to the ground. He was crouched on the shores of a beach, the sky bright as he stared into his reflection in a small tide pool by his side. Just a dozen feet away, the waves of the ocean lapped against the sand. He was Adisa again, and there were others next to him, worry etched into the lines of their faces.

"This will be quick," the young Adisa said. "You won't suffer."

"I . . . I don't understand," a man insisted, lacerations crisscrossing his skin, his wet blond hair limp and bedraggled. "We mean you no harm. Please, sir, we need assistance. Our boat, the engine failed and—"

Uzochi felt the clatter in Adisa's heart, the way the future elder steeled himself before responding.

"We will not be sullied," Adisa said before he entered the sailor's mind, finding the section of his memories that contained his sighting of Nubia, his approach to the shore, his plea for help. With his gift, Adisa grasped those sections of the man's memories, captured them, and released them into the ether, the sailor becoming a dead-eyed, blathering thing placed in a small boat and pushed back to sea by winds generated by a pair of elementals.

And as he sat within Adisa's consciousness, Uzochi realized that the elder had done this time and time again, confronting bedraggled seafarers who'd reached Nubian shores seeking aid, conquest the last thing on their minds, their eyes clouding over and clearing after having their memories erased.

Adisa peered down at the tide pool. "We will not be sullied," he repeated, speaking to his reflection as a crackling scarlet storm appeared above his head, maniacal laughter swirling around him. The elder sent his telepathy forward again to his own reflection, ready to erase memory from yet another mind.

With a gasp, Uzochi lurched forward. He was back in his living room, pain in his arms and head. Had he been thrashing about? He panted, cold beads of sweat dotting his forehead.

Uzochi tried to control his breath as he sat with everything he'd just learned, with what Adisa and the chorus of elders had shared. All this time, they'd been trying to reach him, trying to send him a message about the danger sitting right in front of his face.

Goddess . . .

Uzochi bounded out of bed, crouched down to the floor, and shook his father. Siran rose immediately, like a man used to waking up at a moment's notice in case he had to flee. He turned to Uzochi, trying to blink himself into lucidity.

"Son . . ."

"Dad," Uzochi whispered, his voice panicked as he tried his best not to wake up his mom in the other room. "You were right. Adisa was trying to reach me, to send a message. It's this ancient Nubian, Liv'e. I've encountered him before, at the Swamp . . . when I was with Lencho at the Swamp. The seawall . . ."

But before he could get the words out, a bright news banner flared to life in the corner of the room. Uzochi quickly remembered that he'd fallen asleep with the holo on. The words BREAKING NEWS flashed at the bottom of the projection, and Uzochi had to hold up his hand to shield his eyes from the glare.

The Helios News anchor sat at his desk, reading the news, calm as ever, even though Uzochi had to keep himself from yelping in alarm when he read the scrolling banner at the bottom of the holo.

. . . SANDRA ST. JOHN, INTERIM DIRECTOR OF ST. JOHN ENTERPRISES, VOWS RECKONING FOR NUBIAN ATTACK . . .

Chapter 21

Sandra

Sandra's heels clicked against the polished floor, the only sound that echoed through the large foyer. She made her way to the podium that her father always used when giving a press conference at the main HQ of St. John Enterprises. She caught her live image in the large holo that shimmered above her head, allowing reporters at the back of the gathering to see her more clearly. Her new title as St. John Enterprises interim director was perched right above the holo. She knew that those who were gathered this morning would be a bit more deferential to her, lacing their words with care considering that her father was on the brink of death. Plus Sandra was making news as one of the youngest corporate leaders in the history of North America. The media vultures would want access to her new life, anxious for any scoops they could get. She would use their misplaced sentiments to her advantage. Sandra was someone who'd endured a long, humiliating battle and managed to come out triumphant on the other side.

She knew that soon the word "interim" would no longer appear in front of her title.

Several members of her staff stood off to the side of the stage, Vriana among them. The Nubian girl was dressed simply, her braids in an intricate updo that only someone like Vriana would know how to create. The white of Vriana's sheath dress looked marvelous against her glowing brown skin, just as the blackness of Sandra's pantsuit made her crimson lipstick and hair all the more striking.

She was ready.

"Friends," Sandra began. "I cannot begin to tell you what it means to be speaking to you this morning. True, I have faced extraordinary grief these past few days, but your comforting words and deeply felt support have buoyed me during grave, difficult times. I'm sorry to report that there's been no significant change in my father's condition, that he remains in a coma and we continue to do everything in our power to improve his condition. We have no information to share at this time about the cause of his collapse, though we're able to report that his body went through complete tech failure. Something practically unheard-of in the sky city."

She heard gasps and grumbling among the reporters. Sandra tossed back her hair, looking meaningfully out at the audience, allowing them to digest the news. She took in the slightly stunned look of the gathered newshounds, realizing that they weren't just reacting to news of Krazen's tech failure. They'd never seen Sandra St. John speak with eloquence and gravitas, had never seen her present herself as someone who could be more than the bouncy, flirty lapdog of her father.

"Friends, we have so much work to do together," she continued, holding out her arms. "Our streets are flooded with threats. Opposition against the beautiful world that St. John Enterprises has created mounts every day. But rest assured that I will continue my father's mission, doing everything in my power to be the leader you need in this moment. Though Krazen's bid for mayor has been derailed, his vision lives on through me, his dedicated staff, and you, the good people of the Up High, who deserve to have your lifestyle protected at all costs."

Several drone cameras whirred above Sandra's head, hovering in place. Everyone in the foyer was silent.

"I'm encouraged to know that, even amid the tragedy of my father's condition, the city is taking steps to ensure our safety, to provide the order that our beloved warden would want for all of us. The Paranormal Registration Act has passed, and our militia, your beloved St. John Soldiers, will be at the forefront, making sure that gifted Nubians present themselves to the proper authorities. It is with a heavy heart that I reveal to you that I was among the militia who were attacked at Starlight Greenhouse. That *I* was attacked by a trio of Nubians with special abilities who wished to send a stark message: The Up High is in danger. The opportunities we've worked so hard to create for ourselves are at risk."

The audience gasped again, just as Sandra knew they would. With that, another holo appeared above the stage. Whereas videos of the greenhouse incident already circulating on the holos and social media focused on the attack against the soldiers, this clip showcased Sandra and Vriana being approached by a trio of Nubians. And then, Sandra being hit and crumpling into Starlight's plush grass. She could feel the energy from the crowd, their discomfort and surprise. She hated presenting herself in such a way, but it was necessary so she could do what she had to do.

"It gives me no joy to share this moment with you, my friends. And as you can see, I am fine, despite the viciousness of this attack. But as my father had maintained, as we saw with the destruction of the Carter-Combs Theater by Nubians left to their own devices, we won't be safe until these beings are under our control. As interim director of St. John Enterprises and therefore head of the militia that provides security for our city, I assure you that we will *not* be frightened by these wild assailants. We will not accept such violence. We will find those responsible and see to it that they suffer the consequences for what they've done."

Sandra allowed her words to sink in. Her eyes swept the crowd. Before, she'd been so desperate to discover her own potential Nubian ability. To display the kind of power that could make others bow. But now, she saw what true power was. With her words and authority, she was the one who could corral the fears of others, who could shape their imaginations as she saw fit, her press conference broadcast for all of Tri-State East to see.

"I'll be working with the city council to provide full enforcement of the registration act," she finished. "All Nubians will be under our authority, of this I assure you. My staff will provide a description of our protocols that will be distributed shortly by cloud to implants and external files. Good afternoon and thank you for your time."

Sandra turned around and walked from the podium, ignoring the throng of questions and shouts that she knew would rise. It was far more compelling for her to leave them wanting, to leave them clamoring for more of this self-possessed young woman they were meeting for the first time.

She got into a waiting car, sending a message to Vriana via personal comm that she would touch base with her that afternoon, to stay safe. Militiamen were looking everywhere for Lencho, though Sandra forbade them from distributing his photo across the holos as the primary suspect in the attack on her father. Instead, Sandra had them flood the holos with select photos and videos of the Children, including Uzochi Will and Zuberi Ragee, shifting the focus to them. After all, Sandra didn't need the Up High to think that one of the Nubians her father had recruited to keep them safe, especially one seen prancing and preening at his rallies, was the very one who might've put him into a coma. That wouldn't remotely fit her plans. And so the boy needed to be found, subdued, and made to have a nice conversation with Vriana.

Sandra had the driver take her to the specialized rehabilitation center where they'd moved her father. She soon found herself walking through sleek, silver-gray corridors, following the attendant who guided her to Krazen's room. Once again she heard the click-clacking of her heels against a metallic floor. Sandra looked at the large man, not discerning any change in his appearance, the beep and whir of the machines that were keeping him alive providing the sort of symphony that she hoped she wouldn't get used to.

"Ms. St. John?"

Sandra turned around to see a brown-skinned woman walk in sporting a short afro and a prominent implant along the right side of her head. Sandra had noticed that among some medical professionals, their implants were more conspicuous than your average sky city resident, as if they wanted the world to know they were cybernetically enhanced.

"Dr. Marshall, I presume," Sandra said as she extended a palm. "Pleasure."

The two women shook hands. "Ms. St. John . . ."

"Call me Sandra."

"Ah, okay. Sandra, I just wanted to say that I'm so very sorry. This must be tremendously hard, and please know I'll do everything in my power to expedite your father's recovery. We'll get him out of here, I promise."

Sandra held up her hand. "Dr. Marshall, spare me. I've done my research, and I know you're at the top of your field as a general practitioner, especially when it comes to how the body interacts with cybernetic implants. It's one of the reasons why I've hired you to care for Krazen. I also hired you because several sources informed me that you believe in the power of currency and have a malleable spirit. That you understand how to be discreet, like so many other Up High physicians." She tilted her head and tapped her left wrist three times in slow succession, clearly working an implant. "So, now that I've deactivated all cameras and mics in the room, let's get down to the most important question. Exactly how much currency do you need to ensure that my father never wakes up again?"

Chapter 22

Uzochi

Even with everything that had recently happened to Nubians, Uzochi sometimes felt like the most naïve boy in all of New York. He knew there was no way that what had gone down at the greenhouse would go away quietly, knew he would have to deal with the repercussions from their mission to rescue Vriana eventually. But what he hadn't expected was for Sandra St. John to place a target on each of their backs during an early-morning press conference.

Krazen's daughter had undergone a remarkable transformation, appearing for all the news holos as an avatar of decorum and competent leadership, like she'd been groomed over the years to take over the reins of power from her father at any moment. That was odd enough, but when she'd called him and the others out as "wild assailants" who would face serious consequences, well, that made him jump. Right after her speech, Helios News had displayed photos and short videos of several of the Children, including some who weren't even at the greenhouse. The broadcasters had made sure to include images devoid of smiles and carefree laughing. They seemed to be school pictures where Abdul was sneering, or Sekou was mean-mugging the hell out of a camera, or Tasha was twisting her lips in a rare scowl. It was so unfair, to see them portrayed in a way that didn't remotely capture who they really were.

Of course several images of him and Zuberi were in the mix, Zuberi looking particularly aggressive with her various fighting-form moves. They'd also included a short clip of Uzochi from the fight at the Carter-Combs Theater right before it was destroyed. He was haggard and covered in soot, screaming something, looking crazed. In the public's eye, a deranged, dangerous Nubian for sure.

All of this spun before Uzochi, a jumbled mess that mixed with the revelation he'd just had before Sandra St. John and her damn press conference had wrecked his world.

Liv'e was Up High, the great Nubian threat that Uzochi had been too distracted to see clearly. Not only was he Up High, surrounded by Sandra St. John and her army, but he'd hidden himself in another powerful Nubian.

His own cousin. Lencho. Which was nuts.

Uzochi's parents stood behind him as he reviewed Sandra's press conference for the umpteenth time, trying to make sure he'd memorized everything she'd said. She wasn't calling for the immediate arrest of him and Zuberi and Tasha, wasn't calling for the public to join in a manhunt, but she did say they'd suffer the consequences. What did that mean? Would she just bring them in through enforcement of the registration act? Were militiamen out and about now, looking for them?

His mother placed both of her hands on his shoulders, her way of letting him know *I'm here*. He could feel it with his empathy, coming from her in waves, her unflinching love and care.

"I'm happy I called out of work," she said. "We'll figure this out, dear heart. But Uzochi, your situation, our situation . . . it's become dangerous. Our neighbors in the building have always been good to us, but someone is sure to notice your picture on the holo. What if they decide to try and make a citizen's arrest or some such nonsense?"

"Indeed," Siran said, his hand under his chin as he stared at Uzochi, almost as if he was studying his son. Which felt creepy. It wasn't the first time Uzochi had noticed that look.

"I think . . . I believe we need to get you to the Jungle," Siran continued. "We need to be among our people, receive counsel from the elders and figure out the wisest course of action. It's our way."

Uzochi nodded, trying to process everything that was happening, consoling himself that at least he'd be closer to Zuberi if he was at the Jungle. They'd been texting each other frantically all morning once the press conference hit the airwaves, writing that everything would be okay even if neither one of them really believed it. He wanted nothing more right now than to be close to her, to feel her energy, to be inspired by her fierceness and courage and fortitude. He was such a jerk for turning her away. An idiot. He would make it up to her every day, for as long as he needed to, as long as she would let him. He would—

"Son," Siran said, interrupting Uzochi's quiet spiraling.

"This other thing you mentioned. About Liv'e. I know that what this Sandra St. John has done is terrible, but your explorations of Adisa's consciousness are a priority as well. I am sorry, we must investigate."

Com'pa shook her head. "Uzochi, what you said earlier, are you sure?"

Uzochi placed his hands at the back of his head, not believing what he was about to say, especially as he was still putting the pieces together. "Ma, no, I'm not sure, to be honest, but I think I've figured it out." He hesitated. "I'm trying to trust myself, to trust my gut. If I'm really our people's catalyst, then I need to do that more often, right?"

Com'pa tilted her head, giving her son a bittersweet look. "You're right."

Uzochi swallowed and continued. "Okay, so months ago, when I entered Lencho's mind at the Swamp seawall, I witnessed his expression of the kinetic, how his powers manifested in his soul. It was like this red, super-crazy storm . . . really scary. In all the dozens of Nubians I've helped awaken to their gifts, I've never seen an expression of the kinetic that looked quite like that. Violent, almost like it was mad at the world. I mean, different kids have different inner expressions of the kinetic, some more energetic than others, but I'd never seen one like Lencho's. I thought it was an indication of how powerful his gift was, or maybe even that he was the next catalyst for Nubians, not me." Uzochi looked over demurely at Siran, his cheeks flushed slightly with guilt. His father said nothing.

"But in my explorations of Adisa's consciousness, of

Nubian history, when I learned about Liv'e and who he was and what he'd done . . . he was always surrounded by this crazy crimson storm, the same storm that I saw in Lencho. That I *felt* in Lencho."

"Okay, so say you're right, son. How is this possible?" Com'pa asked. "I've heard the story of Liv'e, like most Nubian adults. But he waged war on our people eons ago. He was supposed to have been killed in a great, final confrontation. Even if he did somehow manage to survive the battle, how would he still be alive today? That would make him more than *two thousand years old*. And how would he have managed to travel over here to New York, with us?"

Siran spoke up. "Com'pa, as catalyst, I carry ancestral memories within, just like Uzochi. Liv'e practiced all sorts of foul magic. This ability to absorb the life and powers of others, this is not remotely connected to the kinetic. Perhaps there was something else in his arsenal that would let his soul endure through the ages. Perhaps . . . he somehow developed the power of possession."

"Really?!? Goddess . . . ," Com'pa muttered.

"This is bad. Very bad," Siran said, fist under his chin, giving that faraway look that Uzochi noticed he adopted from time to time. "If Liv'e is still the same person he was two millennia ago, then his primary desire will revolve around acquisition of power and conquest. He will want to seize everything he can by whatever means necessary."

"Yeah, Dad, I think it's pretty bad, too," Uzochi said. "With all I've been saying here, I'm simply connecting the dots. Think about it. None of the other Nubians who've awoken have a gift like Lencho's, and think about how similar Lencho's and Liv'e's powers are. The power to absorb life essence and energy. I coulda even sworn when I was Up High that I saw Lencho start to absorb Zaire's gift, which would make his power *exactly* like Liv'e's. And Zaire's been saying that Lencho's been acting really off lately, which I agree with if our encounter at Starlight is any indication." Uzochi held his hands out in front of himself, exasperated. "I mean, it's like this horrible danger has been sitting in front of us all this time, and the part of Adisa that's within me is pushing us to recognize it. That's why he's bringing up the parts of Nubian history where Liv'e killed all those people. Those visions . . . they're so bad. And I'm so *stupid*. I should've seen this earlier."

"Son, you are far from stupid, and this was not your fault," Siran said. "And we can fix this. You have done an exemplary job of sifting through Adisa's memories."

Uzochi glared at his father for the first time since they'd met. "Speaking of memory, Dad, do you know how Adisa would sometimes use his powers? What he did to lots of innocent people? I understand now how Nubia's location stayed a secret. Were you . . . ?"

The doorbell buzzed loudly.

Com'pa clenched her fists at her side. "Goddess-damn . . ." She exhaled as she placed a hand on her weary head. "Announcer, who is it? Image of visitor."

A live holo instantaneously beamed into the middle of the living room. A young white couple stood outside, their faces lined with concern.

"I know these two," Com'pa said after sucking her teeth.

"Addison and Mattie, live down the hall. Work as assistant producers at Helios. Very hipster, as people here like to say. They've probably seen your face all over the holos, Uzochi."

He tensed up. "Oh no, you think . . . ?"

His mother shook her head. "No, I don't think they're interested in grabbing you for that wicked witch of the sky. They're probably just checking to make sure everything is okay, if we need help. They're nice people." She gave Uzochi a stern look. "But it's still not a good idea for you to be seen here."

Siran swiveled and pointed to the living room window, the only one in the apartment. "Well, er, this might be extreme, but perhaps with Uzochi's telekinesis we should . . ."

"You will not leap out of a window with my child, Siran!" Com'pa said through clenched teeth just as the doorbell rang again. "Are you mad? We're on the third floor and you're not birds. I don't care what power Uzochi has. It's bad enough he almost plummeted to his death from that cursed Up High. You two stay in here and I'll talk to these morons outside. Go to—"

"Guys, okay, okay, just . . . stop, okay?" Uzochi said. "I have a solution. It's the only way for me to leave the apartment without attracting attention. The streets aren't safe and you're both right, I can't be here any longer."

Uzochi took out his mobile and nimbly texted Zuberi.

Hey, babes . . .

It was the first time he'd called her that. It felt good.

We have an emergency over here at my place. Can u get Sajah?

Chapter 23

Zuberi

The air outside the Jungle was fresh and clean in Zuberi's lungs, the floral scents of Leonard's community garden tickling her nose. She kept her eyes closed, staff in hand, as she reviewed each of the fighting forms, needing to take her mind off that horrible Sandra St. John press conference that had ruined her morning. As she went through each form, her muscles popped and her skin shone in the morning light. She was taking a chance by being outside, as she now thought of herself as a wanted woman, with her picture all over the holos, but she just needed this moment. (Her father, who was currently meeting with the elders about his new vision, would've absolutely killed her if he'd been aware that she'd crept outdoors, even though she was in a little nook behind the Jungle that no one paid attention to.) Who knew when she would see the light of day again if she needed to go into hiding somewhere or always be on the run? With each swing or punch or kick, she tried to channel away her emotions.

She wanted to be in a neutral place of mindfulness, to not worry about Vriana or her own safety, but somehow, she just couldn't get there. Perhaps it was too much to ask, considering everything.

But at least she and Uzochi were talking again, able to soothe each other's nerves during Sandra's press conference. She felt way better than she had a few days ago, though he kept on saying something else was up, which made Zuberi wonder, *What in Goddess's name could be worse than the shit we're dealing with now?*

Only fifteen minutes into her practice, however, she got another text from Uzochi asking about Sajah, needing them to get to his place right away and get him out of there. Zuberi had texted *U bet* and run to the Jungle's main entrance. Thankfully Sajah was doing morning drills with Zaire, Abdul, and Tasha. It was amazing to Zuberi, how Sajah had seemed not particularly happy about aligning themself with the Children at first but had quickly settled in with their own clique, who they practiced their teleportation powers with all the time. In a far corner of the main lobby, which was mostly empty at this hour, Sajah had formed several small shadow portals, and Abdul was sending slim streams of water through each of the apertures, clearly trying to hone his precision with his gift. Tasha had created a massive illusion of a twinkling starlit night sky above them while Zaire practiced jogging in his stone form, sending a rocky, cragged smile over to Abdul with each step he took, not seeming to notice that his movements were causing the entire lobby to tremble. This was now the Nubian way among the Children, to get to know your gifts as well as you could, to become one with your gifts. Adisa would've been proud, though Zuberi believed that Nubians should practice their abilities often to be ready to defend themselves at a moment's notice.

"Sajah," she called out, refocusing on what she'd been called upon to do. "We need you!" Sajah must've already surmised that they would be called into action. When Zuberi explained that Uzochi needed to make a quick getaway from his apartment, exactly where they'd been before, Sajah simply gave her a salute, shouted "On it!" and vanished into one of their portals.

Waiting for Sajah to return soon became the longest couple of minutes in Zuberi's life. She wrung her hands in front of her, not sure what she would say to Uzochi. She wasn't really mad at him any longer, but things still felt awkward. Like they needed to clear the air.

Abdul had noticed her condition and walked over, giving her a bit of a bump with his hip. With the sharp lines of his fade, crisp red sleeveless tunic, arm bracelets, and slim navy jeans, Abdul was the most put-together Nubian she knew outside of Vriana, which was saying something. And Zaire had clearly become enraptured with the dude as well.

"It'll be okay, Beri," Abdul said. "I know you miss him. Sometimes couples fight. Most normal thing in the world, and y'all have been through a lot. It happens."

Zuberi gave the boy a timid smile. "That obvious, huh?" she said, shrugging slightly, relieved that she could talk about Uzochi with someone her age who seemed kind. That she could admit they were a couple. "Yeah, it's not a big deal, and . . ."

A swirl of shadow formed within the pair's sight, and then a large portal appeared.

"Uzochi!" Zuberi shouted.

There he was, crouching, dry-heaving on the floor before her, followed by his father—who looked thoroughly displeased—and then Sajah.

Zuberi ran forward immediately, helping Uzochi up. "Buddy, hey, it's okay. I'm here."

"What did you do to my son?" Siran demanded of Sajah, who threw up their hands as the older man grabbed them by their shirt. "What foul sorcery do you practice? Your gift is clearly *not* Nubian!"

"I ain't do anything, and get offa me, you smelly coot!" Sajah yelled back, wrenching themself away from Siran's grip. "Some people just can't handle my shadow portals, okay? They have a funny reaction."

"Siran, relax," Zuberi said. "Sajah's right. Shadow-walking can feel strange for some reason, you know that. Maybe for Uzochi it's super weird because it messes with his telepathy and empathy. Right?" She glanced over at Uzochi, who gave her a look that said, *I really have no idea.*

Uzochi's father continued to fume, even as some of the other Children gathered to see what the fuss was about. "I have to meet with the elders, but I am far from done with you," Siran said as he pointed at Sajah, turning and stomping out of the lobby. Sajah glowered at the man's back as they stuck out their tongue.

Zuberi hated to admit it, but Siran was right. Something

did feel weird when she was shadow-walking. She'd traveled through Sajah's portals twice now, and each time, the experience left her numb, disoriented.

"Hey . . . babes . . . ," Uzochi said, stooping slightly and looking tired even though it wasn't even nine o'clock.

For a moment, her breath caught once more in her throat, even as she noticed that the rest of the Children crept away, wanting to give her and Uzochi space. All morning, she'd thought about what she would say to Uzochi when she saw him again, trying to ensure that she wouldn't lose her words this time. He turned his eyes to meet hers, and whatever remaining anger she had seemed to evaporate.

"Can I . . . ?" He opened up his arms, his unfinished question obvious.

Oh, Uzochi, she sent to him with her thoughts. *Yes.*

The two leaned into each other, Uzochi's embrace warm and strong, exactly what Zuberi needed more than anything right now.

"I wanted to tell you that I, uh, messed up," Uzochi whispered softly in her ear, his breath light, sweet. "I shouldn't have . . . I made a promise to help Vriana, Beri, and I intend to keep it."

She pulled away from him and glanced up at his future selves, all of whom were fidgeting or fumbling in some way, though one particularly bright phantom was making a move that lit her heart. She folded her arms across her chest, amused.

"And?"

Uzochi sighed again, reaching up to scratch the back of his neck. Zuberi fought the urge to smile. He was squirming from nervousness, and she had to admit, she liked it.

"I was beginning to see things when Adisa's memories arose, you know that," he said. "And now I've seen even more things that've sort of messed me up. And before that, with my dad popping up out of nowhere, and us failing at getting Vriana back . . . I couldn't handle it. I needed a break, and being with Dad was like this unexpected vacation from all the shit we're dealing with. It's no excuse, I know . . . maybe I should've handled the pressure differently. Told you how I was feeling." Uzochi lifted his chest slightly. "I need to figure out what to do with all of this. But I know I need to stand up for all of us. For you, for Vriana, for everyone. I need to be the catalyst y'all deserve."

"You know, buddy," Zuberi said gently, "it would be easier if you let other people help you. Like me. I wouldn't have minded being there with you and your parents after your dad arrived, figuring things out. I would've really liked that."

Uzochi peered down at his sneakers. "I'm not good at that, accepting help. I'm used to figuring out everything by myself. All my hard work with school, I just had to rely on me."

Zuberi chuckled. "I get it. Two fugitive peas in a pod, we are. And I'm sorry, too."

Uzochi recoiled. "Wait, for what?"

"For not being more understanding about what you were dealing with. I mean, your father has basically risen from the dead, your mother seems like she both wants to kick his ass and jump his bones, and I don't know, dude seems pretty intense and kinda difficult. It was just . . . I was hurting so much, and I needed to talk to somebody, to figure things out about Vriana. And you're my boyfriend . . ."

Uzochi's eyes lit up. "Wait a minute, I'm your *boyfriend*?"

Zuberi rolled her eyes, grinning. "Yes, knucklehead, you are. You're my boyfriend, and I really wanted your support, but you were going through your own stuff. I just felt . . . so rejected, by someone I really like.. And it was hard, even though in my head I knew you didn't mean to hurt my feelings. Vriana told me it's important to maintain perspective."

"Waaaaaaaaait," Uzochi said. "How'd you speak to Vriana?"

Zuberi shrugged, placing her hands in her pockets, embarrassed at her slip of the tongue. "I . . . I didn't actually speak to Vri, not really. I just sometimes imagine what she'd say to me if she was here. My way of keeping her close. And I know she would tell us both that we're going through a lot, that we need to give each other some grace and be easy."

She stepped right up to Uzochi then and he took her hands. His palms were warm, his touch like a lightning bolt that went straight through her. She met his eyes, fire dancing behind hers.

"I'm in this with you, okay?" she said. "You can always let me in and tell me how you're feeling, no matter what you're dealing with. And I'll do my best to do the same."

Zuberi wasn't sure who leaned in first—her or him. But what she did know was that, when their lips met, it was bigger than fireworks, bigger than an explosion. Kissing Uzochi was finally finding the rope to hang on to, to keep from going over the cliff, like spotting a shooting star after seeing only empty sky for years. They'd kissed before, and she'd savored every one of those kisses, but this one told him that she wasn't giving up on him. That he wasn't giving up on her, that he meant every word that he said, and that she'd be crazy not to trust him.

After a moment, she pulled back from him. She had to be strong enough to live up to her word.

"So, you were saying that something's up, that you saw something really bad in Adisa's memories?"

"I saw what happened to ancient Nubia," he said. "How it almost all unraveled. Why, I think, our people are so secretive and obsessed with us practicing our gifts."

And that was when Uzochi Will, the official boyfriend of Zuberi Ragee, proceeded to tell her about an ancient Nubian called Liv'e, and how he'd been desperate to conquer their ancestral land, willing to do whatever it took to pull power from the world around him. How Liv'e had risked all of Nubia for it, and how Nubians had lost their lives to stop him. Different parts of Uzochi's story and the history of Nubia in general left Zuberi reeling, especially when he started to share his theory about Liv'e somehow inhabiting Lencho's body. That she found hard to believe, but it was coming from Uzochi, so she had to try.

And then his mood shifted when he mentioned sailors who'd been marooned off the shores of Nubia. She saw his phantoms shift with sadness as he faltered in his speech, and she had to squeeze his hand before he continued.

"They didn't trust the outside world after what happened with Liv'e," Uzochi explained, a hard edge to his voice. "Our ancestors did . . . some really bad things, unspeakable things, Beri, to keep Nubia a secret. People died because of how far they went. How far Adisa went. I mean, he's supposed to be my mentor . . ."

Zuberi saw how the memory of the elder still haunted Uzochi. She let him trail off, and then she ran her thumb over his hand.

"Well," she said, her voice low, "I'm not saying that what they did was right. But when you look at how this place over here has 'welcomed' us, I can see why our ancestors had trust issues. Maybe they just had good sense."

"I get what you're saying, babes, I do. But I mean, it goes deeper than that. This whole idea of Nubian telepaths serving as historians, it's wonderful, but only if we grow from the history that's shared. I personally think our ancestors were really messed up after what Liv'e had done. To isolate yourselves for centuries from the rest of the world? To leave people brain-dead so you can remain untouched? To keep up a warrior class when you haven't been attacked for more than two thousand years? Something wasn't right."

"I . . . I guess I see what you mean," Zuberi said haltingly. "It's almost like . . . there's this pain that they hadn't dealt with."

"Yeah, I think it was trauma," Uzochi said. "Trauma that lasted for generations. I keep on connecting the dots, Beri. Why our parents and other adult Nubians are so secretive, why they alternate between being proud of Nubia and not wanting to talk about it, like there's also a bunch of shame in the mix. I mean, it's crazy . . ."

Zuberi nodded. "It is. But . . . I think we need to take things one step at a time. Between Vriana and Sandra St. John, and now Liv'e . . . we've gotta be strategic and come up with a plan to tackle all of this. Otherwise we'll drown."

"You're right, and I've been discussing ideas with my father. He's with the elders now . . ."

"There's something you need to know as well," Zuberi replied, "with my dad. He has a plan, too, something that I think will help us all out, even though there'll be challenges."

Uzochi exhaled. "Thato is always several steps ahead of everyone. I trust him, babes, almost as much as I trust you."

Zuberi had to admit that at the end of the day she trusted Uzochi as well, even with his foibles and mistakes. She believed in him. She hoped he felt that, even if he always said he didn't read her mind.

"You're not in this alone," she told him, leaning forward to press her forehead to his. "Remember that, no matter what happens, 'kay?"

She kissed him again, because that seemed like the best way to affirm what she'd said. To remind him that, no matter what happened, they were together.

And then Zuberi opened her eyes. She saw that though they had been left alone, there were a few people in the lobby, trying their best not to pry into their conversation. Abdul and Zaire were sitting quietly in a corner, and a couple of adults were coming down the stairs.

She casually took in their phantoms, only to see a woman bleeding from her face, her arms outstretched as she tried to protect one of the Children cowering behind her.

Zuberi straightened up, pulling away from Uzochi. She

swiveled to Abdul and Zaire. In the distance she could see a few of their phantoms being thrown to the ground, Abdul trying to crawl away, his arm hanging limply by his side. One of Zaire's future selves had transformed to his rock form, a series of batons and Tasers descending upon his body.

Her heart raced.

No.

She turned back to Uzochi, only to see one of his phantoms bright and clear, his body curled in a ball as a trio of figures whacked him on his side and head with nightsticks. He was staggering, bloodied. She strained to make out the figures who were attacking.

They were St. John Soldiers.

Goddess . . .

"No . . . ," she muttered. "No. Please, no."

"Babes?" Uzochi said.

"Uzochi," she whispered. "The Jungle, all the people here . . . we're about to be attacked!"

Chapter 24

Lencho

Lencho quietly closed the door to the blood-streaked apartment that had been his home for the past three days. He was refreshed, his head clear. After seventy-two hours of sleep-deprived battle with whatever this force was lurking inside, he'd grown far too tired to put up a fight. He desired peace, a resolution to the torment, an end to the fear. His inner voice had commanded him nonstop to give in, that to do so would yield unimaginable rewards. And so finally, in the wee hours of the night, as a broken, deranged mess covered in shadow, Lencho had done as he was told.

The following morning, he'd eaten a hearty meal and been able to refocus, catching up on what was happening on the news and social media. There were no bulletins calling for his arrest. His portrait wasn't plastered across the holos. There were no special announcements from Sandra St. John asking for his whereabouts, though he did observe from her press conference that she was clearly making moves to rout the Children and take over her father's empire. How fortunate for her, that he'd taken Krazen out. But it was her profiling of other Nubians that really caught his interest, especially Uzochi.

He regretted what he had to do to Edgar Maat, the man whose home he'd taken over, eventually figuring out his name after stumbling across one of the few paper documents he found in the apartment. Lencho had ended up having to drain him for hours on end to keep up his strength, his wonderful might. But the man's demise wouldn't be in vain; such sacrifices needed to be made for those who deserved to rule.

Lencho stepped from the building onto the mostly empty street, having chosen the place because of how sparsely populated the neighborhood was. It was considered poor by sky city standards, a place for those who'd recently ascended and didn't have tons of wealth. Edgar had only had one implant on his body, Lencho realized as he slowly leeched away the man's life. Another lie of the Up High, that all of those who ascended were automatically treated as equals to those born rich.

He stretched his arms and legs, cognizant that he was still in the same outfit from three days ago even though he'd showered. Edgar's frame was too slim for Lencho to fit into his clothes. It didn't matter, not anymore.

Lencho stretched his limbs one more time and then he ran, streaking his way farther south, knowing he would reach his destination in less than ten minutes at his speed. It was unlikely he'd be detected before he got there, though some Up High-ers might have wondered what gigantic thing had just whizzed by them as they walked to work or ran an errand.

Sure enough, he reached the training center that had

practically become his second home in minutes, gradually slowing to a jog. As expected, St. John Soldiers were stationed outside the building. They were concealed in the structure's wings and folds, waiting to pounce on Lencho and surprise him on the off chance that he returned to the building. He was sure they'd surrounded the Divine dorm in a similar way just down the road. Clever, though they didn't realize that Lencho could easily detect the auras and energies of their bodies, which stood out to him like neon lights via his second sight.

Lencho casually approached the gym's entrance, only to hear someone shout, "Freeze!" He turned to see several St. John Soldiers creep out slowly from their hiding places, Tasers aimed straight at him, energy batons out, someone even wielding a slim, strange gun that he thought might house tranquilizer darts. Lencho ran straight to the closest soldiers, grabbed their wrists, and drained them in seconds, the militiamen crashing to the ground. He had no time to enjoy the high that leeching gave him as he turned to the group of soldiers who now surrounded him. He grabbed each person quickly, draining them as mercilessly as possible, never having dared to infuse his body with so much energy, so fast. He refused to limit himself any longer.

He felt a sting on his right shoulder as he noticed two nodes puncturing his skin, a current of electricity flowing through his body. A new type of charge. Wonderful.

Lencho streaked up to the shooter and drained him almost completely of life, exactly what the soldier deserved for daring to shoot him. He turned to the entrance and ran into

the center, knowing he had to reach the others before rein-
forcements arrived. Knowing what he needed to do.

In less than a minute he entered the gym where his as-
sociates trained, all of the Divine turning to him, taking him
in, everyone immediately stopping in their tracks when they
realized who they were looking at.

"Lencho, hey, where've you been?" said the telekinetic girl
whose difficult name he could never recall. She'd spent so much
of her time Up High dully lifting objects with her mind, doing
mindless things like juggling droid kittens for snot-nosed children at Krazen's campaign rallies. A waste of her talents. He
would put them to proper use.

"Hello," he said before he grabbed the girl and started to
drain, taking her life energy, but far more importantly, taking
her gift.

She gasped and dropped to the gym floor. Lencho noted
that the floor was padded, cushioning her fall. A small mercy.

"Ohmigod, what are you doing?" one of the trainers yelled.
"What . . ."

Lencho wanted to slow down and relish the gift flowing through his veins, the first time in centuries he'd had the
ability to move items with his mind. Savoring the varieties of
the kinetic, that would come in time. Now, he had to make
moves.

He pulled at the shouting trainer with his mind, lifting
him up and dragging him forward so that in a second, his
throat was in Lencho's hands. He drained the man effortlessly and pulled two others toward him in the gym. The
telekinetic girl whose power he now possessed could barely

levitate a dumbbell with her mind, but he could lift multiple people at once. He immediately understood the potential of her gift. It had been eons since he'd utilized the kinetic in this way, something he could never forget.

Lencho drained and drained, using his newly acquired power to draw bodies to him, not even needing to streak around the gym to touch people as he thought he might. Those who weren't gifted, who weren't Nubian, he quickly drained, leaving them alive, not having time to fully absorb their essence. For the Nubians, the process was more delicious. He leeched power from that one there who shot electricity from his hands, and the person here who emitted short bursts of flame, and the other one there who'd been learning to create vibrations in the air, or warp light, or manipulate metal. He stole gifts from all of the Divine in the room, taking portions of their life energy as well, leaving a circle of bodies sprawled around him.

It was a portrait of the fallen, a sight reminiscent of when old Nubia was destroyed. A remembrance that, for some odd reason, seemed to be part of him now.

"Bruh, what the fuck?!?!"

Lencho turned to see Aren entering the room, glowering at him, not believing what he was seeing with the array of people laid low.

"Aren, hey," Lencho said, completely calm, as if they were just having another sparring session. "I was hoping to see you."

"Oh man. Man . . . fuck!!!" Aren said. "You've so lost it, bruh. What have you done? We're Divine, we're supposed to stick together. I'm living up here because of you, because I wanted to have your back and be there for you!"

Lencho peered at Aren for a moment, taking in the Divine leader whose ethics he'd always thought of as naïve, ethics that he thought would eventually lead to the boy's doom.

"Whatever it is, let me help," Aren pleaded. "I knew something was going on with you. You've been acting . . . not like you. I'm your friend, right? Divine stick together—"

Lencho looked at Aren pityingly. "We were never friends," he replied. "You know that, in your gut, if you're honest with yourself. I've never liked you, *bruh*. I've never had your back."

Aren recoiled, as if he couldn't believe what he was hearing. And then he remembered who he was. A gang leader who'd earned the right to lead his crew by having the sharpest of instincts, assessing situations with lightning speed.

He had to take Lencho out.

A flash of platinum light exploded from Aren's hands, partially blinding Lencho, who barely managed to cover his eyes in time. Lencho felt his body heat up, knowing that Aren was sending forth a rapid series of radiant bursts, one of the standard attack patterns he'd practiced when training. Lencho couldn't open his eyes or he'd be blinded, but he had to move quickly.

He sensed Aren's body with his mind, pulled Aren to him with a shot of telekinesis, just as he'd done with the others. As he flew closer, the Divine leader must have extended his leg, for Lencho felt a foot smash into his jaw. Lencho blindly tried to grab the other boy, his eyes still shut tight to prevent blindness as he felt the bursts of heat surrounding him, knowing that when Aren fought, he fought like a devil and wouldn't back down.

Searing pain engulfed Lencho's left shoulder. He released his hold on Aren and opened his eyes. He looked down to see that a portion of his shirt was smoking, that a chunk of his flesh was bleeding and charred, badly burned.

He swiveled to see Aren crouching down on one knee, his right pointer finger smoking as well.

Lencho tried to understand what was happening.

Aren . . . he'd done it. Created a laser.

Lencho pushed through his discomfort and again used his telekinesis to grab the other Divine boy, gripping him hard. Aren cried out in agony, too undone to emit another laser or barrage of light. Lencho pulled him close, grabbed his wrist, and drained. He drank deep, letting Aren's gift of light jolt into him.

Yes, the familiar voice said. *Yes!*

Lencho became aware of the muffled sound of someone screaming, and he realized, when he opened his eyes and looked down, that the sound was coming from Aren himself.

The former Divine leader looked desaturated, gray around his eyes and forehead. Weak. Powerless. So beneath Lencho, where he deserved to be. Lencho flung the boy's arm away from him, letting him collapse in a heap on the floor, struggling to breathe. Lencho flexed his fingers, his hand starting to glow with the gift he'd fully drained. The pain in his shoulder meant nothing.

"You're crazy," Aren gargled from the ground. Lencho was impressed that the boy was still conscious. Aren, ever strong and tough.

A laugh bubbled uncontrollably from Lencho's throat, the same laugh that had haunted him for three days in the apartment of Edgar Maat.

"You know, I thought the same thing, that I was crazy," Lencho said, crouching over the Divine leader. "But once I embraced what was inside . . ." He stood up. "I'm good."

Lencho turned and strode out of the gym, leaving Aren and the others powerless among the machines.

Chapter 25

Sandra

As she looked through the window directly across from her gigantic desk, the afternoon sun illuminating a newly installed aquarium, Sandra stifled a yawn. She had to admit, fatigue was catching up to her. She'd only gotten an hour's sleep the night before the morning press conference, too amped up by the future that lay before her, too consumed by all that needed to be done.

She'd added several plants to her new office—she'd officially stopped thinking of it as her father's office now—with a cluster of endangered Australian orchids adding much-needed color to the space. She'd put in an order for a few other plants to be sent over, aware that future visitors might snicker behind her back, saying she was trying to make her office look like the second coming of Starlight. But maybe it wouldn't be that big a deal. Tropical office plants were a big trend among Up High-ers. Some of the haters from the lower city claimed this was because sky city dwellers needed something to make them feel connected to nature, since their lives were nothing but steel and glass and body devices. Sandra actually thought the haters had a point.

She had her personal comm on, waiting to hear back from the lieutenant in charge of the expedition to the Jungle to round up Nubians, specifically the Children, of course. She'd considered activating a holo and following one of the militiamen's body cams to see what type of progress they were making minute by minute. But no, she needed to trust that the squads she'd selected would do their job. They were professionals, top of their class. She wouldn't make the mistake of micromanaging them, not like Krazen.

Immediately after the press conference, she'd zipped down to the lower city in a small motorcade and conferred with the city council, explaining that her St. John Soldiers were ready to enforce the registration act immediately. As the head of St. John Enterprises, she had full authority to send forth the militia to go after the Children in the Jungle, as it was public knowledge that that was where they were mostly residing. Some of the councilmembers had looked at her askance, saying they needed far more time to prepare the necessary paperwork and establish check-in centers. Getting everything in order would take at least a month. Sandra balked.

"Yesterday evening, I directed my soldiers to work through the night to clear out two large St. John Enterprise armories in the Midtown section of the lower city," she said. "These spaces can now serve as check-in centers for gifted Nubians, complete with tents and bathroom facilities."

"Wait . . . tents? Is that really necessary?" one of the councilmembers asked.

Sandra nodded. "It's my presumption that those who register will be at the centers for some time," she responded. "And we're not animals. All of those detained will be treated with respect, given what they need to live with dignity. The protocols of the act are clear and my militia is ready to enforce the law."

Vriana had sat by Sandra's side with a cadre of soldiers as she spoke. Sandra wondered if she would have to use the Nubian's gift to make the politicians a tad more compliant. But thankfully, though they had stunned looks on their faces, they seemed more than willing to follow her plan. The law was the law.

She wouldn't waste any time dillydallying with getting Nubians under her thumb. The Children and the gifts would be the cornerstone of her empire. Yes, some of them would undoubtedly fight back when detained. But any act of violence would be caught on camera via her soldiers' body cams or accompanying drones, which would negatively impact whatever public support they had. And she had to be ready for what might await. Would she need to have a speech prepared for the Children about the wonders of the Up High and how fortunate they were to have the opportunity to ascend? Or would it just be easier to have Vriana sweep into the check-in center and use her persuasion, making everyone who registered immediately compliant? Sandra thought the latter option would be for the best, and was even considering having Vriana use her persuasion on members of the Divine already Up High. Everyone would fall in line. A dream.

There were other things Sandra had to plan for as well.

For appearances' sake, she had decided to see her father and his doctor at least twice a week. During her next planned visit, she would have Vincent anonymously call Helios News, giving them the scoop on when Sandra would be arriving at Dr. Marshall's clinic. She would carry with her a bouquet of orchids from this very room, the devoted daughter spending time with her comatose dad even as she learned how to run a corporation and enforce a new law. Yes, she would control the narrative about her life, the way it should have always been.

Beside Sandra, Vriana was focusing dutifully on her coursework while humming another popular tune from the R&B girl group Complete.

"That's really electric," Sandra commented. "You should record your own version of that."

Sandra had been encouraging Vriana to monetize her talent for singing, as the girl's beautiful voice would no doubt be a hit with those living Up High. But, as always, Vriana demurred at the suggestion.

"Not everything needs to be bottled and sold, Sandy," she said, using the nickname that still made Sandra bristle. "Some things are just meant to be enjoyed for what they are, you know? You need to appreciate that, considering how hard you work."

Sandra wanted to roll her eyes. She'd changed Vriana's memories, but her innocence about the world remained. Not finding a way to monetize and exploit one's talents was sheer idiocy to Sandra.

"So, uhm, I've been thinking about your dad," Vriana

continued, placing her pen down by her tablet. "In one of my psych books, I read that people in comas can hear when they're being spoken to. Or at least that's what some researchers say. I think we should go to Krazen tomorrow, maybe read to him from one of his favorite books, or put on holo-shows that make him laugh. It'll speed up his recovery. We could—"

Sandra heard a ping on her comm and held up her fingers to Vriana, her sign that she was receiving a call. She remembered to lightly tap the right side of her temple for show, and then one of her militia leaders appeared before her, the man put in charge of rounding up Nubians at the Jungle. Lieutenant Hall.

He looked perturbed.

"Ms. St. John," the lieutenant said. "I'm afraid we may have received . . . inaccurate reports. The Nubians aren't at the designated location. The Jungle is abandoned."

Sandra blinked, looking from the holo to Vriana, who was watching with rapt interest.

"What are you talking about?" Sandra snapped. "It's well known that's where they've been holed up since they abandoned the Swamp. Do you . . . do you have the wrong location, maybe?"

Lieutenant Hall shook his head slowly. "No, we verified and reverified the address. We checked the building from top to bottom, even checked out several of the surrounding buildings where we'd received reports that Nubians also resided. All empty, Ms. St. John, though there're clothes and food items left behind that indicate people were living here. There were also a few non-Nubian residents on the premises. When we asked them about any sort of Nubian whereabouts, they either ignored our questions or said they'd never heard of these people."

"WHAT?" Sandra yelled, startling Vriana.

"Ma'am, it's obvious they're lying. We have documentation of lower-city residents interacting with Nubians extensively over the past few weeks, but I'm not sure what we can do about that. Even if they know where Nubians went, these people aren't breaking any laws." The soldier removed his beret and scratched his head, embarrassed. "Ma'am, I'm sorry to tell you, but the folks you're looking for aren't here. They've vanished."

Sandra tried to absorb what she was being told. How was this possible? Had someone alerted the Children to her plans? But that would've been unlikely, unless they had some sort of mole among the city council or her militia. And even if they'd been alerted, they had to be somewhere close in the lower city. Thousands of Nubians couldn't have gotten far, not when they were on the run with scores of old people and children.

Sandra looked again at Vriana, as if she had some sort of solution to offer. The other girl simply looked back at Sandra, bewildered, and shrugged.

"Ms. St. John," Lieutenant Hall said from the holo, "I'm sorry, but do we have any additional orders? Should our squads return to base?"

Sandra heard her internal comm ping again.

What now?

She activated another holo. Vincent instantly appeared,

her contact from the Divine training center. His face was panicked.

"Ms. St. John, I just reached the gym," he said, his words tumbling forth a mile a minute. "Something's happened. A whole bunch of soldiers were taken out on the steps, and the Divine . . . they're inside, but they're really hurt, and I didn't . . ."

Before Sandra could open her mouth to tell Vincent to slow down, she heard a loud explosion.

"What the hell?!?" she said, abruptly ending both holo-calls as she whipped around.

Vriana uttered a loud gasp.

Something had smashed into her window, the glass splintering before her very eyes.

There was a person floating outside.

"Guards!" Sandra shouted, making a show of tapping the panic button on her desk, which hadn't yet been synced to her body implants. "Guards, get in here now—"

The glass shattered completely. Parts of the office's polymer wall were ripped away as well, sending plants and chairs and light fixtures flying.

There, before her, was Lencho Will suspended in midair, his clothes torn and bloodstained. Clouds of smoke rose around his body.

Sandra quickly trained her eyes. Several of the glass towers behind him were on fire.

An invisible door opened and five St. John Soldiers charged into the space, the standard militia cadre that accompanied

Sandra and Vriana at all times. Lencho turned to the squad and made a slight gesture. The guards were lifted off their feet and slammed hard into office walls, their limbs making a sickening crunch that made Sandra feel ill as they gasped and groaned. Lencho gestured again and the guards rose from the floor, only to be shoved through the very door from which they'd entered the office. As the last militiaperson flew out of Sandra's sight, her wails a shrill, piercing thing, the ceiling caved in behind them.

Vriana started shrieking uncontrollably just as Sandra hurriedly ushered her to the other side of the desk to take cover. She pulled the girl close, wanting to tell her not to freak out, that it would be okay, but truly, Sandra couldn't believe what she was seeing.

Lencho's eyes glowed red, his body pulsing with electricity, his hands aglow. As he floated toward the two of them, entering her office, his lips curved into a grin both suave and cruel.

"Sandra, hello," he said. "Are you happy to see me?"

Sandra balled her shaking hands into her lap. She needed to keep hold of her wits, convey strength. Beside her, she saw that Vriana's mouth was agape as she gazed in horror at her former schoolmate.

"Lencho," Sandra said, trying to keep her voice calm. "Your abilities . . . have changed."

"You could say that," he said.

Sandra took a deep breath. She needed to stall, to buy time and figure out exactly what had happened to his gifts. She saw that his left shoulder appeared to be burned. Had he just been in an accident? Or a fight? Had he just come from the training center?

"Okay," she said. "Okay, let's chat, just you and me. We have a lot to discuss, right? About my father, about when you two last met and what happened right here, in this office. I'm . . . I'm so happy we're talking, finally."

Something dangerous passed through Lencho's red eyes. He looked to the floor, fists tightening, sparks forcefully spitting off him. Sandra had observed Lencho's training often enough to know that when he drained someone, he developed superior strength and speed and endurance. But this was beyond. From what she knew of his gifts, what she beheld now shouldn't be possible.

"I'm not going to play your games," Lencho said. "All of this, it's over."

"I'm not playing games," Sandra said, her voice measured. "I was only thinking that . . . we have an opportunity to better understand each other. Maybe I can listen to what you've been through and we can move forward with a mutually beneficial plan for all gifted Nubians. You and I . . . we've always been underestimated, haven't we?"

She smiled at him, trying to reconjure the way he'd looked at her when he'd first arrived Up High. Like she was magic, something he desperately needed to possess to be worthy of ascension.

"Sandra, just like your father . . . always scheming, always seeing me as your tool. I'm not falling for your nonsense anymore," Lencho said.

"Okay. Okay, then . . . what do you want?" Sandra asked, her throat dry, her heart racing wildly.

"Your power," he replied with an air of nonchalance. "And authority."

Sandra didn't know what to say, only just noticing how Lencho's speech had changed, how his lower-city accent had vanished. In her bones, she knew this wasn't going to end well, that she and Vriana needed to run. She needed to activate one of the office's hidden escape hatches embedded in the walls before Lencho handled them like rag dolls, like he'd just done with her guards, or touched them and drained their essence, leaving them immobile and unconscious.

From the gigantic hole in the window, Sandra heard people yelling. Sirens wailed in the distance.

Sirens. When was the last time she'd actually heard sirens Up High?

Suddenly, Vriana scrambled forward. "Leave us alone!" the Nubian girl shouted, swiftly approaching Lencho even as her body trembled. "Go somewhere far away. LEAVE THE UP HIGH!"

Vriana wasn't using the syrupy-sweet voice that had previously swayed the minds of several councilmembers. Her tone was harsh, nasty. As her words floated through the air, Lencho jerked back and stumbled to the floor. He shook, his fingers digging into the office's thick white carpet.

Sandra breathed a sigh of relief as she watched the boy falter, as she felt the waves of energy emanating from Vriana. The girl had used her gift in anger for the first time. Sandra ran to Vriana's side, desperately clutching her shoulders. "Yes," she whispered. "Don't stop, Vriana. Use your gift. All of it!"

Vriana nodded even as she cried, her face covered with tears and snot as she tried to be brave. "Leave us alone," she repeated, her voice slightly hoarse from her screaming. "Get out of here, you. Leave the Up High!"

Yes, the two of them could handle this troublesome idiot, Sandra thought. She would call a full regiment of guards right away to take him out. She would win. She would always win . . .

She looked down and noticed that Lencho's fingertips were once again glowing.

"Get down!" Sandra screamed as she pulled Vriana to the floor. Several lasers flew from Lencho's fingers over their heads, ricocheting off the walls and ceilings, the smell of burned metal filling the space.

Sandra grabbed Vriana again and ran to the nearest wall, reaching the exact location of one of the escape hatches. The entrance to the portal appeared.

"Come on," Sandra said to Vriana as she pulled the girl into the small pod embedded in the wall. Lencho had begun to rise from the floor, having managed to push past Vriana's power of persuasion.

His face . . . he was furious.

"Get in now!"

Sandra knew she only had seconds, trying her best to remember the codes that would both close the hatch and send them on their way through the system of chutes and tunnels that lined the building.

A large pile of debris rose from the floor and shot toward them.

Shit.

Right before they would have been crushed, Sandra was able to shut the portal and launch the pod. She heard a loud boom, the sound of metal crashing against the wall, the two girls barely getting away in time.

The pod was shadowy and hot, its horizontal movement bumpy and rough for what was supposed to be advanced emergency transport. A low red light illuminated its walls, eerily reminding Sandra of Lencho's eyes. Vriana leaned over and buried her head in Sandra's shoulder, violently weeping.

"Shh . . . shh . . . we're going to be okay . . . it's going to be fine," Sandra whispered, keenly aware that she was lying to the other girl, feeling more confused and alone and afraid than she ever had before.

Chapter 26

Zuberi

"Auntie, please rest . . . it's going to be okay," Zuberi said as she held a feeble elder by her hand, helping the woman settle on a low, dusty crate, lamenting that she didn't have time to properly wipe it down. Her head spun when she considered what they'd managed to pull off in such a short time.

Zuberi was surrounded by scores and scores of Nubians bunched together, a few kids crying as their parents tried in vain to console them. Most of the adults simply stood around, looking dazed and shocked as they took in the dark, cavernous space that was part of their new home. The former airplane hangar was a small component of the sprawling military base that everyone had just been transported to. Her father was running around, crazed, having other members of his hastily put-together team do a head count.

In a corner of the hangar, she was heartened to see Beka hovering over Sajah, who was sitting on the floor, their eyes closed, head leaning against the wall. In less than an hour, the teleporter had just moved thousands of Nubians from their location in SoHo to the abandoned military base right at the border of Tri-State East, in a rural area between New York and Pennsylvania. Beka tenderly held Sajah's hand. Zuberi couldn't hear what the elder was saying, but she could see her lips moving. She was sure Beka was whispering words of thanks and care to the teleporter after what they'd just pulled off.

After Zuberi had seen waves of Nubian phantoms being taken down by St. John Soldiers, she'd acted fast, alerting the elders. Her father declared that they had no choice but to implement his plan now, to have the Nubian community migrate from New York to a locale he'd surveyed as safe. As an independent security specialist, he did, after all, specialize in contacts with people who had access to abandoned military bases that belonged to the former United States. And Fort Chisolm, where they were now, was one of them.

Even with the registration act looming over everyone's heads, Thato had wanted to initiate the move slowly so as not to draw undue attention, with a few families already prepared to relocate. However, when Zuberi had told him they needed to flee right away, the notion of a gradual move flew out the door. Instead, they'd needed to rely on her, Uzochi, and Sajah to get everyone out. Uzochi had been able to see the exact location of the base in Thato's mind and sent the location telepathically to Sajah, who then opened portal after portal after portal. Zuberi had run around the Jungle like a madwoman, Sajah right on her heels as she told every Nubian she encountered that they had to leave now, that St. John Soldiers were coming, that they were planning to enforce the registration act immediately. So many of her people looked confused

and terrified, with lots of adults completely put off by the prospect of having to rush into a thick cloud of shadow.

"WE HAVE NO TIME!" Thato had thundered at them.
"GO!"

Uzochi had sent his thoughts to as many people as possible,
telling them to trust him, that they were going someplace safe.
Zuberi had practically pushed several of the elders into Sajah's
portals, feeling terrible that she was forcing them to shadow-
walk but believing that the alternative would be far worse.

After they'd gotten everyone out of the Jungle, she and
Uzochi and Sajah had run to the adjacent buildings where
Nubians also resided. Uzochi immediately sent out his telepathy to locate as many of their people as possible, while
Sajah looked like they might pass out at any moment from
opening so many portals so quickly. Zuberi had run through
buildings and hollered and pleaded with whatever Nubians
she could find, a few so frightened by her hysterics that they
jumped into Sajah's shadow portals without thinking. Some
of the non-Nubian neighbors even promised to help, that
if St. John Soldiers were descending on the neighborhood,
they wouldn't say anything about Nubians teleporting away.
Zuberi had been so relieved, shocked that she was feeling
gratitude toward groups of people that, just months ago, she'd
wanted nothing to do with.

Finally, Uzochi had declared that he'd scanned the area
several times and couldn't find any minds that he could identify as Nubian. And then Thato had run over to them on the
street, declaring that he'd spotted a large cavalcade of militia
vehicles heading their way. He'd waved his arms frantically,

yelling, "Go . . . GO!" She and Uzochi had looked at each other, grabbed hands, and stepped into Sajah's portal, her father dashing through right behind them.

And now here they were, in a part of the country they were completely unfamiliar with, disoriented and irritated and anxious, but together. From what Zuberi understood of the registration act, the St. John Soldiers were probably only coming for the Children. But there was no way they were going to leave adult Nubians behind to be harassed at will by the militia, to potentially be taken in, detained indefinitely and interrogated.

She wasn't that sad to leave the Jungle, even if she had grown somewhat used to it over the last couple of months. The larger issue now was that Nubians were on the move again. Was this to be their permanent fate, to be nomadic, to never have a place that they could fully call home?

Zuberi walked out of the hangar, catching her father's eye as he gave orders to several others. He gave her a slight nod and she blew him a kiss, wishing once again that she had Uzochi's telepathy so she could send to him and say in his mind, *Thanks, Dad.*

Zuberi walked out into the fields of grass that covered the area, dandelions everywhere. She thought it was odd to see flowers sprouting so abundantly in early autumn, wondering if it was another sign of how the climate crisis had altered the land, until she remembered from her biology class that dandelions flowered in both spring and fall. She took in the huge expanse of terrain that surrounded her. Zuberi had never been in the middle of such emptiness, such openness, even though lots of buildings dotted the landscape. Fort Chisolm covered hundreds of acres, a far cry from the megabases that her father said existed in the US at one point but still pretty huge from Zuberi's perspective. Chisolm could house thousands and had clean running water, but it hadn't been used in decades, something that definitely showed in the layers of dust and grime covering every corner. In one of the base's mess halls, her father had discovered tons of ready-to-eat packets, but they had expired years ago. A whole bunch of Nubians succumbing to food poisoning? Not a good look. Plus, even though the area was remote, anyone who drove by might wonder why suddenly there were a whole bunch of Black folks wandering around an abandoned military base.

But they had contingency plans. At Beka's direction, Tasha was walking around studying Fort Chisolm, knowing she might be called upon to create a camouflage illusion at a moment's notice so that, to casual observers, the base would still appear deserted. And thankfully Leonard would be able to provide everyone with food if he worked day and night. But it would still be hard living, having a legion of people getting used to being in a completely foreign space, isolated from civilization and living together in barracks. And there were other Nubians still scattered throughout the city, who were at work or living outside SoHo and therefore vulnerable to the registration act.

As soon as he'd arrived at Fort Chisolm, Uzochi had pulled out his mobile and called his mom, telling her what had happened and where they were. He was freaking out, as Sajah was too burned out to open yet another portal, but Com'pa promised she would be fine. She would call in sick to work, prepare her overnight bag, and stay with a friend for a bit, just in case St. John Soldiers came knocking at their apartment.

Zuberi made her way through the fields of the base, taking a walk by herself to clear her head, something she'd begun to realize she needed to do whenever she'd experienced something extremely stressful. She lost herself in the dandelions and surrounding green until she spotted Leonard a good distance away, crouching in the dirt with his purple Mohawk in the center of his garden. His gift was so remarkable to her. In just half an hour, he'd created a large oasis full of plants leaning over with tomatoes and carrots and apples and grapefruit and papaya, his pockets always full of the seeds he'd need to propagate certain foods.

They really had a chance of survival, because of him. She wished for telepathy again, so she could send her gratitude. Instead she just waved at Leonard, aware that shouting his name probably wouldn't be a great idea just yet. Leonard looked up, frowned, and flipped Zuberi the bird.

Well, that was certainly unexpected, she thought as she turned around, realizing that the boy probably wanted to be by himself, disgusted by the recent turn of events. He had been leaving the Jungle, on his way to an all-day music festival, when Zuberi grabbed him with practically no explanation and pushed him into Sajah's portal. And now here he was, stuck with having to provide nourishment for thousands of Nubians, having no say in the matter. It wasn't remotely fair.

Zuberi sauntered several dozen yards west before stumbling upon a sight that brought her joy. There was Uzochi standing in the middle of a circle of people, the Children sitting around him cross-legged at rapt attention. Abdul and Zaire were slightly off to the side, with Sekou lying in the grass beside them. Zuberi knew that he had sent forth his soul from his body, that he was flying in the ether and scanning the surrounding area to make sure the coast was clear.

Uzochi had mentioned that he would gather the Children, see how they were all feeling, and talk about how everyone could care for each other while contributing to the survival of their community. As she walked closer, she observed him, how gently his hands moved when he spoke, how patiently he listened to Tasha's and Veronique's questions, how he wasn't barking orders or making demands or telling the others how they needed to toughen up. She could feel the waves of care he sent out to the group with his empathy, not needing language to let the others know, *I'm here . . . I got you.*

He glanced up and spotted Zuberi walking over. Uzochi immediately stopped what he was doing to give her the cheesiest of smiles and a gigantic, goofy wave. The other Children looked over at Zuberi, a few of them teasing her and crooning, "Ooooooooooh." Her cheeks became flushed, but she didn't mind. Not really. Uzochi was her dude, and she was proud.

"Uhm, I think we're set," he said to those who'd gathered. "Check in with the adults, see what they need, and maybe relax? We'll each have our assignments starting tomorrow, and we've been through a lot, so let's just take it easy for the day. Cool?"

Most of the others drifted away, heading back to the hangar or the barracks, Zuberi presumed. Uzochi ran up to her and gave her a big hug.

"Hey, goddess," he whispered. Zuberi's heart fluttered at hearing another of Uzochi's terms of affection. She loved it.

"Hey," she said. She pulled away and took his hand. "Wanna walk?"

The two strolled for a bit, saying nothing, just content to be in each other's presence, Uzochi purposely enveloping them in sensations of peace and serenity. They found a particularly plush patch of grass in their wandering and Zuberi led them to sit there, in the field just off the main part of the base. Uzochi lay on his back, and she lay back, too, the two intertwining their fingers and staring at the clouds in an increasingly overcast sky. As she squeezed his hand, a canopy of dandelion petals swirled above her in an undulating figure eight.

"That's new," she said with a smile as she sat up, looking at Uzochi. Then she began to cough as a couple of dandelion flowers got stuck in her mouth and throat. "Where'd you learn that?"

"I saw it in Adisa's memories," Uzochi admitted as he released his telekinesis, the flowers floating down around the two of them. "It was too beautiful not to try, but, uh, I think I messed up."

He projected into her mind what he saw—her locs and clothing completely covered in white fluff. She looked ridiculous.

Zuberi giggled, not caring about her appearance, spitting out more dandelion and brushing the seeds from her nose.

"Actually, this looks kinda nice," Uzochi said. "The seeds of the flower, and your glow."

"My . . . glow?" Zuberi said.

"Yeah. My dad, he said the kinetic is all around us. That catalysts are way more sensitive to its expression and have a deeper sense of control, but any of us can tap into the kinetic, really. I was trying last night, back home . . . but now, I think I see it a bit, surrounding you."

"Yeah?" Zuberi laughed nervously this time, not sure how to respond. "Makes sense. You know, I wonder if I'm witnessing the kinetic when I see those different types of glows associated with Nubian gifts. Remember, that's how I realized you and Lencho needed to merge your powers to save the Swamp."

"Wow. Yeah, I mean, that really does make sense." Uzochi paused, his gaze full of tenderness. "Oh, Beri, I love your laugh. I wish . . . I wish we could laugh more."

"Me too," she said. "It's just all been so relentless, right?"

"Yeah," Uzochi said, sorrow in his voice. "But you were great back there at the Jungle. All those people you saved. I think maybe we'll be okay."

"For now, yeah," Zuberi said. "But this isn't a permanent solution, you know what I mean? Sandra and her goons are going to be searching for us, and we're still legally within the bounds of Tri-State East. I mean, we could just go over the border and be in the US, but who knows how we'll be treated there. And living out here, so isolated . . . it's gonna get to some people. Do you know that Leonard just, like, flipped me the bird?"

Uzochi's mouth dropped. "Really? He's usually so cool."

"I know. I mean, it was kinda *extra* but I get that he's really pissed. At the Jungle, he just wanted to grow his flowers and fruits and listen to his electropunk music, not become the sole food source for thousands. My dad was brilliant to set this up, to get us here, but I'm not sure it's sustainable."

"No, maybe not, but it's given us a reprieve," Uzochi said. "We have a safe space, at least for a bit. We can recharge, not have to worry about being on the run in the city, figure out how to get Vriana and mobilize against the registration act."

"And we'll have help, thank Goddess," Zuberi added. "Our neighbors in the Jungle actually had our back, were planning to stand up to the St. John Soldiers for us. I mean, can you believe it?"

Uzochi gave Zuberi a sarcastic look that said, *Of course I can.* Her dude, ever the optimist.

The two soon rose and made their way to the hangar. However, as soon as Zuberi walked in and saw the look on her father's face, she wished she'd stayed in the field.

"Oh *Goddess,* what is it?" Zuberi asked, her stomach plummeting, not even wanting to observe her dad's phantoms to answer her own question. "What's happened now?"

In response, Thato held up a small holo-projector. The sight of Central Park filled Zuberi's eyes.

The park was filled with smoke, with fire, with massive trees ablaze and dozens of people running in terror from the elevator towers that loomed over Sheep Meadow. The sky city above seemed to be raining glass and mortar to the ground.

She grasped Uzochi's hand tighter, unable to believe her eyes.

Something was happening to the Up High.

Chapter 27

Sandra

As Sandra's legs moved faster than she would've thought possible, she began to wonder if this was what being at war was like.

The sky was filled with billows of black smoke as she and Vriana raced through the city streets. All around her, debris rained down . . . dust and rubble and glass. The shrieks coming from people were practically nonstop, some running for cover while others just peered up at the sky, shocked, never having experienced an iota of violence in their shiny, perfect lives. And others sprinted through the streets as if their feet were on fire, creating more obstacles to dodge in the chaos that blocked Sandra at every turn. She could barely breathe, coughing from the ashes in the air. All she could think about was that she had to get as far away from Lencho Will as possible.

Sandra dared to turn around, just for a moment. Sure enough, the boy was still floating high overhead, partially obscured by smoke. At this point, Sandra had no doubt that he was following her and Vriana, that they were his primary targets, even as he shattered building windows or tossed flying vehicles down to the ground or uprooted bushes and trees with the slightest of gestures.

Pandemonium—purposeful pandemonium, she realized—to strike fear in people's hearts.

When she and Vriana had hurtled to potential safety in their pod, Sandra had activated her comm right away and reconnected her calls with Vincent and Lieutenant Hall, telling them the Up High was under attack. To the lieutenant, she'd declared that all units were to return to the sky, were to engage with the Nubian Lencho Will and take him down, immediately. Backup units from New Jersey and Connecticut should be called, too. Lieutenant Hall had scoffed, wondering if that was overkill, if all of this was really necessary to take down one pesky Nubian. "You have no idea, Lieutenant!" Sandra had screeched. "You need to get here . . . now!"

The escape pod had stopped its trajectory in two minutes, depositing the two girls in a nearby parking lot, which was considered best for quick getaways. But Sandra thought accessing one of the St. John vehicles and taking to the sky wouldn't be a good idea, making her and Vriana an easier target for Lencho. And even if she kept whatever car she took low to the ground, the prospect of being mangled in a smashed vehicle wasn't appealing. So she'd run into the street, feeling like a fool as she and Vriana hid behind as many of the Up High's ubiquitous shrubs as she could. "Stay low . . . and quiet," she'd whispered to Vriana. "We have to get to the elevators, get to the lower city." Sandra felt like a fool for whispering, thinking that surely Lencho couldn't see them or hear their words from where he hovered.

But then she spotted him high above, peering straight down at them; she could swear she felt his anger from hundreds of feet in the air.

"Shit!" she swore. "We've gotta run."

And then she'd dragged Vriana and sprinted, not worrying about finding a car or tree to hide behind, daring to look back occasionally. She could see that St. John Soldiers were engaging Lencho, a couple of helicopters and an aerial van circling his position. She heard the click of powerful Tasers placed on the underside of the helicopters and the odd *shoom*-ing sound of the van's electromagnetic cannons, something she only really recognized from militia training videos she'd occasionally watched growing up. Using heavy-duty weapons was forbidden in the Up High except in the case of major emergencies. This most certainly qualified.

When one of the helicopters started to twirl like a top, spinning out of control, plunging into a tower, Sandra's fears were confirmed—there was no guarantee that she and Vriana would live to see the next day. She looked away just as the second helicopter met a similar fate and the aerial van retreated. She had wanted to scream, to rip her hair out. She had grabbed the reins of her father's empire a mere two days ago—two days—and this was what had she been reduced to, a harried, battered thing scuttling for safety. It wasn't right, wasn't fair.

Sandra's heart filled with hope as she panted, her lungs

starting to burn, when the massive elevator towers came into view. Throngs of people surrounded the cluster of elevators that would descend to Central Park, pushing and shoving, some physically fighting with the St. John Soldiers trying to impose order. People stuffed themselves into elevator cars that would take them to the lower city for safety, the same lower city they routinely spat upon as being so beneath them.

Sandra slowed down, just for a moment. She and Vriana wouldn't make it to the lifts, not with all those people in the way. No one would care at this point that she was a St. John. Maybe she could grab a couple of militiamen and demand that they clear a path for her and Vriana. But would that work with a shouting, maniacal crowd? Maybe she could . . .

"Sandy," Vriana said, pointing up. "Ohmigod . . ."

She looked up, only to see Lencho rapidly descending, coming straight at them.

Shit. Shit . . .

Another aerial van swooped down upon the boy, the rapid *shoom* of energy cannons filling the air again. Pulses of energy crackled around Lencho in an orb, never reaching his body, as if he was surrounded by some sort of invisible field. Was he using telekinesis, like his cousin? Even with her comprehensive examination of Nubian gifts, Sandra still didn't consider herself an expert on what they could do.

How in the world was Lencho utilizing this type of power?

With a haughty stare, he lifted his head and the aerial van stilled. The vehicle crumpled in the air like a crushed aluminum can and plummeted to the ground, exploding with a fiery boom upon impact and knocking both girls off their feet.

Sandra groggily attempted to lift herself off the ground and screamed when someone touched her arm. She pulled away, moaning in fear. It was Lencho. He'd reached her. He was about to drain her, to make her pass out . . .

No.

No. It was Vriana. The girl was helping her up.

"We have to keep moving," Vriana said, her voice steely, tough. "Get up. We're not fucking giving up."

Sandra nodded, knowing there was no use trying to control her trembling or put on a front. They had to run into a building, find cover. She could access another escape pod, though it would be risky to do so if the building's interior was badly damaged. She could . . .

Lencho descended before them, alighting on the ground and blocking their path as his eyes glowed red as blood. Hatred flowed through Sandra for this boy who'd come to her home and left nothing but chaos.

Vriana grabbed Sandra's hand then and squeezed. Sandra peeked over at the girl, expecting her to be on the verge of falling apart, but she was staring at Lencho defiantly, steadfast, as if she wouldn't grovel no matter what he did to her.

And neither would Sandra.

She pulled Vriana close. "Run faster than you ever have before and take cover somewhere," Sandra said, speaking quickly. "You might feel really funny for a moment, but don't look back. Don't come out until we're gone, until you can make it to the elevators. Get whatever help you need."

Before Vriana could respond, Sandra pushed past the girl and ran to Lencho. "HEY!" she screamed. "So you want me?"

Lencho moved back, startled by Sandra's outburst.

Sandra reached deep down into her body, remembering what she was made of, what she could do.

She activated as many of her implants as she could, sending forth an array of humongous holos all at the same time, surrounding Lencho with videos of a death-metal rock band performing to a roaring crowd of thousands; historical war footage from Ukraine, tanks rolling, buildings being bombed; blaring lower-city hover-car traffic; simulations of the bombings of Hiroshima and Nagasaki and so many other scenes of terror and destruction, a gigantic holographic skyscraper in fact seeming to fall right on Lencho. She turned up the color saturation and audio as high as they could go, the brightness blinding, the noise deafening. She barraged him with all of these images and more, sending forth more than a dozen of them simultaneously. Lencho turned and turned, bewildered, disoriented.

She couldn't stop. She wouldn't stop. Didn't matter if she was blinding herself as well, if her eardrums felt like they were about to burst. Sandra interfaced with a vehicle that had been turned onto its side by the explosion, causing it to come alive and race toward Lencho. The car slammed into Lencho's body. The boy flew through glass, entering the lobby of an office building, only to fly back outside seconds later, his feet not touching the ground.

He was somehow still functioning, even after being hit by a car.

Sandra sent another wave of holos at him before she felt something hard and unseen slam into her as well, sending her sliding down the street on her right side. The images and videos faded away as she struggled to rise, but she gave up, the pain in her body too much to overcome. Her chest rose and fell. She was hurt, dizzy, and uncertain about the condition of her implants.

She scanned the area as best she could, trying to ignore the few people who were running by, no doubt headed to the elevators. No one stopped to help her up or see if she was okay. Vriana, nowhere to be found.

Be safe, my friend, Sandra thought. *And I'm so sorry, for all of this madness. Be free . . .*

Sandra smiled even as she tasted blood in her mouth and struggled to keep her eyes open. She was about to be a prisoner, yes. Or maybe she was about to die. But she had managed to do the right thing for this girl who'd shown her nothing but kindness during their time as friends.

Lencho hovered over to where Sandra lay, looking down at her pityingly, his silence unnerving.

"I asked you before . . . what the fuck do you want, Lencho?" Sandra said, seething, not having the energy to play nice any longer.

"I already told you," he said in that new, disconcerting voice of his. "How much pain and death could've been avoided up here if you'd been willing to listen? I simply want your power and authority. And your sublime voice."

Chapter 28

Uzochi

In Uzochi's mind, he was Adisa, learning how to swim.

The waters he was being held over were clear, a beautiful, crystalline blue. Two great, warm hands were wrapped around his small form, keeping him just above the ocean as if he was a bird looking down at his own reflection. As the hands bounced him in the air, he was brought closer to the water, so close that he wriggled his tiny toes at the edge, a laugh bubbling up out of him at the coolness. Then he was lowered even more, so that his legs met the water, too, and he was able to kick and splash. All around him, others frolicked on the beach as the warmth of the sun beamed down on them from a clear sky.

Even though decades had passed since the creation of the memory, Adisa's feelings of trust and invincibility shot through Uzochi like a bolt of lightning. He felt the elder's love for his people, for his homeland, as warm and vibrant as the sun had been on that day. Even as the memory faded, Uzochi still felt like he could grasp its contours, could hold on to those feelings of paradise to buoy him during harrowing times. He realized that even when Adisa had a harsh message to convey, he always led with these idyllic memories, as if to make sure Uzochi experienced beauty with the pain.

But he couldn't linger in the sun, not when there was a specific purpose to his mission, to go back to the time of Liv'e's attack.

Uzochi concentrated and found the golden thread that he'd started to use to help him navigate Adisa's memories. He imagined it to be a part of the elder leading him to where he needed to go, though he also noticed that the thread's shimmering luster reminded him of the glow he saw surrounding Zuberi. The thought helped soothe his nerves as he swiftly glided along the thread, going to the part of Nubian history he would've preferred never to visit again. He moved past the fires and corpses and raging, red sky that overtook the capital city of his ancestral land, finding himself pulled to a particular moment.

A statuesque, slim man in robes of black, arms bare, approached a woman who reclined on a couch, surrounded by an assortment of other Nubians who casually watched the exchange. She was the most beautiful woman Uzochi had ever beheld besides Zuberi, her braids long and flowing, adorned with cowrie shells and some sort of iridescent trinkets. But then Uzochi took a closer look and realized that he was mistaken, that her hair was naturally aglow with twinkling pinpricks of light. Her presentation was just . . . celestial. It had to be an expression of her kinetic gift.

Several other Nubians carried packages that the man

gestured to grandly before turning to the reclining woman, who regarded him with an air of patience and slight annoyance. The man in black bowed to the woman and took her hand, grazing her fingers with his lips. She seemed taken aback and tried to pull away, only for the man to hold steady. The woman began to struggle. Other Nubians took notice, some rising from where they stood.

Pain, nauseating, crushing pain, emanated from the woman. And breathlessness. Like she was suffocating . . .

And Uzochi felt her pain in his own body, couldn't breathe. Felt his gifts leaving him. His heart . . .

"Uzochi!"

His eyes flew open. The room was dimly lit, but late-afternoon light was creeping in through the open window. His nose had just been filled with the scents and perfumes of what he thought must've been a palace or temple, but now, they were replaced with the odor of dust and musty air. He was at Fort Chisolm.

He sat up, feeling an ache at the back of his head, and saw his father looking at him with concern. Even though he'd told the Children to take it easy after the ordeal of getting to the base, Uzochi had felt antsy, like he had to do something, like he had to find some more answers about Liv'e. Though he had no proof, he was sure that the pandemonium happening Up High was the Nubian sorcerer's doing. He could feel it. And so he'd found a corner in one of the empty barracks, sitting on the floor cross-legged, and entered a trance, having realized that he no longer needed to go to sleep to travel within his own consciousness. The process was similar to when he entered other people's psyches and helped them awaken to their gifts, except this time he was entering his own mind.

"Was it Liv'e?" Siran asked, his hand on Uzochi's shoulder, giving the trademark father-son shoulder tap that Uzochi had come to appreciate. "Tell me, son. Every vision matters. I saw you meditating here and had my suspicions about what you were doing. You screamed out. I thought it best to wake you."

Uzochi nodded and gave his dad's arm a light punch. (Was that the coolest way to show his father he was thankful for him having his back?) "Yeah, uh, Dad, appreciate it. And yeah, I definitely saw Liv'e . . . I think when he first returned to Nubia, with this woman who was so regal. She had to be that light catalyst the ancestors spoke of. Her name's Jalisa, right? I think that . . ."

Uzochi's voice trailed off when he saw Thato and Zuberi approaching him and his father, their looks stern, his empathy immediately picking up the concern radiating from their bodies.

He shot up from the floor. Was it his mother? Had she been taken in by the militia?

"Sandra St. John has been speaking on the holo-news," Thato said grimly. "Come. A few of us have gathered to watch the telecast. You should see this." He shook his head. "I am so very sorry, young one, that your short time on this earth so far has been filled with such challenges."

Uzochi was quick to get to his feet. He'd been wondering when they would hear from the princess of the sky ever since they first saw the Up High raining fire. But what was she saying now? And why did Zuberi and Thato look so somber?

Uzochi, his father, Zuberi, and Thato all went to join the elders in a room that was mostly bare, that he thought maybe had served as a common area at one point. Someone had placed a holo-projector on the floor, several Nubians having had the good sense to grab any devices they could before jumping into shadow portals. He saw that quite a few of the Children stood by: Sekou, Sajah, Tasha, and others. One look around the room showed Uzochi plenty of grim expressions, but he turned his attention to the holo shimmering in the center of the space.

The camera zoomed back, and there from some undisclosed location was Sandra St. John speaking, her gaze lowered as she read from a tablet. Uzochi could see right away that this wasn't the usual Sandra St. John known to grace the holos. She looked completely disheveled. No, actually, she looked badly hurt, her face covered in bruises and blood, her clothes torn. And her body was trembling as she looked down at the screen that lay in front of her.

That was when he noticed the words of the Helios News banner at the bottom of the holo.

... *SANDRA ST. JOHN CALLS UPON NUBIAN*
** *TEEN UZOCHI WILL FOR HELP* ...**

What?

Zuberi gripped his hand tightly.

Goddess . . . , he sent to her.

It'll be okay, buddy, she sent back to him. *Don't freak out.*

"They've been playing her speech on a loop," Thato said. "Listen closely."

"My neighbors in New York and all of Tri-State East," Sandra said, her voice quavering. "I come to you today with a grave plea."

She glanced behind her, at someone Uzochi couldn't see because they were out of frame, before returning her gaze forward to the camera.

"I am begging today for Uzochi Will, the true catalyst of his people, to come to Central Park to render aid."

Uzochi blinked at the screen as Sandra took a dramatic pause. Well, that wasn't what he'd expected.

"She has to be kidding, right?" Zuberi scoffed. "After all her and her dad have done to Nubians—"

Thato cleared his throat, nodding at the holo. Zuberi closed her mouth, but Uzochi couldn't help but think she had a point. Why would he help Sandra? Especially when, as far as he could tell, at least one threat against Nubians had now been neutralized.

"Lencho Will has decreed that he will continue his decimation of the Up High unless Uzochi Will—a member of his biological family—comes to speak to him in Central Park tonight at eight p.m. sharp."

Whispers instantly ignited among the elders, but Uzochi kept his eyes on the screen, watching Sandra speak.

"Uzochi, if you are the catalyst you say you are, who your people have declared you to be, then you will meet your cousin at the Sheep Meadow elevator towers of Central Park. He'll be waiting. I beg you, lives are at stake."

And then Uzochi understood. This wasn't Sandra St. John asking him to come to the park. It was Lencho who was making the ask.

The clip looped back to the beginning of Sandra's speech once again. Beka bent down and turned the holo-projector off just as Zuberi and Siran said at the same time, "It's a trap."

They were right, of course. Uzochi knew what his cousin wanted, or really what Liv'e wanted. The same thing he'd wanted that day in the greenhouse.

Uzochi's gifts for himself.

"This is too dangerous," Beka said, turning away from the projector. "I do not carry the stories of our ancestors within my memory, but I know our history well. This is one of Liv'e's oldest tricks. He will drain your gifts, Uzochi, and as the catalyst, your connection to the kinetic will increase his power tenfold. You mustn't go."

Uzochi said nothing, but completely agreed with Beka's assessment, remembering what he'd just witnessed with ancestral memories of Jalisa. It was Adisa's warning, he was sure of it, telling him what would be in store for him if he confronted Liv'e.

"Our catalyst is safe and sound here," agreed another elder. "There's no reason for him to put himself in danger, not for these people who've routinely treated Nubians worse than dogs, who drove us away to this barren place."

"Exactly," agreed a third. "And with him safe—"

"I," Uzochi said, his voice loud and firm as it cut through the chatter, "will make my own decisions."

The room went quiet. Uzochi kept his eyes steady, feeling the burden of the collective breath everyone had taken. Zuberi was watching him, and he remembered her words from that time soon after they'd lost Adisa. She'd told him it didn't matter whether or not he was truly a Nubian catalyst—what mattered was that he was a better leader than Lencho could ever be. And over time, he'd come to understand that part of being a leader was taking personal risks for his people.

Uzochi breathed in and out. He steadied himself and looked straight ahead, finding his father watching him. Siran was standing in the corner, gazing upon his son, his emotions closed.

"I can't sit by while Liv'e hurts people and wrecks their lives," Uzochi said. "I just can't. I know the people of the Up High have pretty much ignored Nubians or treated us like dirt, but I won't stand by and watch them be terrorized—and killed, for all we know. And if I don't step up now, how many more people will suffer? Liv'e will go after folks in the lower city next, and some Nubians still live there, including my mom. And yeah, we don't owe any of those other folks anything considering how poorly Nubians have been treated, but is that the right thing to do? Just walk away?"

Uzochi noticed that his words caused some of the adults to look down, hints of shame in their shoulders. He took in a deep breath. "I've been sitting with our history and learning things that really bother me . . . and we can't keep on isolating ourselves from other communities because they've somehow hurt us, or because we think we're superior to them with our gifts and traditions. The more I learn about our history, I don't know, maybe the whole point of us being Nubians and being deeply connected to the kinetic is that we're supposed to help others when we can." He swallowed. "Even if they're a real pain sometimes."

More silence, but Uzochi felt the swell of the emotions filling the room in place of words. He felt pride, fear, and even hurt. But instead of focusing on others, he zeroed in on the steady rhythm of his heart. His conviction.

"Yeah, well, man, if you meet up with this whacked-out Liv'e dude, you aren't going alone, either," Sekou said, stepping forward. "Your boy's with you. The Children are with you."

"Absolutely not!" said Beka. "A whole bunch of gifted Nubians appearing on the scene is the last thing the situation needs. Liv'e can immediately drain each of your abilities with a touch, adding to the roster of gifts I suspect he's already absorbed from the Divine. Having access to a catalyst's power and a host of awoken Nubians . . . the danger is unimaginable."

"Precisely," agreed another elder. "Besides, the Children are still relatively untrained in the use of their abilities. If this is Liv'e, as Uzochi and Siran assert, then he's extremely well versed in the kinetic and other forms of sorcery. A direct confrontation would be remarkably unwise."

"Pardon me," Abdul said, stepping forward as well. "I don't mean any disrespect, but what would be 'remarkably unwise' would be to send Uzochi in there alone. Nope. No way. Not going to happen on my watch."

"Mine, either," Zaire said, rushing to Abdul's side. "Not after what Uzochi has done for me. For us. I got you, Uzochi. *We* got you."

Harsh whispers swept the room then, but several other Children stepped forward—Tasha, Sajah, even Veronique—declaring that they, too, would go to the park with Uzochi.

Uzochi's eyes landed back on Zuberi and her father, who stood beside her.

Thato stepped forward, immediately causing the room to fall silent.

"Brethren," he said. "I have brought you here to safety, and for that, I am immensely grateful for the grace that we've been given, to live our lives unconfined. But I cannot promise that we will always be safe."

His gaze tracked the room as he made eye contact with each elder.

"These are *our* children," Thato continued. "And they are declaring that they wish to stand by the person who stood by them during the challenges of their awakenings, who allowed them to gain a deeper understanding of their gifts and themselves. Who allowed all of us to reconnect with our glorious, complex heritage, our ways that we thought had been forever destroyed. If young Uzochi wishes to confront Liv'e, as is his right, then so be it. And if the Children want to accompany their revered catalyst to the field of battle, so be it. And I will most certainly be there with them." Thato turned directly to Uzochi. "But let us take a moment, young catalyst, to strategize. To contemplate how we can outwit Liv'e and drive him from our lands." Thato swiveled. "Siran, do you agree?"

Uzochi's father had been leaning on the wall, still quiet. He looked at Thato and simply nodded, a cipher, before walking forward. "Where my son goes, I go," he declared.

"And there you have it. We are with you, Uzochi," Thato said.

Upon hearing her father's words, Zuberi was beaming. Then Uzochi watched as she stepped forward and raised her staff.

"I am my father's daughter," she declared. "This goes without saying, but there's no way I'm staying behind when someone threatens us, when someone dares to threaten *my* guy. I'll proudly fight beside Uzochi Will, our beloved catalyst!"

The room exploded with cheers from the Children, and Uzochi's heart thundered in his chest. Not with fear or dismay, but with the knowledge that his people were there for him, that they'd genuinely appreciated all that he'd done for them, for their community.

His friends had his back and he would not fail them.

Chapter 29

Zuberi

After sitting with her father and strategizing for the past two hours, after trying to send Uzochi as much support and care as she could while she sat by him, going over yet another set of plans that involved the damned Up High, Zuberi was ready for what would await them at the park. She was never one to back away from a fight, so she had entered that zone of calm deliberateness, of embracing what was to come with steady resolution. The warrior's path, her father had called it, the few times he'd noticed his daughter entering such a state.

Zuberi realized she was probably heading to the biggest fight of her life, but there was nowhere else she could imagine herself being. Not with Uzochi in such potential danger. But still. Sitting with what Liv'e could do and what he could reduce Uzochi to . . . Zuberi didn't know what to think about that. And the more she'd learned from the holos about what was happening with the sky city, how the main streets were burning, how several buildings were badly damaged, and that a wave of refugees were making their way down to Manhattan, the more she'd had to steady her heart. Sandra St. John was sitting by herself on that Helios News holo, which meant that maybe Vriana was somewhere safe, that maybe she was hiding or had made her way to the lower city. She had to be okay.

Zuberi was headed to the just-reactivated mess hall to grab a glass of water when she saw a figure standing by one of the sinks. She immediately had a strange sense of déjà vu, considering her last encounter with the man at the Jungle.

Kefle was standing there with his arms crossed, a cup of tea brewing in front of him. He was wearing gray-and-black fatigues that showed off his muscular form. In the hubbub of getting to the military base, Zuberi had completely forgotten about Kefle, not thinking about his whereabouts. But of course he was here, having been hanging around the Jungle of late. Escaping her notice, he'd probably just hopped into one of Sajah's portals when the impromptu evacuation of the Jungle got underway. It was strange to see him after finding out that Liv'e was controlling Lencho. For a moment, Zuberi considered what the man might be feeling.

But she pushed such thoughts aside. Dealing with this aggravating dude was the last thing she wanted at the moment, not when she needed to remain focused on the coming fight. Then something crossed her mind.

It was time for answers, especially about a certain Nubian catalyst she didn't fully trust who was about to accompany her people into battle.

"Kefle, hey," Zuberi said, wasting no time with formalities. "I need to know, about your brother. What's the deal? Why are some of the elders still so standoffish with him? I'm about to head into what could be a major fight with this dude. I need to know who he really is, and why you're always giving him such a hard time. I know you said you don't want to talk about catalyst BS and Nubian history, but, considering what we're about to get into, I'm owed the truth."

The man considered Zuberi as he picked up his tea, taking a long, slow sip before setting the cup back down on the counter. "Okay," Kefle said. "You want the truth . . . here it is. Our former revered catalyst Siran was a prodigy with his gift, able to manipulate the weather in all sorts of wondrous ways. He was in love with his power, in love with his connection to the kinetic, far more than he ever cared about being a brother or husband or leader. Com'pa is a forgiving, loving woman, and she adored my brother so much that she overlooked his faults, but I saw Siran for who he was. How he exploited his role as our catalyst."

"What do you mean?" Zuberi asked, suspecting she wasn't going to like what she was about to hear.

"Catalysts are able to draw upon the kinetic and other Nubians' access to the kinetic as they see fit," Kefle said. "It has long been a Nubian tradition to build upon one's power through play and experimentation, to push oneself to the very limits of one's gift to reach the next level of power. Siran wanted to exist as a supreme elemental, one who could practically become as one with the winds and rain and lightning. To protect Nubia, he would say, but really, such strivings were for his own ambition. He tapped into our people's connection to the kinetic to create the massive storm that he would need to engage with and control to reach the next level of his power."

Zuberi's insides froze. "Wait, massive storm, as in the storm that sank Nubia?"

Kefle rolled his eyes as if Zuberi was an idiot, far too slow to understand what he'd been getting at for weeks now. "Yes, Siran caused the storm that swept away our land. In his quest for power and perfection."

"Wait . . . what?" Zuberi said.

"It's taboo to talk about. Adult Nubians pledged that we needed to let go of the past. Still, some of us have harbored a grudge, that his exercise in power, though within his rights, caused the destruction of our lands and collective loss of power. And for what?" Kefle shook his head and scowled, like talking of the past had left a sour taste in his mouth. "Siran will help Uzochi because he's obviously not going to stand by and watch his son face a danger like Liv'e by himself. But I also believe he's been consumed by guilt for what he's done, the pain he's caused to so many. I know my brother . . . for all his haughtiness and self-involvement, he genuinely cares about his people. He's trying to make amends. I see him struggling with having a more humble, less exalted role, but he'll do right by us and your little boyfriend, don't worry."

Zuberi just listened, taking it all in, having to grapple with even more Nubian secrets. She silently pledged to herself that when all of this was done, she was going to have a long, serious talk with her father.

"Okay," she said. She took in Kefle's clothing and checked out his phantoms, realizing that he was planning to travel to the park as well. "Okay, I guess that sounds right to me. And so you're coming with us because . . ."

"Because Lencho is my son, you fool," Kefle barked back. "Do I even have to respond to such an inane question? What would you have me do, stay behind and watch him be pummeled? Or worse, live as an ensorcelled monster? I must do what I can to get him back . . . His mother, I was just on a call with his mother, who's still in the city." Kefle paused and looked at the floor, Zuberi realizing it was the first time she'd seen the man show anything that even slightly resembled guilt. "Siran isn't the only one who's made grave mistakes," Kefle continued, his voice faltering just a bit. "The degradations I have endured in this vile place, Zuberi. Royalty treated like scum. But it's no excuse. Perhaps . . . if I had been better to Lencho, he would not have been so susceptible to . . . to whatever is happening to him now."

Kefle raised his head and stared hard at Zuberi, his old grizzly self back, the moment of vulnerability gone. He charged over to her, grabbing her by the shoulders.

"So, girl, if you're ready to fight for your beloved catalyst, let's fight," he growled. "It's time to reclaim my son."

Chapter 30

Lencho

Lencho realized all too late that he no longer had a voice. He had a speaking voice, of course, one that now sounded weird and old-timey as he barked at Aren or Sandra, but it wasn't his voice. Not the one that mattered. His voice had become submerged by this thing that had taken hold of him, this being whose name sounded something like Liv'e or Livay who held memories that didn't make sense, terrifying memories of crumbling towers and wailing, hurt people Lencho assumed were Nubians. Lencho had been so tired at the apartment, had just wanted peace, not realizing that when he let Liv'e take full control, he wouldn't let go. That the mayhem left behind at the gym was only the beginning.

He tried to ignore the carnage that had overtaken the Up High, the fires that seemed to be burning everywhere, the line of vehicles overturned and smoking on the streets. He tried to ignore the panicked man who was hunched into a fetal position by a car, his body trembling, his droid canine completely still. He tried to ignore the crying child he saw just a block away, the little girl frantically shaking her mother, who lay limply under a hyacinth tree, petals drifting everywhere.

This isn't right, he wanted to tell this disgusting thing who'd taken control of his body and mind. *This isn't fuckin' right for you to do this, not with my body, my gift.* But he had no voice. He felt it becoming smaller, harder to find. A once-roaring fire reduced to an ember. Something soon to be snuffed out forever.

If he had known it would all come to this, he would've fought harder.

His movements, too, no longer his own, he looked down at Sandra. He had tied her up with cord that he'd manipulated with telekinesis. She was seated on the floor of one of the St. John aerial vans that he had crashed to the ground, the driver up front either dead or unconscious. Sandra's usually perfect hair was limp, her clothes dirty. She caught him watching her and glared.

"Answer me, Lencho, why am I even here?" she demanded as he stepped up next to her in the van.

He knew what she was really asking. Why had he left her alive? Lencho had to give it to the girl. She had gumption. Tenacity. Always did, he now realized, though she kept it hidden. How many people would still have the audacity to be giving orders if they'd found themselves in her position?

"You're an insurance policy," Lencho heard himself say. And that was why, even though he could easily discern that Sandra had changed, he'd decided not to treat her like the Divine, decided not to drain her. "We need to make sure Uzochi shows up and behaves," he continued. "And we need to make sure your militia will fall in line, to me, that I won't have to deal with their attacks while I take what I need."

Sandra didn't say anything. She pursed her lips. There were a bruise under her eye and cuts snaking across her forehead. Blood covered her teeth. He'd hurt her bad, when he'd knocked her down with a wave of force after she'd done that wild holo trick. But he'd had enough.

She looked away from Lencho.

"Inform your militia that I am now an ally and that they'll be expected to defend me against any attacks, whether from Nubians or gangs or other renegades in the city," Lencho said. "Tell them they are to do what they've been trained to do as St. John Soldiers."

Sandra's head snapped to him.

"Do it," Lencho demanded again, his voice harsh. "Now! Use your implants or a projector if you have to. Or your life, along with the lives of so many who live in the sky, will be forfeit."

He watched her swallow as she looked past him, quickly weighing her options and considering the possibilities, what Sandra always did.

In the end, she tapped her wrist and activated a holo, speaking to the image that blinked to life in front of her.

"Lieutenant Hall . . . ," she began.

Lencho savored the look of shame that overcame her as she spoke, as she followed his instructions to a T. He savored her shame and then, deep inside, felt shame himself for doing so.

He stepped back out into the hellish landscape that had become the Up High. He looked out over the destruction, hearing the cacophony of wails and screams. If any of the militia was aware of his current position, they'd ceased their attacks for some time now, perhaps realizing the futility of their actions. And now when they reappeared, they'd be on his side.

Liv'e wanted to show people here the true meaning of power, just as he had all those years before in Nubia. To create mayhem and sow fear so that people knew, when they beheld him, when they beheld Lencho, that they should cower and beg for mercy.

It wouldn't be long now before he would meet Uzochi in the park below. After thousands of years, to once again drain the abilities of a catalyst. To become practically unstoppable. More people would attempt to bring him down, and certainly some Nubians would put up a show of force, but Liv'e had learned his lessons well, had had thousands of years to think about his mistakes while observing this new era, this new land. Within days, the entire city would be in his hands. There would be partnerships to negotiate, practicalities of rule to work out, but it would be done, this he was sure of.

Only the beginning, true. But the beginning was Liv'e's favorite part.

Chapter 31

Uzochi

When Uzochi stepped forth from one of Sajah's portals, trying to hold it together as his telepathy and empathy went crazy while shadow-walking, he was greeted by a sight that harkened back to a scarlet memory that actually wasn't his. People covered in soot or blood stumbled through the park, crying, holding on to each other for support, begging whatever St. John Soldier they could find for assistance. Uzochi looked up, only to find that one of the elevator towers had been damaged, smoke and flames pouring forth from a scraggly crater that had been formed. And the howls and wailing that filled the lawn, nonstop . . .

Uzochi had only recently felt the collective anxiety of his people when they had to flee the Jungle, but the emotions that swept over him here defied description. The pain and terror and rage . . . the unmistakable rage, and the thoughts that floated through the air . . .

Those vile Nubians! We should never have let their kind ascend . . .

Nubians destroy everything they touch . . . where will I go? . . .
I have to get away . . . he's crazy, that Black beast . . .

And so it went.

As Siran, Kefle, and a line of adult Nubians came through Sajah's portal right behind Uzochi, he felt deeply aware of the collective hopes and fears of those who'd accompanied him to the park. Their emotions were raw, tangible things, something to cherish, speaking to the beauty and resilience of his community, no matter what other city dwellers thought of them.

Uzochi continued to scan his surroundings until he settled on his target. There he was, people pointing and shouting at the sky as Uzochi's cousin and Sandra St. John floated down from the heavens, eventually coming to rest among a contingent of vans and tanks that belonged to the city militia.

With each step Uzochi took closer to Lencho, moving deeper into the park, he felt the emotional weight of what he was confronting. But something else permeated the air, something different. Underneath the raw, wild emotions, there was something he couldn't explain. It was like a stickiness on the walls, a sludge that seemed to drag everything around him down.

"You're not imagining it," a ragged voice said beside him, and Uzochi turned to see Zaire. The giant of a boy was looking out at the park as he strode forward, already transformed. His earthen body was slightly hunched forward as if he was prepared to run away at any moment, even though he was the largest, most intimidating entity on the field by far. Abdul stood next to him, constantly flexing his hands, the telltale sign that the elemental was ready to conjure winds at any moment.

"You feel it, too?" Uzochi whispered. Many other Nubians, mostly adults, were behind him, spread out in pairs as they spoke in hushed tones, assessing the situation. He knew that Zuberi and her team would be arriving at the other end of the field far more quietly and surreptitiously than Uzochi.

"It's what I felt living in the sky," Zaire said, tilting his chin up. "Every night, I went to sleep, and it was like something was pushing down on me, taking my breath. I thought it had something to do with the air up there, like it was in short supply or something because we were so high up." He shook his head. "I know that sounds stupid."

"It doesn't," Uzochi said. "Zaire, I think . . . I think this is what Liv'e is . . . It's like, despair. Everywhere." *Liv'e*, Uzochi thought at once. Again, he didn't fully understand how this Nubian legend had come back to life, but he knew what he was feeling now, like someone was trying to choke the life out of the city.

Zaire nodded. "It took me a while to piece it together. To realize that it felt like . . . like I was being haunted or something. Like there was some sort of spirit, everywhere. All of us Divine, we were constantly on edge, starting to bicker, even though Lencho was the nuttiest by far. We could tell after a while that something wasn't right." Zaire shook his head. "Uzochi, the others up there, my old crew. Aren . . . I haven't been able to reach them. What if they're . . ."

Uzochi touched Zaire's rocky form, as did Abdul. "Don't think that. I have faith they're still here."

"But without their gifts? Y'all said Liv'e probably stole their powers already," Zaire said, his voice quivering. "I know this is still new for us, but I can't imagine living without my gift."

Uzochi nodded and noticed that the gathering clouds were gray, wispy. A threatening tempest. Zaire looked up as well. Was this a natural storm, or had Lencho absorbed the power of an elemental Up High?

Uzochi gathered himself, glanced over at his father, and then turned to look straight at his cousin, their eyes meeting across the park. Sandra St. John sat behind him on the ground, a stoic, deadened look on her face. He saw his cousin's energy lapping around him, like smoke tethered to fire, burning deep red. But laced in that red . . . Uzochi noticed something else for the first time. Something gray, like decay, streaking through the color.

Uzochi touched the minds of the Nubians around him, and then he and his squad walked forward. The closer they moved to Lencho, the heavier the feeling of doom and suffocation. And the way Lencho was looking at Uzochi . . . even from this distance, there was no denying the rage and fury. The hunger.

Stay where you are, Uzochi sent to his squad, holding up his hands for emphasis so that they didn't press forward. He sent out a warning to the Nubians farther away on the field to hold as well. In truth, different members of the Children were scattered throughout the area. Sekou and Veronique were directly outside the park. Sekou would send his astral self out to scan the premises and get a sense of what was happening Up High, while Veronique would be on standby in case anyone was badly hurt and needed her healing gift. Zuberi was with her dad, and Tasha was somewhere nearby, completely camouflaged with her illusions, their ace in the hole who would jump in where necessary.

Uzochi turned to his father. "I'll try to appeal to Lencho," he whispered. "He's strong. Wickedly strong, in fact. I should know. I bet he could throw Liv'e out if given the chance—"

"Liv'e is an extremely powerful entity, Uzochi. An ancient entity," Siran said. "I am not sure how he managed to possess your cousin, but it is unreasonable to expect that Lencho is a match for him."

Kefle grunted, turning suddenly on Siran. "Don't you say that shit about my son."

Siran glared at him. "You think I would lie to you, brother? Liv'e is the most powerful Nubian—"

"I'm going to try to speak to him," Uzochi cut in. "As we discussed."

After giving his father and uncle pointed looks, Uzochi started to walk toward Lencho, the others staying behind as they'd been instructed to do. In less than a minute, Uzochi stood face to face with his cousin, the air around them thick.

If Uzochi hadn't believed before that Lencho was possessed, he most certainly did now. Flanked by St. John Soldiers, Lencho practically oozed power, the emotions vibrating off his body the most repellent thing Uzochi had ever experienced. Contempt, condescension, self-absorption . . . madness. All swirling around Uzochi like a toxic cloud. Uzochi started to recoil just as Lencho's grin broadened to maniacal proportions.

"So you came to parlay," Lencho said. "Very wise."

"Lencho," Uzochi said steadily, realizing that Liv'e had changed his cousin's style of speech. "I've come to talk. And now that I see you, I know the truth. This isn't you."

Lencho laughed, the sound carrying through the park, even amid the turmoil of those fleeing the sky.

"Cousin, this is me," Lencho said. "This is who I've always been, though you've all been too blind to see it. Everyone has always wanted to fall at your feet, haven't they? Straight-A Student Uzochi. Preceptor's Pet Uzochi. Our Honored Catalyst Uzochi. Uzochi this, Uzochi that."

He took a step forward and spat on the ground.

"You're a small boy for a small time. And I want to thank you for your ignorance and obnoxiousness," Lencho continued. "I was underestimated, and now look what I have. Look what I've claimed within the span of a day. I have power the likes of which you could never dream of. I didn't just move Up High, Uzochi, ascend, as you people say here. I conquered it. And that's just the beginning."

Uzochi took a measured breath, realizing that the person he was speaking to was far more Liv'e than his cousin. "I can't allow that. And Lencho, if you're in there, you can fight this, you can push Liv'e out. I know what's happening, that this isn't really you. We have a real chance here for unity, for everyone in the city to work together. We're here for you."

A shadowy look took over Lencho's face. "So . . . you know what I am. Good. No need for pretense." He took another step forward, nearly closing the gap between them, but Uzochi threw up his hand.

"Lencho," Uzochi pleaded. "I *know* you're in there. I know he has your mind. But I'm here. And I refuse to let you go."

With that, he threw his consciousness forward, finding the landscape of Lencho's mind just as desolate and decaying as Central Park. Upon first glance, Lencho's psyche appeared to be a dilapidated structure that had been burned out from within, filled with sludge and mystical symbols that he couldn't decipher. Despite the initial shock, Uzochi refused to be defeated. He knew he could find Lencho. He knew—

Hello, Uzochi Will. I've been waiting for you.

Uzochi gasped as, suddenly, he felt a hand on his throat. And it wasn't happening in Lencho's mind, he realized. No, the feeling was too sharp. And the pain . . . it tore through him like a hot knife as his consciousness ricocheted back into his own head.

Lencho's hand was around his neck. Somewhere, someone was screaming.

"Look at your so-called catalyst!" Lencho bellowed.

Uzochi struggled to breathe. His chest was heaving. He tried to get back to Lencho's mind but suddenly felt a heaviness pressing against his skull. All he saw was stars, and he tasted nothing but ash.

Was something burning?

Was he . . . was he on fire?

Uzochi's eyes were blurred, but he forced himself to focus. Forced himself to see his cousin and how he glowed. Not just red, he saw. No. Now . . . now he was glowing blue.

Behind Uzochi, the screaming had intensified. He watched,

dizzy and shaking now, as St. John Soldiers jumped to action. They were firing long-range Tasers, he realized. At the Nubians. The Nubians who were fighting to get to Uzochi. He heard them now, his father and uncle, Zaire and Abdul and the others . . .

Was his father coming? Would his father save him?

"It doesn't matter who comes for you," Lencho crowed, drawing Uzochi's eyes back to him. "They'll all die."

Uzochi struggled against Lencho's grip, only for Lencho to drop him suddenly without a word. Uzochi hit the ground, heaving, feeling weaker than he ever had.

"You're powerless now," Lencho said. "Your gift . . . your sweet, exquisite gift . . . is in my hands."

He laughed as Uzochi struggled to stand before hitting the dirt again. He'd never felt so weak, so empty, but he refused to believe his cousin. It was impossible. It was—

"You're nothing, Uzochi," Lencho said, kicking him back to the ground. "And now, as nothing, you will end."

Chapter 32

Zuberi

For so many years of her life, Zuberi had trained beside her father. But she'd never actually fought in battle beside him, much less a battle that was started because the enemy had opened fire with no warning. And it was all the worse when said enemy was unexpected, as no one had realized that Lencho would have St. John Soldiers and their Tasers and batons and tanks to back him up.

Zuberi was so proud to see her dad in action as he effortlessly dodged and dispatched anyone who came at him, his staff thicker and more jagged than hers, almost akin to a long, massive club. She saw what he was doing, creating a moving perimeter around her, a safety zone, so to speak, so she could try her best to go through with the plan. Everyone had figured that Lencho, or Liv'e, or whoever he was at the moment, would be so focused on absorbing Uzochi's gift that he wouldn't be paying attention to what was happening around him, which would be the perfect time for a unified strike from all the Nubians on the field. A reasonable gambit, that is before they realized that a whole league of militiamen would be working for Lencho. When Zuberi spotted Sandra on the battlefield, it all made sense.

He's somehow got this bitch on his side, Zuberi thought as she flipped over the head of an attacking soldier and knocked another one out with her staff. Anticipating the moves of her opponents was child's play as she locked into their most prominent phantoms, sometimes even goading militiamen into initiating an attack that she'd glimpsed in one of their future selves. Zuberi believed she would be fine, but she tried her best not to think of Vriana and where she might be, praying that she'd found a little bunker or something in the sky and kept herself safe while the city around her went mad.

Then she twisted her body, looking for Uzochi, her heart almost breaking through her chest when she saw him on the ground, writhing in pain.

No.

Shit, shit, shit . . .

Uzochi was down, which meant that Lencho . . .

No, she had to stay focused. She had to figure out a way to get to him.

Before Zuberi could finish her thought, she noticed that Sandra was running away from Lencho just as one of the militia tanks on the field wheeled around, aimed its slim cannon, and fired. Lencho turned just in time to deflect the energy pulse with some sort of invisible field, flipping his wrist as the tank was raised off the ground and tossed upside down, causing the earth beneath Zuberi's feet to tremble.

Had one of the militiamen decided to turn on Lencho

midfight, seeing that he was a crazy loon? Or was he following Sandra's orders to turn on him?

A St. John Soldier ran forward, Zuberi able to see from a phantom that he was about to Tase her as she crouched low and swung her staff against his knees. The man crumpled to the ground, crying in pain.

A couple of Nubians had reached Lencho. A burly woman with a staff of her own was about to cuff him good in the noggin when she dropped her weapon and clutched her head, falling to the ground.

Zuberi turned again to Uzochi, sending her thoughts to him, praying to Goddess that he could hear her voice with his telepathy if he hadn't been drained.

Don't give up, babes . . . I'm coming.

Chapter 33

Uzochi

As he watched the smoke from the Up High elevator towers that continued to fill the sky, Uzochi was wholly prepared to accept his fate. He was barely conscious, though pleased that he could still feel the histories of Nubia in his soul. His eyes fluttered closed and he saw the shores of his ancestral land. He saw Adisa with other Nubians, laughing, crying, training, living. He saw the near utopia that his people had lived in, and he wondered if he might see such a place in the afterlife. Did his people return to a different sort of paradise when their lives ended? He wasn't sure. Nubians and their secrets.

It didn't matter, though. Anything would be better than this. Uzochi felt his muscles atrophying, his throat becoming dry, ragged. He realized that Lencho had grabbed his arm again. He wasn't merely going to drain Uzochi's power. He was coming for his life's essence. Uzochi would be nothing more than a husk soon.

"Uzochi."

He heard his name shouted on the wind, like a faint call

that was too far to answer. All around him, he felt the movement of others, of those fighting for him. He had been foolish to bring them here, to think that such a basic plan could work. He knew that now. Lencho's powers were too great. He should have recognized that, and perhaps he would have been able to spare them, given them a chance to come up with another strategy, or remain safe at the base.

These are bad thoughts, Uzochi decided. He didn't want to die thinking of the bad. He tried to focus on the good, the pleasant. Memories of Zuberi holding his hand at the Jungle, of her iridescent glow, of her kissing him like she never wanted to stop. He saw his friends learning how to wield their gifts, how the Children had created safe spaces for Nubians and non-Nubians alike. Loving spaces. And he saw his mother and his father, sitting together in Com'pa's apartment after so many years apart.

Yes, those were good memories. He could die with those.

"Uzochi!"

Hearing his name, he cracked open an eye and saw Zuberi flying into battle, anticipating the move of every St. John soldier who stood against her before they even had time to blink. Behind her, Thato moved almost as smoothly, a ferocious physical force against all who stood against him. Then there were the other Nubians: Sajah, who reappeared and disappeared with his shadow portals, scooping up startled St. John Soldiers left and right, and Abdul sending forth a cascade of rock with fire that rained down upon a screaming Lencho. Zaire was there, too, using his rocky arms to push back several St. John Soldiers who were threatening Abdul, trying his best to be gentle and not hurt anyone with his bulk even in the midst of battle. In front of Uzochi, they formed a line that bore down on Lencho.

They're together now, Uzochi thought. *Working together as a team.*

It was something close to the plan. Form a line of attack that would overwhelm Lencho, that would disorient him and prevent him from absorbing power or essence. Do your very best not to touch him, to keep your distance, a crude, contemporary version of the group attack that had bought down Liv'e all those years ago.

Maybe they would have a chance. Goddess, he hoped so.

Uzochi closed his eyes. He was ready to let go.

Suddenly, there was a loud cry, something like a war scream, and Uzochi's eyes flared open. He saw two people shoot forward, Siran and Kefle, with Kefle swinging into Lencho's side with a staff. Uzochi choked, inhaling a sharp breath that seemed to sting his lungs. He looked up, seeing Lencho stumble back, rage curling across every inch of his face.

"You will not take my son from me, you foul hell-spawn," Siran declared, standing beside Uzochi.

But Uzochi's eyes weren't on his father. They were on Kefle, who had regained his footing and charged forward, straight for Lencho again, with a roar like a wounded beast. Uzochi didn't understand what his uncle was trying to do. Kefle had no powers. His gifts had been taken from him, severed all those years ago . . . was he truly trying to fight Liv'e with his fists?

"Remember what we discussed before, at the apartment.

Find the kinetic, son," Siran said, his voice an urgent whisper as he knelt behind Uzochi. "Please. Quickly."

The kinetic? But Uzochi had lost that connection. His powers had been drained. He was nothing, just as Lencho had said. He was no longer catalyst. He was just a boy. A dying boy.

"We never lose the kinetic, no matter the state of our gifts," Siran told him, speaking again as if he could read Uzochi's mind. "I promise, son. You are a catalyst, and it is always there for you. For us. Find it now. Believe in yourself, as I believe in you. We can do this together."

Uzochi opened and closed his eyes and then opened them again, struggling to see past the dizzy shapes that swooshed before him.

But there . . .

Just ahead, he saw a golden, glowing thread that flared out into thousands and thousands of webs.

The same thread that guided him through Adisa's consciousness.

The same glow that surrounded Zuberi at the Jungle.

The kinetic.

"You and I will always be able to find the symbol of our birthright," Siran said, his words urgent. "Can you grab it, Uzochi? Can you place your hand in the ether and hold on?"

Could he? He wasn't sure, but if his dad believed in him, he could try. He lifted his hand, reaching forward. He brushed the golden thread with his fingertips, a thread that seemed so bright, so strong, that he wondered how he had ever missed such a thing. And then, with his father beside him . . .

Yes.

His fingers clasped the thread.
Yes.
It was real.
The kinetic.
In his hands.

Chapter 34

Lencho

Lencho observed the man he knew to be his father whacking at his side repeatedly with a Nubian staff, feeling a sense of distance from what was happening. There was no real pain, his body so tough from repeated absorptions that striking him in this way wouldn't matter. He remembered his history with the old man who stood before him here. He was breathing hard, wearing himself out, and Lencho felt both glee and pity to see his father in a weakened state.

"Get the hell outta my son!" Kefle snarled.

Lencho understood what his father was saying, appreciated the concern, but it was too late. Liv'e had just absorbed the gifts of the latest catalyst of their people. Already he could feel the sorcerer using Uzochi's telepathy to touch the minds of everyone close by in the park. Would he start to induce madness? Cause excruciating pain? The possibilities . . .

"Lencho," Kefle said. "I know you're in there. This fucking monster has nothing to do with you. You're far better than this. Stronger than this."

Lencho would once have done everything in his power to prove his father right after hearing such affirmation from Kefle's lips. But he was an ember now, not even that.

A laugh bubbled out of Lencho's mouth, even though he hadn't wanted to laugh.

"You would try to persuade him?" Lencho asked, even though he didn't wish to speak. "I see into his heart, into his memories. He hates you, and with good reason. Just because you pulled him out of the ruins of that theater doesn't mean he's yours once again. He has countless terrible memories to counter that one moment of grace you showed him. You cannot suddenly decide you want to be a good father after years of terror and abuse. You cannot save him."

Lencho watched the war of emotions flash across his father's face. There was something inscrutable there. Something . . . something almost broken.

Something like ice stung Lencho's heart.

He was truly trapped.

He would soon be no more.

"Brother, now!" Kefle called out, breaking Lencho's thoughts. Liv'e's madness flooded through him again, pushing him to the floor of his own mind.

Lencho raised his hand, redness clouding his vision. Without another thought, a beam of hot white light exploded from his hand, going straight through Kefle's chest.

Chapter 35

Zuberi

The moan that erupted from Zuberi at the sight of Kefle stumbling backward was inhuman. Time seemed to come to a standstill, her eyes unable to look anywhere but at his searing wound. Above his head, she saw his phantoms flickering, the slightest wisps of a man, barely visible through the grayness that stretched between them all.

But then the world seemed to change, shifting from gray to something otherworldly, lit by some incredible light at the center of the park.

Uzochi was standing—Goddess help her, he was standing!

He wasn't glowing the usual blue that she associated with his use of the kinetic. Now he was a triumphant bright gold, standing beside Siran, illuminating his father.

No, Zuberi realized, it wasn't just Uzochi glowing. Siran was glowing, too.

"Impossible," Thato murmured, coming up beside her. "How could Siran . . . Goddess, are his powers restored?"

Zuberi watched the future selves of Siran and Uzochi

begin to whir, moving at such a breakneck pace that she could barely discern one from the other. It was as if their phantoms had a million possible futures, each fighting with the other to emerge as the dominant force.

What was happening?

Uzochi was alive. Alive and fighting.

"Together!" Uzochi called out, and Zuberi watched as father and son threw their arms forward. Several of their phantoms did as well, and Zuberi watched the two catalysts grab at something she couldn't see.

Until she could.

Suddenly, Sheep Meadow was lit up with thousands of golden threads, pulsing and burning with magnificent light. It flowed throughout the park, searing through the oppressive foulness that had settled into the air, a collective gasp rippling through the crowd.

The kinetic, she realized. It was flowing into all of them, giving bodies an ethereal light, the Children shining the brightest. And Uzochi was controlling the flow.

Uzochi rose, and Zuberi watched Lencho crumple to the ground as his connection to the kinetic was severed by his cousin, a scarlet-gray cloud spewing from his chest. Her heart gave a quiet pang as she saw him hit the grass just beside Kefle, two fallen men.

Was it really over?

"Hey, Zuberi?"

Zuberi turned, not quite believing what she was hearing, not quite believing what she was seeing.

OhmiGoddess . . .

It was Vriana, standing in front of her in a bedraggled, torn dress and frayed braids and makeup askew.

OhmiGoddess . . .

"Vri, is it really you? You know me?"

Vriana shrugged her shoulders and gave her friend a bashful grin as she nodded. "Yes, I know your trifling ass all too well, Ms. Fighting Forms every morning at seven a.m. You miss me?"

Zuberi started to cry as she ran to her friend and threw herself into a hug. "Oh, Vri, how'd you get here?"

Vriana pulled back, her eyes full of tears as well. "Sandra, she put herself on the line for me when Lencho was after us. Sent me running, told me to get to the elevator towers, to get away from Lencho, who'd lost his *damn mind*. It was so scary, Beri. The chaos and pandemonium, people stuffing themselves into the elevator cars to actually descend. Can you believe it? There were so many people crowded around the towers that I just ran into an empty storage closet at a car repair shop across the way and hid for hours. Once things calmed down a bit, I got myself down here."

She found her bunker, Zuberi thought. Of course she did. "But . . . but how do you remember . . . ?"

"You mean how am I myself?" She tapped the implant on her temple. "I really don't know what to tell you. It's just, it's like whatever story was being pumped into my brain suddenly stopped. I'm not sure why . . . I mean, I don't think it was tech failure, like what happened to Krazen. It happened a little before I first got to the elevators, right after I left Sandra."

"Okay, okay," Zuberi said as she gave her friend another hug, tears streaming down as she repeatedly thanked Goddess in her heart. "And we're going to have someone get rid of that nasty implant they gave you with the quickness."

"What happened down here?" Vriana whispered as she took in the carnage sprawled across Sheep Meadow. The pitter-patter of raindrops began to echo through the field. "Was this Lencho, too?"

"Oh, girl, I don't even know where to begin," Zuberi said. And then, across the way, she spotted Uzochi, who was some distance from her and Vriana. Zuberi's eyes locked on his, her heart elated, and she smiled, knowing that soon his arms would be around her. Only then did she look beside him, her gaze falling upon Siran.

Most of the future selves that hovered above Siran had become faint, with one single phantom taking center stage in Zuberi's line of vision. She watched this future self strike down several of the elevator towers that led Up High, thick thunderbolts flashing in the air around him. And then the phantom shifted, facing down something, or someone . . .

Her lips had started to form a warning, but already, she saw Siran rising into the sky, something that should've been impossible, unless someone else was hoisting him up with their gift.

She looked above, and the clouds turned a deeper gray as rain began to pour down.

"No," Zuberi whispered as she took Vriana by the hand and started to race forward, realizing what was happening, realizing that another malevolent force had been sitting in their midst all along. "I fuckin' knew it. No!"

Chapter 36

Uzochi

"Uzochi? Hey . . ."

He wasn't sure how he'd gotten back to school. Though, now that he thought about it, this didn't look like good old HS 104, with its ancient tablets and sticky floors and dingy walls. Here, the walls were painted a light brown, and several windows looked out over beautiful greenery. There were plain desks—no tech—and the smell of spices that he couldn't identify drifting through the air.

"Uzochi, eyes up here, please."

He turned to the front of the room. There, leaning against a podium, was Adisa as Uzochi had known him in life, his salt-and-pepper hair wiry and free, his red daishiki extravagantly embroidered. The elder's eyes shone bright in the light of the room. A soft smile played on his lips.

"There you are," Adisa said. "I wasn't sure if you were with me."

Uzochi didn't know what he was talking about. In fact, he wasn't sure of anything at all. This was no memory, for Uzochi had never been in a place like this before. And when Uzochi had explored Adisa's memories, he'd almost always done so as Adisa. But now . . . now, Uzochi was firmly himself, completely confused.

"I need you to take a deep breath," Adisa said. "You've touched the kinetic, and that is no small feat. During the journeys into your soul, you found all sorts of ways to interact with such a primal force, visualizing it as my voice, as a golden thread . . . so thoughtful, as always, preparing for the struggle to come. I'm proud of you. You continue to understand your potential as a catalyst. Liv'e, in all of his years on this plane, has always focused on acquisition of power, never bothering to understand how to directly hold the kinetic in his soul, never understanding how this would leave him vulnerable to someone like you, Uzochi. A testament to his corruption."

Now Uzochi was sure that it was he who was going crazy. How could memory man Adisa be speaking to him about things that didn't happen during the real Adisa's lifetime?

"I would guess that I'm a bit of a combination of what has been and what is yet to come, my dear catalyst," Adisa continued, as if they were having a perfectly normal conversation. "I am made from my memories—now stored in your wonderful mind—and your experiences. I'm neither here nor completely there. I say things I would have said in life, had I been able to live longer."

Guilt flooded Uzochi at that. After all, it was because of him that Adisa was no longer alive.

"None of that," Adisa said. "Feeling guilt over things you're not responsible for, Uzochi. The question now is if you can handle what is to come."

Uzochi stared at the elder. What was to come? He had broken Liv'e's hold on Nubians, restoring their stolen gifts. He had felt that, as sure as when the kinetic appeared before him. By seizing control of the kinetic, Uzochi had severed Liv'e's ties to Lencho, and—

"Ah," Adisa said. "But the kinetic cannot be controlled, Uzochi. You're thinking of it the wrong way. The kinetic is something with which you play, with which you dance, perhaps even manipulate from time to time . . ."

Uzochi blinked. "I think I understand, Baba."

Adisa smiled. "I am here to remind you that there is more journey to come. Much more. Your gifts are back, but who will you be as you use them, for yourself, for your community? This is the test you must face."

Uzochi didn't fully understand, but Adisa was slipping away, flickering in the light of the room.

"Baba, I'm not sure about what you're saying," Uzochi said. "My powers—"

"It is sometimes far too easy to let a dream eclipse reality," Adisa said, his voice suddenly sad. "Especially when we constantly look outside ourselves for the love we need. I am so very sorry, Uzochi. I am sorry that the part of Nubian history that brings you shame is what will serve you well on this day. And I'm sorry for my imperfections."

Uzochi's eyes flew open. He was in Central Park, and rain was beating down on his cheeks. His body, so tired and depleted before, now felt wondrous, alive. He instantly knew that his gifts were restored, his mind bubbling with the thoughts and feelings of those around him.

He spotted Lencho on the ground, his stomach churning at the sight of his cousin laid low. Tentatively, Uzochi reached out, scanning Lencho's mind for signs of Liv'e, but there was nothing to be found of the ancient Nubian.

Yet Liv'e's impact was not completely gone. There next to Lencho was Kefle, a gaping hole in his chest. Uzochi thought he might drop from grief then and there, for from his uncle he sensed . . . nothing.

Trying his best to focus, Uzochi continued to sweep the area with his mind, finding the world around him in chaos. Most non-Nubians were continuing to flee the park, the pouring rain adding to the hysteria.

He shook his head, turning back to Kefle and Lencho. His uncle's soul was gone, but Lencho . . . The boy was still, and Uzochi felt that his mind was in disarray. So much would need to be repaired.

Still unsteady on his feet, Uzochi turned to look at Siran, noticing that that his father was glowing from his connection with the kinetic as he stared at the elevators. He followed Siran's gaze and saw that smoke continued to billow into the air from the damaged tower. Hadn't he realized what had just happened to Kefle?

The rain began to pour as a series of gusts bore down on Uzochi.

Siran continued to watch the damaged tower as he said, "Even amid this carnage, it's time for us to create new dreams, Uzochi. Ones where all Nubians will benefit from ascension."

Uzochi reflexively nodded, though not quite sure what his father was saying. "Uh, Dad, actually, what d'you mean?"

Siran turned to his son, his demeanor stoic. "You fought well, Uzochi. Your connection to the kinetic . . . is impressive. I would've expected nothing less from a catalyst. And it was exactly what I needed."

Uzochi was confused. The emotions peeling off his dad didn't seem to convey gratitude and appreciation, like his words. Uzochi instead sensed a high degree of self-regard. Of . . . arrogance?

Siran began to rise from the ground.

Uzochi looked around, trying to figure out what was happening. Was his father being lifted by someone's telekinesis? No . . .

His father's gift had been restored.

"Dad!" Uzochi called out, smiling. "Wow! Your gift!"

Siran looked down upon his son. "Liv'e had transformed himself into a demonic creature for the sake of conquest, but he was right, my son. Nubians do deserve to rule the sky, to rule the world. The Up High will be ours. Our people will never be subjugated again by these fools." Siran closed his eyes and raised his head toward the sky. "And now, thanks to you, I am restored."

Uzochi recoiled from the sight of his father as he struggled to make sense of his words. What did he mean, Nubians deserved to rule the sky and the world?

"You wouldn't do that!" Uzochi shouted over the gathering winds, refusing to believe what he was hearing. "I know you."

Siran gave Uzochi a sad, almost mocking grin. "Do you?

You have the power to look inside my mind, and yet you never have. Well, go ahead, Uzochi. I know how important your precious ethics are to you. You have my permission. Look into my mind."

And so Uzochi did as his father commanded.

Siran's inner expression of the kinetic was the first thing he saw, a sparkling blue orb where pulses of energy constantly shot back and forth, seeking, searching, filling the abyss . . . ever restless . . .

And then Uzochi flew more deeply into Siran's psyche, wasting no time in taking it all in as he observed the battered, bruised man who'd washed up on Ghanaian shores, and how his father was slowly nursed back to health by a local physician. And how the physician and his father eventually married and had two children of their own, twins who were now ten years old. And how Siran, even with his new family, even with a stable, somewhat fulfilling life, had taken it upon himself to leave Africa and travel to Tri-State East once he'd heard news of the awakenings. For he'd never forgotten who he was, had never forgotten his birthright and the power that flushed through his veins, that power that could be his again if he worked with his catalyst son. For if they touched the kinetic together as two catalysts, if a more freshly empowered, trusting Uzochi catalyzed Siran, well . . .

Tears streamed down Uzochi's cheeks now. He didn't need to look in his father's mind any further.

Uzochi was simply the means to an end, for Siran to reconnect with the kinetic.

"Oh, Dad," he whispered, realizing that Siran could care

less about him and his mother, could care less about his dead brother, not now, not when his gift was restored. His primary reason for reuniting with his people.

Siran looked down at Uzochi as he rose higher and higher, rain pouring, thunder booming, lightning streaking the sky.

"Join me, Uzochi!" Siran shouted out. "Our rule in the sky would be glorious."

His father was planning to soar to the Up High to finish what Liv'e had begun.

"No," Uzochi said again, more to himself than anyone else. "Oh, Dad . . ."

And for the first time in his life, Uzochi used his mind to throw out a wave of solid force, a wave intended to strike his father down.

Siran was thrown a few feet in the air and then used the wind to steady himself, gesturing slightly and sending a mighty gust toward his son. Uzochi threw up a telekinetic field to deflect the blow but still found himself thrown head over heels through the park, colliding with a humongous tree. He slid down into the dirt and mud, dazed, wondering if he'd broken anything, realizing that the winds were raging so badly that he could barely stand.

Several militia vehicles that were still in the park toppled over, the drivers scrambling to get out. People were maniacally holding on to whatever they could find, with one man swept into the air as he cried for help.

Dad, Uzochi telepathically sent to his father, *you've gotta stop this.*

"Hey!"

Uzochi turned to see Zuberi and Vriana—Vriana was back?!?—coming toward him, barely managing to remain upright considering the winds. Zuberi was using her staff as an anchor to hold steady in the mushy earth, Vriana's arms locked around her waist. Uzochi tried to steady himself as well, tried to stand up straight though it was nearly impossible.

Several of the other Children were right behind the girls, everyone grabbing on to trees and bushes as best they could. Sajah, Zaire, and Abdul slowly made their way over, with Zaire using his massive rock form to shield everyone else from the gusts.

Zuberi, Uzochi sent to her. *My dad, he's . . .*

She just shook her head and grabbed his hand. "I know, buddy, I know. His phantoms, they told me everything. I saw it all . . . And you know what you have to do. I saw that as well, among your phantoms. And I'm so sorry that it's come down to this, but we're here for you." Zuberi leaned over and kissed Uzochi tenderly on the lips. "And I love you."

With that, Zuberi turned to the others. "Let's hit it!" she yelled. "Remember what I just described."

And the group ran closer to where Siran continued to rise and rise into the sky. Suddenly Uzochi's father was engulfed by an orb of smoky shadow, shocked to find himself only a dozen feet or so from the lawn's surface. One of Sajah's portals, the bane of his existence.

And then Zuberi threw her staff at Siran like a javelin, the elemental barely having time to dodge the attack just as Abdul sent forth a massive stream of rock and water. Siran was struck down, tumbling into the mud. Zaire pounded both of his fists into the earth, opening a fissure that would have swallowed Siran whole if he hadn't created another gale to carry him aloft. And Abdul sent forth another stream of rock and water, which Siran dodged, only to find himself being thwacked repeatedly along the head by Zuberi's staff, and dodging another one of Sajah's portals.

Suddenly a humongous swarm of bats engulfed Uzochi's father, the man letting forth an audible shout of dismay for the first time. Uzochi didn't understand . . . bats? In gale-force winds. And then he understood, feeling her presence with his mind. There, holding on to a tree for dear life, was Tasha, having been camouflaged on the battlefield all along.

Siran pushed his way through Tasha's illusion, confused, looking at himself, checking to see if he'd been bitten or scratched. And then, perhaps the most powerful of the Children stepped forward and threw out her hands and shouted, "Please, come down, sir! Join us, be our friend!" And Uzochi saw a wild grimace take over his father as he struggled to resist Vriana's persuasion.

Siran flew higher into the sky just as Sajah created several swirling portals around him, his father weaving through the air as only a skilled flier could do.

Uzochi stood there dumbfounded for a moment, trying to grasp what was happening, realizing that his friends had no hope of beating his father. That they were simply distracting him . . .

. . . so he could do what he was supposed to do.

Was Uzochi supposed to use his friends' connection to the kinetic to augment his powers, as Siran had told him was his right to do as catalyst? To subdue him with his telekinesis?

But no, his father would still be who he was.

. . . the part of Nubian history that brings you shame is what will serve you well on this day.

And then Uzochi understood.

He focused his telekinesis once again to form a field around his body, and with this Uzochi levitated, careening and rocking wildly as his father's winds raged. Siran summoned a great gust that scattered most of the Children far across the park, all except mighty Zaire, who remained immovable.

Zuberi ran forward again and thrust her staff into the ground. "Zaire, NO!" she screamed, Uzochi understanding that she was seeing the gargantuan boy's phantoms.

Uzochi read his father's thoughts, no longer feeling like he needed to honor his ethics, and knew that Siran was preparing to strike Zaire down with lightning. To turn his earthen form into a mound of rubble.

Dad, Uzochi sent to his father. *Please, let's end this. I've decided to talk, to hear you out.*

And with this Siran lowered himself to his son, held aloft so regally by the winds while Uzochi could barely manage to keep himself upright with his telekinesis.

"Uzochi," Siran said, his voice a confident, sure thing among the howling wind.

Uzochi looked his father square in the eyes and said, "Dad . . ."

No—he stopped himself. This man wasn't his dad.

"Siran," he said, "I'm sorry."

With all his force, Uzochi threw his mind into his father's and seized his consciousness. He gripped it, holding tightly, corralling everything he could of his father's recollections, from his washing up on the shores of Ghana, to the time he told his brother goodbye during the cataclysm, to the news that he would be a father, to the first time when, as a child, he realized he could use wind to take to the sky and glide over Nubian mountains . . .

Uzochi used his telepathy to gather all of his father's memories into a tidy ball. And just as he had once observed Adisa do, he took these memories, packed them up, and released them to the heavens.

Siran immediately fell from the sky, as Uzochi presumed he would, for his father no longer knew himself to be an elemental, no longer knew he had the power to fly. He no longer knew he was Nubian. He no longer even knew his own name. There'd been no time for Uzochi to be precise with what he erased.

Uzochi used a telekinetic field to catch Siran before he hit the ground, and when his father landed, he called out his name even though he knew he didn't remember it any longer. His father would never remember him again, and so Uzochi fell to his knees, even as the rains subsided and the winds died down.

Zuberi ran to Uzochi and held him in her arms as he wept, as the clouds parted and moonlight reflected off a field of grass and debris, bouncing off the towers to the sky that he had once thought would make him so happy. The other

Children slowly gathered around him as well from different corners of the park, all getting down in the grass. He could feel the waves of care that they offered freely. And he was thankful, even though he couldn't move.

"It'll be okay," Vriana said as he cried and cried, heaving, clutching Zuberi, unable to stop himself as he looked at dead-eyed Siran. "Please, sweetie, just go to sleep, just for a little bit. It'll be okay."

And even though Uzochi knew her persuasion was at play, as he began to drift off, he happily let the lie settle him into darkness.

Chapter 37

Lencho

Lencho had always hated funerals. He thought it was one of the few things he and his dad had in common, though in retrospect he realized that probably wasn't true, that they had far more in common than he cared to admit. Lencho remembered when his mom's cousin had passed and she had been all torn up about her husband's refusal to go to the funeral.

"Why are we gussying ourselves up because someone died?" Kefle said. "They're gone. They're not coming back. Let's not create a big ordeal." It was one of the few times his mother, Leeyah, had gone at it with his dad, declaring that she would permanently walk through the door if Kefle didn't pay his respects the way any decent human being would. Her father had relented, Lencho having enough sense even at ten years old to know that his father would be a lost, starving puppy if his mom left him.

Lencho had agreed with his father's sentiments at the time, but probably not for the same reasons. To Lencho, he'd lost a day to someone he didn't really know. His time could have been better spent focusing on his favorite holo-series or picking up a game of ball with the neighborhood kids. But they'd attended the services, and when Lencho had stood with the casket in front of him and Kefle beside him, he'd turned to see that his father's eyes were narrowed, the slightest hint of glassiness to them.

Now, a bit older, wiser, he wondered if maybe his father had hated funerals because his brother never had gotten a proper one. There had been no body to bury, and now they all knew why. Or maybe his father hated funerals because they made him feel things that Kefle Will didn't want to feel. Lencho would never know. Lencho wasn't a telepath or an empath or anything else like that, but beyond that, his father was gone. He would never get the answers to the questions he hadn't realized he held inside him.

The biggest question Lencho had that he would never get an answer for was why his father had died trying to save him, to have his heart and lungs pierced, to be thrown around like a rag doll by an ancient Nubian force. Kefle hadn't been a good father, had never been particularly self-sacrificing. He'd been an abusive asshole who'd hurt Lencho in ways he might never recover from. Lencho had known that, even when Liv'e had tried to suffocate all the life and memory out of Lencho's mind. He had still felt the sting of his dad's hands and insults when he was becoming nothing but a wisp of a soul. Which was why it had been so confusing to see his dad fight for him. It was why Lencho stood at Kefle's grave at Fort Chisolm not knowing what to say.

Earlier in the day, with the morning sun robust and bright,

a host of elders and a few of the Children had gathered around Kefle's grave, basically a modest mound of upturned earth with a headstone created by Abdul. Leeyah stood behind her son, and Uzochi and Zuberi stood right by him as well. There had been words from Bekah, and even a short song of remembrance from Vriana, Lencho not having had the slightest idea that the bubbly girl had serious pipes. And then people had slowly started to drift away. His aunt Com'pa and Zuberi said they would take a walk with his mom, who was as silent as ever, not shedding one tear over Kefle, telling Lencho everything he needed to know about their relationship at this point. That only left the two cousins, both boys standing around, glancing awkwardly at each other.

After a couple of minutes, tired of standing, Lencho had just said "Fuck it" and plopped his ass in the grass. Uzochi, being ever so thoughtful, had sat on the ground with him. Lencho knew that the polite thing to do would be to make small talk with Uzochi, not to leave him in silence as they sat, but he just didn't have it in him to bullshit, not right now. He was struggling with his new reality, with having a mind that felt free after weeks of dealing with this . . . crazy thing. They still hadn't figured out how Liv'e had entered Lencho's mind or how his power had come to be activated within Lencho's body. It was nuts, but Lencho was happy that fuckin' dude was gone, even if it meant he no longer had a kinetic gift to call his own.

He was also going to have to make peace with his new living arrangements. With Lencho's face all over the holos as the Nubian who had caused massive damage and loss of life in the Up High, he would be arrested on the spot if he was to pop up in New York, right after, of course, people threw up their hands, screamed, and ran for their lives. Folks were accepting that they now had superpowered Nubians living in their fine city, but telling these folks that an innocent Nubian had actually been possessed by a maniacal parasitic sorcerer who was thousands of years old, which was what had caused such mayhem . . . nope, wasn't going to fly. So Lencho had to hide out on the base. Would he ever be free to go where he chose? It was practically the same thing as being imprisoned.

"Hey," Uzochi said, finally breaking the silence and Lencho's brooding. "How are you, dude?"

"Oh, considering my dad is dead, that I'm responsible for dozens of deaths and millions of currency in damage and I'll never be able to step foot in my hometown again, feeling really great, cuz, thanks for asking," Lencho said, not bothering to look Uzochi's way. "Listen, you don't have to sit with me. I appreciate what you did . . . what the others did . . . but I'm not the best company right now. I don't want to piss you off, I don't want to be rude, just keeping it real."

"It's okay," Uzochi said. "I just wanted to sit with you, Lencho, even if you have nothing to say, even if you don't want to talk. But I do want to apologize."

"Apologize . . . for what?" Lencho sucked his teeth. "After all the crap I've just done, man . . . stop bullshittin' . . ."

"It wasn't you, Lencho, what just happened. It wasn't, we know that, even if the world doesn't. And I'm apologizing about being a jerk back at 104."

Lencho scrunched up his face. "Wait, you're bringing up high school drama now? After what we've just been through?"

Now it was Uzochi's turn to look into the distance. "Lencho, I've always been jealous of your swag, charisma, and strength, how all the kids always flocked to you at school, how you could navigate the streets of the Swamp and other parts of New York, easy breezy, no prob." Uzochi gestured to Lencho as he spoke and then to himself. "Lencho Will, perennially electric swag king of the lower city. Uzochi Will, Up High obsessed preceptor's pet who's also a dateless loser. I was jealous and didn't know how to admit that, so instead I acted like a condescending, hoity-toity jerk instead of being there when maybe you needed a friend . . . you know, considering everything you were coping with. I didn't know how to admit what I was feeling, not before my own awakening, but I do now. You've been dealing with a lot of shit on your own for years now, and it wasn't cool. I should've been there way earlier." Uzochi gave a short nod. "I can't change the past, but I can do the right thing now. And I'm here. Whenever you want to talk, whenever you're ready."

Lencho just stared at his cousin, realizing that Uzochi now not only looked different—with his hair all out and wild in a fro, something old Uzochi would've never done—but also *seemed* different. More confident and aware, more genuine . . . definitely less hoity-toity.

He turned and once again looked into the distance. "Okay, cuz, cool. I'll sit with all you've said. But if you're cool with just sitting, not really talking, that's where I'm at now. You feel me?" Lencho paused. "And I'm sorry about your dad. I heard what happened."

"I feel you," Uzochi said. "And about my father, thanks,

Lencho." Uzochi grew silent, still. Lencho could tell that it would be best not to push him on the subject, at least for now. "Uhm, just one more thing," Uzochi added. "Did you know that you'd awoken to your gift?"

Lencho swiveled back to his cousin and glared. "Man, what you talking about? I didn't have a gift. That draining shit was from that crazy sorcerer."

"No, Lencho, I'm not sure how it worked, but so much of what Liv'e could do was piggybacking on your awakening. I think, from what I see of your power, that his presence was a corruption of what's naturally yours. Your power . . . it's there. And it's beautiful. I can show you."

"Well, I'll be," Lencho said. He looked at the bright sky and then at his father's headstone, realizing he hadn't the slightest idea what Kefle's gift was when he lived back in Nubia.

"Okay, Uzochi, why the hell not? Show me."

And with that Uzochi entered Lencho's mind, gently guiding the representation of his cousin's psyche to see his personal expression of the kinetic, a rich field of glistening, multicolored stars going back as far as the eye could see, an entrancing, majestic expression.

Your gift is the ability to absorb solar energy, Uzochi sent, *whether from the sun that's the center of our solar system, or from other stars that are light-years away. You can hold and manipulate energy with your body, Lencho. But not life energy, not from people, the energy of the stars.*

Lencho opened his eyes to see that his entire body was

glowing, a sense of rejuvenation and rebirth cascading from the crown of his head to the soles of his feet.

He looked down at his hands one more time and then closed his eyes and let his mind wander, allowing his body to commune with the sun, as was his birthright.

Chapter 38

Sandra

Sandra had begrudgingly come to accept that the sky city would never be the same. The process of rebuilding? Easy enough, something that could be done quickly considering the amount of currency that flowed through Up High channels. But that wasn't the issue. People were spooked. Two thousand residents had revoked their ascension status in a matter of days, opting to pack up and move down below. And more departures were on the horizon.

"It's too dangerous to live up here, not unless there are real evacuation protocols," one woman had uttered tearfully to Helios News, a hover platform full of luggage behind her. "If there's another attack, I will not suffer through the madness of getting to the lower city via the towers."

Yes, Sandra realized, some people were moving because of such practicalities, but others simply couldn't walk Up High streets without being reminded of how a floating madman almost took their life, or, in a few horrible cases, actually took the lives of their friends or family members. The Up High was now entering its postsiege era, reporters proclaimed. Change was in the air. The age of descension had begun, at least according to one popular journalist. Sandra shuddered at the thought.

After a day of recovery in a med center, Sandra had checked herself out and gotten back to work, handling calls from St. John Enterprises shareholders and militia leaders and government officials and newshounds. She simply went to her office and closed the door, noting the quick patch-up job that had been done to her windows and walls, and dug in. Sandra knew she looked a mess on her holo-calls since she didn't bother to hide her injuries, but she didn't care. Glamming up could become a thing again when her business was back on track.

And so it had been to her surprise when Vincent, working as her primary assistant now, had pinged her personal comm to say that a Nubian from the lower city was requesting a meeting ASAP. A Zuberi Ragee.

Sandra wasn't sure what the girl wanted, especially considering that Vriana had been sent back home with a free mind, but her intuition said she needed to take the meeting immediately.

Within three hours of Vincent's altering her schedule to accommodate Zuberi's request, the door to Sandra's office opened. In walked the strident girl she'd last seen kicking behind on Central Park grass, the same girl who'd struck her down at Starlight.

"Please feel free to have a seat," Sandra said to Zuberi, but the girl didn't move. She simply stopped in front of Sandra's desk, hands behind her back.

Sandra knew Zuberi had no weapons, that she'd been thoroughly scanned before being allowed entry, and that she was completely surrounded by two dozen St. John Soldiers right outside the office if she tried anything. But Sandra felt uneasy. Memories of the greenhouse still stirred within.

"Fine," she said with a roll of her eyes. "Stand. How can I help you, Zuberi?"

"Are we being recorded?" the girl asked.

Sandra tilted her head. "No. We are not. I disabled any lingering surveillance tech before you walked through the door, as I do with all meetings."

"Good, because I'm going to say things that you'll probably want off the record," Zuberi replied. "I have two major demands. Firstly, I want you to develop a number of initiatives for lower New York and the rest of Tri-State East. I want you to actively funnel currency to help nourish and protect underserved communities, providing everything from scholarships to job opportunities. Considering all the Elevation your dad pumped into the city for years, all the lives he fucked up, it's the least you can do."

Sandra remained still, her face a mask. "And your second demand?"

"Second, I want the registration act completely done away with. Lean on your city council members to revoke the law immediately with a full set of apologies, letting the public know that Nubians are to be left alone. It's bad enough our community's going to deal with all sorts of sick fallout from Liv'e's attack, and we'll need the government having our back. Do whatever manipulative thing you usually do to get your way. But the law needs to be sacked, ASAP. And while it's still in place, I expect that there'll be no active enforcement of the act from your mangy St. John Soldiers. Gifted Nubians will be free to live in the city without fear of detainment."

Sandra raised an eyebrow. "And why, exactly, would I agree to these demands, Zuberi?" she said, purposely dragging her voice to sound bored, to mask her anxiety. "You're awfully sure of yourself."

"Because, after all the problems caused in the sky by a crazy, gifted, rampaging Nubian, I don't think you want the people currently rebuilding their homes up here to know the truth about the woman in charge of their security operations and so much of their commerce," Zuberi said. "That she's a crazy, gifted Nubian herself."

Sandra could feel the color draining from her face, her eyes widening for a second before she pulled the mask back into place.

"Vriana figured it out, about your powers," Zuberi continued. "Most of you Up High-ers, you need to manually activate your implants to make them work. But Vri said she saw you sometimes project holos from your eyes or open doors with none of those crazy tapping moves, as if you were able to handle everything with your mind. And we figured it out. Your gift, it's the ability to interface with devices. No hands. You were the one who freed Vriana from that implant you had placed on her. And during the battle in the park, you made one of your militia tanks shoot at Lencho . . . with your mind."

Sandra remained silent. She would neither confirm nor deny this wretched girl's claims.

"So?" Zuberi asked.

"So," Sandra said, "the terms of your deal sound fine to me, Ms. Ragee. I'll make it so." She would play it calm, cool, and keep it short, giving nothing away. "Anything else?"

Zuberi took in Sandra again, no anger or glee to be seen, just a steely resolve. "Nothing else. But keep in mind, I'm not the only one who knows your secret. If anything happens to me that smells like one of your schemes, or if you ever, *ever* come after Vriana again, I assure you that others will jump through hoops to make sure the world knows your secret."

Zuberi turned and made her way to the door, not seeming the least bit intimidated by the group of soldiers waiting outside. Before exiting, she turned to Sandra and said, "Be well. Try to be kind. And maybe think about who you really are." And then she was gone.

After the visit, Sandra didn't have much drive to do work or take calls, feeling like she had no choice but to reflect and own up to her mistakes. So she sat in her office and stared out the window, surveying all the damage her home had endured, losing track of time. She swiftly interfaced with all the devices surrounding her, a daily ritual that she found comforting, the whirs and clicks of machinery a balm to her spirit. She'd thought she was being so careful, remembering to engage in the theater of pretending to activate her implants manually when she hadn't needed to do so for weeks now, as she'd awoken to her gift of technopathy soon after she'd taken Vriana Up High. And that was the thing, being with Vriana constantly, the girl becoming like a second shadow . . . Sandra had started to get careless, to forget to do her standard tap on the wrist here or slide on the temple there that she was always so mindful of in public. She hadn't believed the chipper girl would notice, but apparently she had.

Sandra thought it was an indication that she still had a soul when she'd used her gift to deactivate the Conway Protocols in Vriana's implants. She figured the girl might not survive Lencho's attack, and if that was the case, she deserved to be free. Maybe such a gesture of kindness would make up for the sin of initiating Krazen's tech failure just days earlier. It was only through divine coincidence that, at the very moment she stood near her father's office and reached out with her gift to shut down his implants, Lencho had been having his own meeting with Krazen. The deranged boy had thus inadvertently taken the blame for something he had no part in, though she had little sympathy for him. Some of the Divine and the Children were declaring that he wasn't responsible for his later actions, that he'd been possessed by an evil spirit, this Liv'e, as Zuberi had just said. Such a load of bull. Lencho Will, with his different personalities and shifting gifts, was a psychopath. Wherever he was, she hoped he never set foot on the Up High again. Sandra only had room in her life for one madman—her father—who was still under Dr. Marshall's care, peaceful, alive, and out of the way.

Zuberi Ragee had advised her to think about who she really was, as if she was saying something profound. What ignorance. Sandra St. John had been doing exactly that for far longer than Zuberi could ever imagine.

Chapter 39

Uzochi

"All right, babes, love you too. See you soon."

Uzochi sat on the crumbling steps of the Jungle, tucking his mobile away, thankful that Zuberi had called to say that her trip uptown had gone well. She'd become in demand of late at cultural centers as a guest teacher focusing on self-defense. The Nubian warrior girl who was an expert in her people's unique form of martial arts. The local celebrity who'd fought to take down the lunatic who'd caused so much destruction just two weeks ago. It was great, to see Zuberi getting well-deserved praise from so many people. And he was heartened to see that she seemed less consumed with the idea of bringing the Up High down—maybe because it was currently in such a state of disarray—and much more interested in advocating for different communities in the lower city. She seemed more at peace, even with the turmoil they'd just survived.

In general, so much of what had happened with Liv'e was a mixed bag for Nubians. Some of the public hated them more than ever, claiming they were all menaces who should be locked up. Others came to their defense, pointing out that a large group of Nubians were the ones who'd defeated the maniac who'd caused so much mayhem. But there were still questions, even among the allies: Where had this attacker, Lencho Will, vanished to? And could the Nubians who'd been recruited for the St. John militia ever be trusted, considering one of their own had gone rogue?

Uzochi often thought about how he could fix such problems, especially if it involved his cousin and other awoken Nubians. But he'd reached his limit. Going to see his father for the past few days in that filthy lower-city med center, a vegetable who at best could one day learn how to do basic things like eat or use the bathroom by himself . . . that was a lot. Constantly consoling his mother, whose guilt was eating away at her for not giving Uzochi the full story around how ruthless Siran could be . . . again, a lot. Grieving for Kefle and helping Lencho slowly come out of his shell, just being around for his cousin . . . a lot. He could feel it in his body that he had to be still, let others take the lead for a minute. That he needed some quiet time for himself and with Zuberi, so he could rest and finally think about his future. He'd let the administrators at HS 104 know that they could validate his class credits, and so he was now officially a high school graduate. He definitely wanted to head to college, but he would need time to figure out what that would look like while serving as a Nubian catalyst.

Several of the Children burst forth from the building, giggling about the drama on some gaming holo they'd just watched. Zaire and Abdul brought up the rear as they walked in lockstep, arm in arm. Uzochi appreciated seeing the boys so happy as they got to know each other, especially Zaire, who'd gone from being quiet and withdrawn to bouncy giddiness on the regular. (Uzochi lamented that most people on the street seemed to think that Zaire was Abdul's security detail instead of his date, but every relationship had its challenges.) With the registration act officially rescinded, many Nubians at Fort Chisolm had declared that they wanted to return to New York, that the city was their home, warts and roaches and rats and all. They didn't want to relinquish the special community they'd started to build.

After much deliberation, Beka and the elders had relented, though many Nubians still decided to stay on at the base, including Thato, who believed that their people would always need a secret refuge should shit ever hit the fan again. And so, using Sajah's portals, scores and scores of Nubians moved yet again, Uzochi and Zuberi among them along with most of the Children. Fort Chisolm was only a quick shadow-walk away.

The smell of basil mixed with other herbs reached Uzochi's nose, a telltale sign that Leonard was working in his garden around the corner. It had been a relief that, after he'd grown several gardens at Chisolm by himself, others would be able to produce whatever fruits and veggies they needed on their own, Leonard only needing to appear at the base from time to time. The Mohawked boy had literally skipped and danced as he shadow-walked to get back to SoHo, Sajah almost believing that Leonard was going to kiss the ground upon his return.

Uzochi rose off the hard stone steps and walked inside the Jungle, wanting to stretch his legs for a minute. He was heartened to see his newly formed soul/mind group sitting in a little circle, communing with each other telepathically with Sekou reclining off to the side, no doubt astral surfing somewhere. They were the small group of telepaths among the Children that had awoken, five in number. Though none had powers of the mind as robust as Uzochi's, they each had their specialties, including one excitable kid who could broadcast their thoughts to lots of people at the same time. Uzochi had known that, if Nubians were going to live openly and freely in SoHo, they had to acknowledge that there was always the chance that someone would come after them, that they needed to have a line of defense even if the St. Johns were no longer a threat . . . for now. And so there would always be a rotating shift of Nubian telepaths scanning the surrounding area to warn of danger. Uzochi wished things were different, but he knew he had to be realistic. Nubians could be part of the larger world, fine, but his people still had to protect themselves as best they could.

Right next to the meditators, Tasha was running an art class. A whole bunch of neighborhood kids sat with sketch pads and paints or pencils as she ran through basic drawing techniques with an illusion of a giant canvas that she slowly filled in with lines and color. And Vriana wasn't far behind as she gave a social worker a tour of the building, the two chattering away about what it would take to open an intervention center for kids facing abuse at home. Uzochi thought of his cousin back at Fort Chisolm and how much he'd approve.

Uzochi stood there for a moment, taking in his community as he thought about what they'd accomplished. Siran had seemed so proud that his son was capable of telekinesis, but Uzochi knew he was a person of heart and spirit, that empathy and telepathy were his most cherished gifts by far.

With that in mind, he gathered up the disparate emotions of everyone in the Jungle . . . their hopes and doubts and awkwardness and giddiness and pride and fears and tenderness and insight and desire for connection, *especially* the desire for connection . . . bundled them up, and sent them through the hall on a magnificent, gentle wave for everyone to experience. And as he felt their awe and wonder reflected back at him, he sent to Nubians and non-Nubians alike, *Please remember, this is who we are.*

When Uzochi walked back outside, his steps slow and measured, he saw the person with whom he had his own appointment coming down the block. He'd discussed the idea at length with Zuberi and Thato and some of the elders, and they'd decided that he should do what felt right, even though he was nervous.

As Cassandra Johnson made her way toward him, Uzochi could see that the majestic presence she exuded as a contributor to *World Village Report* wasn't some sort of studio trick for the holos. It was really her. Uzochi immediately felt at ease about his decision.

They had agreed that for their meeting there would be no cameras, no multiple interviews, just a casual talk, so Professor Johnson could listen and ultimately present a related story in the way she thought best. Uzochi knew there were aspects of Nubian history that would remain a secret to the larger world for now, that were too outlandish and hard to believe. But sharing some of the basics . . . who Nubians were, where they came from, what the awoken could do . . . that was fine. He thought it was time, that Nubians had to start to take control of their own story before someone did it for them, like Krazen and Sandra. That Nubians also had to embrace that their story had forever changed.

"Good afternoon, young man," Professor Johnson said as she approached the steps, clad in a blazer and dark blue jeans. "Would you by any chance happen to be Uzochi Will?"

Uzochi immediately perked up and extended his hand. And then he smiled, imagining he was hearing Zuberi's or Vriana's voice in his head—or Lencho's—telling him that it wasn't a test, that he had nothing to prove. To just chill and be himself.

Uzochi felt himself relax. And he breathed.

"Professor Johnson . . . hey," he said, instead giving her a casual, friendly wave. "I am indeed Uzochi, and it's an honor to meet you."

He extended his arms in a wide, grand arc. Maybe he looked silly, but that was okay.

"Welcome to Nubia."

EPILOGUE

To be disgraced . . . yet again . . .

Liv'e's consciousness floated through the thick air of the lower city, aware that he couldn't survive long unless he found rest in another body. And soon. He had thought that his days of torment were over, that he would no longer have to move through the world as a wraithlike, pitiful thing. Lencho's mighty form surely could have been his for decades. But the pleasure of having a body that he controlled again, of feeling the varieties of the kinetic thrum through his veins . . . it had left him sloppy. Overconfident, delirious, becoming something akin to a fool . . .

He had always prided himself on his cunning, a man far ahead of his time. Upon leaving Nubia, Liv'e had decided that there was too much of the world to experience to allow himself to succumb to something like death. And so he had studied endlessly with a secret society of sorcerers from Europe and Asia, learning not only how to draw life essence and kinetic gifts from others but also how to enable his soul to live free of his body. Some Nubians had possessed variations of this ability through the ages—that overbearing child named Sekou being the most recent example—but none had enhanced their gift the way Liv'e had. None could send their soul outside their body indefinitely without fear of dying. Liv'e had made sure that he would endure, whether his body was alive or not, though the cost was high.

And so when ancient Nubians had managed to defeat him, destroying his form, Liv'e's spirit had survived. Using sorcery that defied the kinetic, he inhabited other bodies, reducing his consciousness to a small, easily ignored dot, one that would escape the notice of the more powerful telepaths of his ancestral land. For millennia, he hid in the minds of countless generations of people, preferring to inhabit those who were more outward-facing in their personalities or expression of the kinetic. They would be less likely to take notice of this sliver of a thing residing in their consciousness. And this was how Liv'e had lived for more than two thousand years, a true ghost of his former self, slowly going mad as he experienced the mundane lives of dozens of others. No control of his movements, no control of his destiny, his existence the very opposite of why he'd abandoned Nubia in the first place. The cost of his arcane explorations far too high. He would not know greatness, would not be recognized for his triumphs. He eventually realized that his spirit was starting to shrivel away, death on the horizon. After eons of pain, he welcomed it.

It was only through celestial fortune that he had decided to occupy the body of a royal, Kefle Will, one of the least introspective Nubians he'd encountered in all his days. Kefle had survived the great cataclysm, getting himself to New York with other Nubians, eventually creating a home for his wife and son. He had even managed to find decent work amid the prejudice Nubians faced, though the realities of his diminished station in life had left him a violent, angry thing. Liv'e eventually had enough of Kefle's toxicity, finding the mind of his son a more hospitable place to hide.

The old sorcerer had thought that the age of Nubians was over, that they would quietly integrate themselves into the filthy, waterlogged city across the sea where people grasped for dignity's leftovers. To Liv'e's shock, a new catalyst had arisen, the most powerful catalyst he'd observed in thousands of years. A catalyst who'd awoken young Nubians to their gifts left and right without noticing, who'd awoken Lencho's power at their vile high school, who'd reinvigorated Liv'e's own disappearing abilities and psyche . . .

Finally, Liv'e had felt like himself once again.

It had been nothing to corrupt Lencho's gifts, to manipulate the boy's pain and anger, to alienate him from his allies in the sky and sow confusion and destruction as he began to drain . . . as he began to *live*. In Liv'e's mind, the Up High would have made the perfect seat of power, a reflection of what he had dared to achieve all those years ago.

A palace in the sky . . .

But he had been sloppy, too quick, too thoughtless. Of course someone like Uzochi, even powerless, would have understood how to manipulate the threads of the kinetic and wrench that thread from Liv'e's hands. Once defeated, he'd had no choice but to leave Lencho's body immediately. A telepath as mighty as Uzochi, deeply probing his cousin's mind, would have seized him with little effort.

Though Liv'e found himself drifting again, he reminded himself that he was far from a wraith, thanks to the revered catalyst of New York. Liv'e had hopped from consciousness to consciousness postbattle until he found himself in lower Manhattan, at the place Nubians called the Jungle, reaching the child known as Sajah. Yes, this one was feisty, perhaps dangerous to inhabit, as they tended to look both inward and outward with their mind. But Liv'e would make himself tiny, Sajah a prize too tempting to pass up. The young Nubian's portals were laced with energy from a shadow realm that most certainly was *not* of the kinetic. Liv'e liked that. This energy felt familiar, reminding him of his experimentations from so long ago.

Sajah would do.

And so Liv'e had entered the child's mind, insignificant, microscopic, aware he would have to avoid Uzochi's telepathy at all costs. He would find out what entity the teleporter was in communion with, find out what opportunities for conquest still remained beyond the kinetic.

Liv'e could wait.

ACKNOWLEDGMENTS

Thank you once again to my copilot, Clarence A. Haynes, for taking this journey with me to bring *Nubia: The Reckoning* to the masses. The late-night phone calls, the plotting and strategizing, the brainstorming, all on a super-tight deadline . . . we did it.

To our editorial team at Delacorte Press: Krista Marino, Beverly Horowitz, and Lydia Gregovic, your patience, professionalism, and dedication are a blessing. To my agents, Todd Shuster and Erica Bauman at Aevitas Creative, thank you for your time, superb talent, and guidance. I also can't forget publicists Josh Redlich and Cynthia Lliguichuzhca, along with the entire marketing team at Delacorte Press . . . applause and kudos for all the hard work that you do. And to the pair of visionaries who've crafted the cover for the Nubia series, artist Adeyemi Adegbesan and designer Casey Moses, I can only echo the nonstop praise your work has received from booksellers, general readers, and critics alike. An honor to work with both of you.

And finally, to my three beautiful children, thank you for inspiring me to construct this story specifically for the likes of yourselves that will be enjoyed by many generations to come! I love you beyond this world. To my wife, family, and close friends, thank you for your unwavering motivation and support.

Always walk in truth, remember to laugh, and most importantly, lead with love!

ABOUT THE AUTHORS

Actor and producer **OMAR EPPS** was introduced to audiences as Q in Ernest Dickerson's film *Juice,* opposite Tupac Shakur. He has gone on to star in the beloved romance *Love & Basketball,* as Dr. Eric Foreman on *House,* and as Darnell on *This Is Us.* He is the author of the memoir *From Fatherless to Fatherhood* and the coauthor of both novels in the Nubia series.

CLARENCE A. HAYNES has worked as an editor for a variety of publishers, including Penguin Random House, Amazon Publishing, and Legacy Lit, an imprint of Hachette Book Group. He has edited top-selling fiction titles like *The Hundredth Queen* and *Scarlet Odyssey,* as well as *Washington Post* bestseller *The Vine Witch* and its two sequels. He is also the author of the nonfiction work *The Legacy of Jim Crow* and coauthor of both novels in the Nubia series with Omar Epps.